BO

MW01128452

FICTION
The Pistol
Outlaw

The Montana Saga
The Rebels - book one
Pardners - book two
T.S. Grounds - book three
Home Ranch - book four

Riverboat Trilogy
Fort Sarpy - book one
Upriver - book two
Captains - book three

Books of Short Stories
Tales
Arikara and Lord Guest

Sharpshooter Trilogy
Sharpshooter
The Hunters
Legacy

NON-FICTION
History of Early Rosebud

This novel is a work of fiction, written in the
vernacular of the day. No offense is intended
to any person of any religion, race or nationality.

DEDICATION

Our father, William James Lloyd, almost 98 when he died, was a lifelong hunter and fisherman. He wasn't a trophy hunter, though he hung horns when he got them. Rather, he liked to put meat on the table, and my earliest memories were when he came back from a successful hunt, helping him to clean the game and then presenting it to my mother to work her cooking magic.

Growing up, his father left the family of eight children when Dad was five years old. As a boy, he remembered his oldest brother, then the bread-earner of the family, giving him an old .22 and a few shells and telling him to go down along the river and shoot something for the family to eat. If he didn't connect, sometimes the family was without meat. He always prided himself on using as few shells as possible to get the game down. He passed his love of the hunt and shooting on to me and my brother, Dan.

Dad was a career Navy man, retiring from the service as a Lieutenant Commander, a mustang officer who had worked his way up through the ranks, helped along by a world war, and a couple smaller conflicts.

He loved to shoot and was an excellent marksman. He was on the battleship Texas rifle team as an enlisted man, and garnered several trophies from the experience.

I wanted to get this book done, as he was yet an avid reader and always said he enjoyed my books. Sadly, he never got to read it. I dedicate this novel to his memory. Dad, we certainly had some great hunts together.

PART I

Chapter 1

Sleet rattled heavily against the whiskey bottle window and the wind moaned at the walls of the stout little cabin. It wasn't those sounds of the winter which had descended upon the mining camp that brought Ben Hite's head up from the nap he'd been having in front of the stove, though. Something else was out there, the sound faint but—it had pierced Ben's slumber and sharpened his keen hearing as he waited to hear the noise again. There, it came as a scratching above the wind and the sleet.

He got up and walked to the heavy door, started to lift the bar, then turned back and took up a pistol lying on the rough table. As always when he had a gun in his hands, he checked to make sure it was loaded and ready to fire, though he knew it was. The door swung back on the forged hinges and he confronted an animal right there in front of him. *A big . . . dog?*

Ben brought the Colt up and nearly shot the creature, then let the hammer back down as he saw the animal was just standing there, looking at him. Seeing his attention on it, it turned, looking back over its shoulder, as if beckoning him to follow.

"What the hell?"

Still looking back, the dog, which Ben now saw was a Pit bull of goodly size, mostly brindle but with a scarred, white head, ran a few steps off to the southwest, then returned, whining, coming closer and seemingly agitated.

"What you want, old fella? Ye want me to come?"

Hite stepped out into the harsh bitter cold, trying to gain some night vision. The sleet was swirling through the trees close by, the snow deepening from the foot or more that had been laid down during the night and day before. He shivered. *"Should have thrown on a coat,"* he thought. He tucked the pistol under his arm to keep the powder charges dry, the cold steel making him wince even through the thick wool shirt.

"Huh. Now where did it come from?" Ben wondered. *"And where was it goin'?"*

He knew most all the people in the little camp and couldn't remember any of them having a dog like it. That kind of creature was mostly owned by some sporting man who promoted dog fights, a saloon man usually. Out some 20 yards from the door, the dog waited, shivering.

Curious, he turned around and went back in the cabin to grab his coat, throw on a beaver hat and gloves. Tucking the pistol in a big side pocket, he went back out, carefully shutting the door to keep the warmth in. The moonlight shining through the trees gave enough light for him to track the animal's progress. Then he saw it in front of him, the dog seemingly waiting for him to catch up before going on. Hite followed, wading through deepening snow as he went downhill toward a copse of trees by the creek. The dog went into the trees and Ben followed, touching the gun in his pocket. He'd been ambushed before and was leery.

Out of the wind somewhat and with snow piled up against the lower branches of a big nut pine, he saw the dog stop and turn, facing him. Over its back and under the boughs, his disbelieving gaze took in three, no, *four* white faces looking over a tattered blanket at him. The eyes of the youngsters seemed huge in pale emaciated faces that spoke volumes of the cold and hunger they'd lately been fighting.

"For God's sake!" Ben Hite was flabbergasted. "You kids! What in hell are you'all doin' out here? Where's yore folks?" He rumbled.

Silence. He saw now that they were near frozen, unable to respond to his query. First things first: He'd best get them back to the cabin. The dog nuzzled them as he gathered two little ones up in his big arms. The largest, a girl, got to her feet with difficulty, the smallest one, a baby, still in her arms. It whimpered, the sound small in the shrilling of the wind. She and the dog followed as he waded back uphill to the cabin. Inside, he deposited his burdens on the floor, then went back to help the girl, who'd fallen in the snow, the dog staying by her side. He lifted and half carried her over the threshold, taking the baby from her arms and placing it close to the fireplace. Then he stood at the open door trying to coax the dog in.

It wasn't until the girl called, "Get in here, Maxxus! come on!", that it crept in. Ben closed the door and dropped the latch, then put the plank bar across it. The dog lay down watchfully by the entrance.

* * *

The fire stoked, the cabin grew warm again in a hurry and the girl stood up and helped the little ones take off their coats. One was a boy about six, the other a girl three or four years old. The girl, Ben judged, was a youngster of eleven or twelve. A family. He threw off his own coat and hung it up on a wall peg. taking out the pistol and laying it back on the table.

"Here, give me your duds. We'll hang 'em up."

She handed them over as they came off and then she went to stand by the fire, taking in its warmth. She flexed her hands and he wondered if she had frostbite, if they all were suffering from the biting cold.

"So what happened to yer folks, Gurl?"

"They got sick and died in their bed there in the wagon. Momma one day and Daddy the next. He told us to go to the camp and we did, but no one wanted us. They just said to go away. When we came back to the wagon, it was gone. Maxxus took us into the trees and tried to take care of us. He got a rabbit for us more'n once but we finally ran out of matches and . . . it's so cold!"

She looked ready to break down and Hite said, "Let me see those mitts."

He came close and took her hands in his own big paws and looked them over. Not frostbitten, though badly chapped and sore looking. He turned and got out some salve he kept handy for his own use when the constant work in the cold Wisconsin Creek water cracked and irritated his skin. He opened the tight lid and handed it to her.

The little girl moaned and he went to her, kneeling on the rough unplaned floor to take her small hands in his. She resisted feebly, then let him peer at them. As he'd feared, they showed the beginnings of frostbite, particularly in the little fingers. He slipped off her shoes and stripped her threadbare socks off. Her tiny feet were likewise frostbitten, with some toes turning an ugly blue. Whatever he did would have to be quickly done. He rummaged around in back of the stove and came up with a large pan in which he poured some coal oil from a large tin.

"Come here, young'un, and get your sister's feet and hands to soakin' in this here oil. It'll draw the frost out."

She came and assisted him to prop up the young female who protested as they worked over her. "No, Moira, it stinks!"

He turned then to the boy, who sat up and was watching them.

"Come on, son, and put yer hands and feet in. It'll pull the cold out of 'em."

The boy obeyed and Hite turned to the whimpering baby. He saw with dismay that the hands the little one was waving were blue. He drew the ragged clothes off it and found that the feet were likewise in jeopardy and needed some immediate care. He soaked a rag with the oil and brought it to the child, grasping each extremity as carefully as he could, knowing the hurt the squalling baby was feeling.

* * *

4

Fifteen minutes later, a close inspection of the children told Hite that they required the services of a doctor—a commodity that he knew was unavailable in the camp this winter. The nearest physician was in Bannack, if he hadn't pulled stakes for some other camp. And from what Ben remembered hearing of him, not worth the powder to blow the drunken bum to hell. What needed doing would have to be done by himself, tonight, something he dreaded.

Frostbite was insidious: left alone, it would rot the skin and the flesh, cause the fingers and toes to turn black and break or fall off, with usually blood poison and gangrene a fatal result. Hite was no stranger to the malady and reluctantly turned to the wall peg holding his hoof nippers. Getting the tool down, he got his file and sharpened its edges. As he worked, he explained to the one the others called Moira.

"Gurl, I hate to tell you but we got a bad job in front of us. Your little ones got frostbite in their fingers and toes and are gonna have to lose some of 'em. The baby, too. And we cain't wait, Gurl. The ones that're still black need to come off tonight. You'll hev to hold 'em and I'll do the nippin'." She started to protest but he cut her off.

"No buts about it, Gurl. Jest somethin' has to be done—now. Do ye want 'em to die? Gangrene's a bad way to go. I seen it."

Hite decided that it would work easiest with less resistance from the older ones if they were done first, so Hite called the boy to him.

"Son, look at those feet. You see the black little piggies? They have to come off, boy, 'er you'll git blood poisonin' and it'll kill ye. Now, be a little man an' put 'em up here on the chair fer me and hold on to yer sister."

Trying to distract him, he asked, "So what's yer name, son?"

"My name is. . . Frederick Barnes. Daddy called me Freddy."

"And what about yer little sister? What's her name?"

"Elizabeth Barnes. We call her Betty."

Working fast, he nipped two toes from the boy's left foot and the last one from his right, disregarding yells and the struggle the older girl was having to keep him still. Then, as she held on, Hite poured whiskey on the wounds, which brought a fresh outburst from the hurting child. By the door, the dog got up and growled and the girl shushed it with a hoarse yell.

"Now, the hands. Hmm. Maybe just the little finger on yer left there."

He captured the hand the boy tried to hide in his pants and with another struggle, the blackened finger came off with a snip of the pliers. Hite took it up with the toes and threw them in the fire. He went to a corner and rummaged in his duffle.

"Here, tear this shirt and wrap 'im up."

After seeing the boy bandaged, they turned to the girl who was watching the proceedings, wide-eyed. Wiping tears, Moira gestured, "Come on, Betty, you don't want to die, do you? The man says they have to come off."

The girl shook her head and scrambling to the dog, held on to its neck. Moira came after her and a short tussle ensued, with the dog in the middle. For a wonder, the animal didn't turn on the older one as she peeled Betty off and brought her to the table, where Hite took her feet and examined them. Quick for a big man, he worked the nippers and two toes came off each foot, then a finger from the right hand. The little one fainted. Moira wrapped the extremities in whisky soaked cloth and they turned to the baby, whose name Moira said was Katrina, Katy for short. Hite found himself sweating in the warm room and wiped his forehead with a trembling hand.

"Damn! This is a fix. Looks like both feet need to go but what good is a young'un without any feet? I dunno. Maybe a baby kin recover better than an older kid. If we let it go, the tyke might make it, but I'm not hopeful."

The two peered at the tiny bluish hands and feet of the child and finally Hite put the tool back on the peg.

"Hell, I cain't do it. Too soft, I guess. We'll wait until tomorrer and see then. How 'bout some grub?"

The cabin resounded with the crying of the children and Hite did his best to ignore it, though he finally was able to distract them somewhat by the smell of warming stew he began heating in the pot on the stove. The youngsters were famished and their hurts were overlooked as the stew was ladled out into tin dishes on the table. Hite had four spoons and he gave them out to the children and told them to dig in, breaking up a hard loaf of sourdough bread and doling it out to them to dip in their plates. The baby was a puzzle, though, and they finally solved it by dipping a cloth in the stew and letting it suck the nourishment from its folds. It was so hungry it was distracted from its crying and suckled greedily for as long as they fed it. Then it urped half of it back up and Moira began the task of cleaning it up with the limited supplies Hite had available. Ben cleaned up the dishes after letting the dog lick the leavings in the pan.

Then he dipped some water from the pail and putting the dishes and utensils in the pan, set it on the stove to heat. Dish soap was an unknown, but boiling hot water was a convenient commodity. While the water was heating, he made up a common bed out of the way on the floor by the stove and got the little ones to lay down. The dog came and snuggled up to them and little by little the snuffles and crying abated in the cabin, except for the baby.

Chapter 2

'During the war, the docs used Laudanum. Wisht I had some, the pore little tykes.' Hite mused, sitting in his big chair, baby Katy cradled in his arms. The chair was a homemade affair, one of many that he'd pieced together over the years, made out of willows and hides, usually cowhide but sometimes deer or elk. It sagged but held his weight comfortably. He stroked his heavy beard, trying to think how he might ease the baby's misery. Tomorrow, maybe he'd go down into the camp and see what he could buy or scrounge in the way of medicine.

"Little ones need some clothes, too," he thought.

* * *

Luckily, his poke was heavy. He'd worked his two claims just below the cabin with a thirty foot sluice that had kept him busy as a beaver all summer and fall until ice in the creek and the hard snowfall had shut him and the other miners down. His poke had grown and so had his caution. The last few months or so, miners all over the diggings were being sought out and killed for their gold. It wasn't going to happen to him, if he could help it. He kept to himself as much as he could.

Men down on their luck had approached him wanting work and he could have used them but turned them away. He wanted no one to know his business or learn how good the two claims were. That was almost impossible, though, since the Carruthers brothers down from him were blabbermouths and had let everyone they encountered know how well they were doing.

Then, up above him was Jake Rangeley, who was a drunkard and subject to binges in which he threw his heavy poke on the bar and ordered up drinks for all. It stood to reason if those on either side of him were doing well, he was, too. So he had to be extremely careful, though the Miners Committee had declared there could be no claim jumping because of owners being absent during the winter freeze-up. That didn't rule out being robbed or killed, though, and he knew that many had been so far.

He looked at the girl. She was drowsing in her chair before the stove. He went and tidied up his bunk.

"Hyar, slip in there and try to sleep. I'll sit up a while with the wee one and try to git her to settle down, if I can." She nodded, barely able to hold her head up. Going to the bed, she fell into it and was almost instantly asleep. Hite held baby Katy in his arms and rocked it and gradually the child quieted, no doubt exhausted. Ben was still of two minds about its feet and hands but thought he saw some improvement. No longer was the blue color so prevalent, though the toes of the right foot still were a deep color. He racked his brain, trying to remember if youngsters had some greater resistance to the effects of frostbite. If his memory served, though, it seemed that the opposite was true.

* * *

He sighed and leaned back, the baby silent at last. The cabin gradually cooled and Hite awoke in the early morning hours to the dog shaking itself, wanting out. He rose awkwardly and deposited the baby, still sleeping, on the floor where the dog had been lying, the place still warm. It stirred but didn't wake up, to Hite's relief. Going to the door, he lifted the bar and swung it partly open, just enough to let the dog through, then closed it again. He went, then, to the stove, shook it down, opened the damper and stoked it on the embers left, watching it take off again and almost immediately start radiating warmth.

He was damn proud of that stove, a middle sized Dwyer that had cost him $100 from a destitute late comer who was trying to scrape up enough for a claim up Indian Creek. Hite had never heard whether he'd been successful. But the stove had been a stroke of extremely good luck. Most of the cabins and miner shacks made do with a crude fireplace which were most always smoky and seldom put out much heat, unless the fire was kept high. Then, too, they were a fire hazard, spouting sparks and embers on flammable roofs and Hite had seen the results too many times. Hite himself had barely escaped just such a shack fire and wanted no part of another, if he could avoid it. To him, the Dwyer was worth its weight in gold. Indeed, he'd rather lose his poke than the stove. He'd fashioned a wood box in a corner that he could fill from the outside.

The children were all still asleep, though Hite heard whimpers and moans occasionally from them. He took a treasured big slab of bacon from the cooler and began cutting slices off it and laying them in the big frying pan starting to sizzle on the top of the stove.

The cooler was another of his innovations. In one corner of the cabin farthest from the stove, he'd built a stout lidded box, lining it with tin. With a pail of frozen water in it, it kept his perishables cold and secure from rodents. In it was meat from a quick fall hunt behind his claim, what was left of a big cow elk who'd fallen from a snap shot of his Sharps rifle.

The small bunch, led by the cow, had come down the ridge and jumped the creek right by Hite as he was working. Ben had grabbed his ever-ready rifle and followed them up as they buck-jumped up the steep other side. Cocking his gun, he'd given a sharp whistle and they'd stopped just long enough for a shot. Shot in the heart, the big bullet had rolled the elk almost to his feet. The rest hightailed it before he could reload. Hite had hung the quarters high and covered them with canvas against the camp robbers, both birds and men.

* * *

Now, the big backstrap was one of the pieces left, Ben having saved it for a special occasion. He took it out and worked it up, along with spuds that had come the whole long way from the Mormon gardens in Salt Lake. A feast was what they needed now, for the next day would be torture for the children. The food would help take their minds off their hurts.

He wasn't too worried about the older kids, just the baby. Toes and fingers were mere appendages. You had ten of each. But you only had two hands and two feet. The big pan was cooking, giving off some great odors. The coffee pot was starting to perk with beans he'd ground yesterday. On the floor, he saw some stirring among the blankets. The moans and cries got louder, waking the baby, which started crying. On the bunk, Moira raised up a sleepy head, then seeing Hite at the stove, jumped out and came to help. At the door, scratching was heard and Ben said,

"Let yer old dawg in, Gurl, and then git the kids to the table fer a good feed. Don't hev any milk so coffee'll have to do. It's hot an' ready, so come and git it."

The dog in, they came limping to the table, the baby still on the floor, wailing. Hite dished up, grabbed a slurp of coffee from his cup, then went to the baby. Almost, he hated to see its condition. He looked, though, and was heartened by what he saw. The hands seemed better, white except at the tips of the fingers of the left hand. The feet—well, the left one was turning a shade of cream and red, showing some circulation return. The right still looked bad, though maybe not so blue.

He'd give it some more time, using the coal oil bath. It was all he could think to do. He gave it a soupy rag to suck on and it took hold greedily. Encouraged, he dipped some of the softer portions of the bread that was left into the pan and breaking it in small pieces, fed it sparingly. The baby needed milk but where the hell could he come up with that? As far as he knew, there wasn't a milk cow in five hundred miles. Maybe at the mission at

Saint Ignatious, but that did them no good here, with mountain ranges in between and winter a deadly curtain over all.

But wait—what about the Indians? Hite knew there was a Bannack band down the valley, a few miles on the Jefferson, there on a flat about where the Big Hole ran into it. It was a good winter spot because there were lots of deer wintering in the willows along both rivers. They were supposedly peaceable. The squaws would be used to raising their young ones under primitive conditions. He'd have to bundle the baby up and take it to them. And they would want something in return for their help. What could he offer them? It would have to be something the braves would want and it was against miners' law and whatever law existed in the territory to trade arms or ammunition to an Indian, though some did, he knew. He looked around the cabin.

On the wall above the stove there was a peg on which resided a big .44 Colt Dragoon. The heavy pistol was a war trophy he'd brought all the way with him from Shiloh. Now he turned and took it down from its perch along with a horn of powder and a pouch of bullets for it. He tucked them into a large leather bag along with some jerked meat and another shirt, his last clean one, for a last diaper. Then, to wrap the baby, he took down his fall coat, a blanket coat he'd never liked much anyway, grimy and worn. He tied the sleeves together, then folded up the bottom into a bag and tied the sides. Then he deposited the baby inside. He took another gulp of coffee. This would have to be fast. He couldn't leave the rest of them too long. He believed that he was being watched off and on and his going would alert them to a deserted cabin. At the least, he could expect it to be ransacked when he returned, if he gave them enough time to get organized.

"Listen, Gurl, I'm goin' to take Katy here down valley to the Indians. They'll take keer of her, I believe. They'll know better'n me how to do it. I think though, that some bad men may try to break in. That means you kids may have to fight. Now, I'm going to charge up this old shotgun fer ye. The ten gauge might discourage 'em some—that and my pistol here." He handed her his .36 Colt Navy and then had to show her how to cock and fire it. He then did likewise with the shotgun.

"Now, don't play with the guns and fer the Lord's sake don't point 'em at each other! Guns kin kill ye. I'll be back soon's I kin. Along towards dark, fer sure."

With that, he bundled the baby, still crying, and taking up his rifle, lifted the bar and went out the door.

"Put the bar back down and don't open it fer anyone but me!"

He set a fast pace, hurrying along through the snow as the sun rose over the peaks and reddened the far slopes. In the folds of the coat and tucked in, the baby gurgled and moaned, occasionally letting out a squall. The noise only served to make him keep his speed up headlong down the valley. Now he wished that he still had Flint.

1859 Sharps carbine

Chapter 3

Mid-morning found him outside an encampment by the river. He counted fourteen tipis in two irregular circles, one within another, smoke trailing up from each of them. A horse herd was scattered amongst the willows on the south, half hidden by the mist rising from the river. Dogs had alerted the camp when he was about a half mile out. Eyes watched him come. Several blanket wrapped braves waited for him, their rifles prominent in their arms. A few yards away, Hite stopped and raised a hand in greeting. As he did so, the baby let out a wail. Hite pointed to the burden he was carrying and said,

"I come in peace hoping you might help me with the little one here."

At that, an older brave stepped up to him, grounding his long old Infantry rifle and raising his own hand, he spoke in a deep rasping voice, his English hesitant. "Greetings, white man who digs in the ground, we know you. You have a camp up Big Elk Creek. You have no squaw. How did you get a papoose? Did you dig it out from Earth Mother?"

This sarcastic remark was translated for the others and it generated some chuckles which if nothing else, eased the tension. Hite slipped the coat from the baby's head.

"I found a bunch of kids in the snow who lost their mother and father from a white man's sickness. The others have given up some fingers and toes to the frost demon. This papoose's feet were bad frozen and I, who knows too little about helping it, come to you for help."

The old brave stepped up and pushed the blanket coat aside. He lifted a tiny leg and the baby turned up its cries.

"Hahh! We go to my lodge. My woman, Little Owl, has some skill with medicine."

He turned and Ben trudged along behind him, the others trailing them. At a lodge decorated with mounted warriors chasing recognizable buffalo all around it, he unfastened the round leather door and stepped inside, beckoning Hite to follow. He did and the smell hit him: a combination of wood smoke, unwashed bodies, sage and cooking stew in a large iron pot hanging over a small fire. An old squaw was stirring the concoction and looked up at their entrance.

The brave turned and announced, striking his chest,

"Me Hish-e-waya, Lame Wolf." Abruptly, he gave a creditable imitation of his totem animal, startling Hite and making the baby cry harder. Then he spat a stream of Indian talk at his woman, who got up and ambled over to the squalling baby. She took it from Hite's arm and sat down by the fire to see it better. She grunted and made a face, evidently objecting to its smell, and rummaging in a pack at the back of the lodge, came up with some dry moss, which she used to clean the baby's bottom. Another pack, and she took up a handful of sage leaves to wipe it. Then a close inspection of the feet ensued, after which she stuck first one foot in her mouth, then after a few moments, the other. The baby's cries abated. She did the same with the hands as Hite watched, absorbed in her matter-of-fact expertise. Then she got up and tucking the baby in the folds of her dress, left the tipi.

Meanwhile, Lame Wolf sat down in a lean-to chair by the fire, evidently his favored place, and gestured to Ben to be seated on his right. A scratching was heard on the door and the brave yelled something, evidently an invitation, because some of the same Indians who had seen him arrive, entered and coming to the fire, seated themselves. Lame Wolf looked around and came up with a pipe, which he stoked from a pouch, then lighted.

16

Taking some puffs, he raised it to the different directions of the earth, then passed it to Hite, who did the same, then seeing he was expected to, passed it on. It went the rounds and back to the old Indian, who sucked it and blew smoke until the small bowl was gone.

Then he set it back and said, "The white man has a name?"

"I'm called Hite, Ben Hite."

"Hite. A small name for a big man. The papoose is not yours, yet you have tried to keep it alive, Hite."

"Yes. And I know now that your woman can do a better job of that than I can."

Lame Wolf nodded his head. "Women know those things. Woman things, not man things."

"You are a wise man."

"A man needs a woman. You need a woman to care for the papoose—and the other papooses."

"I hoped to have your women teach me what to do."

"A man who digs the ground all day can't do woman's work also. You need a woman. I have a woman I will trade you. She's still in milk and the baby can feed with hers. Also, she will care for your other papooses. It is good you came here to us, Hite. Better for all of us, Hite."

"Wal now. . . " In his mind all along had been the idea of leaving the baby with the band to take care of, maybe for the winter. *But the old Indian was right about all the work the kids would make. Maybe he did need a woman to take care of the baby, the cabin and do some of the chores.*

"How much for this woman? Is she a good worker?"

"Three horses. Yes, a good worker, if you beat her."

"I don't have any horses. I am a poor man. No horses."

It was true. It hurt him to be afoot, but horses were a liability that took too much care and time away from mining to be worthwhile.

"What do you have then, to trade?"

Hite pulled the pistol from his bag and handed it over.

Lame Wolf hefted it and said something in Indian to the others, who evidently agreed. There was head nodding and Hite heard, "Waugh! Waugh!." The old brave passed it around and each Indian fondled it, evidently wanting it. Then it returned to Lame Wolf, who dropped it in his lap, still keeping a grip on it.

"A gun is no good without powder or bullets."

Hite was feeling easier in the smoky tipi and grinned, "Powder and bullets might be had, if the woman is a good one. A hard worker ."

"She is Gros Ventre. We got her in a raid this summer. Her man was killed and she cut a finger off from each hand in her grief and we had to beat her often to make her do her work. Little Owl and the other women taught her to work hard. I will trade her to you for the gun, but for her child, you will give me the powder and bullets. A good trade."

"Let me see this woman."

Lame Wolf got up and went to the door, called out in Bannack and presently his wife came back, with another woman in tow, a young squaw carrying a papoose on her back and still suckling the infant Hite had brought. Hite saw that she was tall, taller even than the braves by the fire. His eyes were drawn to her hands and sure enough, she had fingers missing from each of them, the ring finger of her left and the little finger on her right. The hands still looked damn sore. Her black eyes flashed in the fire's light and Hite got an impression of defiance in them, quickly suppressed. He stroked his beard in thought. Likely she would be gone for home the first night away from the Bannack camp. He'd have to see about that. The baby needed her milk and he could damn sure use her help. "What is this squaw's name?"

"She is called "Sic-coo-lum—Buffalo Guts.""

Hite brought forth the powder horn and the bullet pouch and handed them over. Lame Wolf received them with satisfaction, then barked some Indian at Siccoolum, who merely looked bored. To seal the bargain, he brought his pipe out again, and this time, Hite stuck his hand in his bag and came out with a small bag of tobacco, all he had in the cabin.

"For you and your braves, Lame Wolf."

"White man's tobacco!"

It made a hit with the men and the atmosphere grew congenial. Hite smoked, then thinking of the cabin he'd left, explained his hurry. The men agreed he needed to take the trail for home. Lame Wolf barked at Siccoolum and she rolled a robe with a few things from the packs that Lame Wolf's woman gave her, then slung it on her back beside her infant. She was ready.

* * *

They made good time on the return trail, Hite taking the baby and offering to carry her heavy robe, too, but getting a shake of the head. He set a fast pace but she had a stride that matched his and had no trouble keeping up with him. A half mile from the cabin, he heard the hollow boom of the big ten gauge, handed off the baby to her and began a hard run, cussing himself because he'd taken too much time at the Indian camp.

A turn of the creek and a slight rise of the hill brought him in sight of the cabin. A man was on the roof and Hite saw at a glance that he was stuffing the stove pipe with something to smoke out the kids, who were evidently still inside. Another man was down by the window, two others standing over him, and even from where Hite had stopped, he could hear their angry shouting. He took several deep breaths, judged the distance at three hundred plus yards and raised his sight to match it, then knelt in the snow. The man on the roof was an easy target and he touched off as the barrel came steady in his hands. The big rifle boomed out and the smoke fanned away from Hite's front. The figure doubled up at the shot, then rolled off into the snow at the back, his limp form telling Hite he was dead.

Those in front whirled around and one raised a pistol and fired in his direction, the bullet whizzing over his head. Hite dropped the breechblock and calmly stuck in another paper shell, pulled the lever closed, then sighted again. The rifle blasted and the shooter toppled into the snow. The other one ran for the trees. Hite let him go. Behind him, the woman came up, which surprised Ben. He had thought she might take cover when the bullet whipped by them, or maybe choose freedom for herself. He'd thought he might have to run her down. But here she was, and she followed him as he went forward, the rifle ready in case the one who'd run decided to get brave and come back to shoot it out. Guns being fired off evidently didn't upset her too much.

At the cabin, he checked the man he'd downed there. He was dead, a bearded gent Hite didn't recognize. Ben had to yell several times before Moira opened the door. He was delighted to see she had the shotgun ready, though her eyes were wide and red from the smoke. The dog, Maxxus, was right by her side, alert and growling. Inside, the smoke hung heavy, though some of it exited from the window that Moira had blown out with the ten gauge.

He went out and around the back, where the snow was piled high enough to get on the roof, as the dead man had. He was lying sprawled in a heap and Hite barely spared a glance at him as he scrambled up and removed the coat that was draped over the chimney. Getting back down, he turned the body over and saw it was Jack Gibbons, a loafer from the camp that always seemed to have enough money to stay drunk much of the time. Hite had refused him a job two months before. The bullet had taken him high in the chest and blown a hole out his back that had taken some of the lung with it, the blood staining the snow a bright red.

Going to the front again, he saw that the woman, Siccoolum, had waited outside the door, both babies still in her arms. Ben went in and with Moira's help, they worked to clear the cabin. The girl and boy were coughing and Hite was going to get them out into the fresh air but then remembered the dead men. He went out and grabbing both by the collar, pulled them over the snow into the trees a ways. The action had been quick enough that he hadn't had the time to think of the consequences of the shootings but reviewing it, he didn't know what else he could have done.

"They was trying to break in an' shot at me an' all I did was defend me and mine."

* * *

That thought settled his mind and he went back in and shooed the kids out to take a breather while they finished freeing the cabin of the smoke, and then he hung a piece of elk hide over the window. Once that was done, he got everyone back in and acquainted the children with Siccoolum. She stood there silently while they took her measure. Hite noticed that the two little ones seemed more interested in asking Moira about the "bad men" and where they had gone, than the tall Indian woman. Their sister replied,

"Mr. Hite shot at 'em and they're gone."

Ben knew, though, that she had seen the dead ones in front and had decided to spare them the details.

The cabin interior was crowded, though perhaps no more so than an Indian tipi, Hite thought. "Hyar, Siccoolum, spread yer robes over there by the wall and we'll have sump'thin to eat."

Getting the last of the elk out of the cooler, he stoked the stove and made sure it was drawing, then slapped the pan with some bacon grease, laid in as much meat as it could take and set some coffee on. That pan went quick, Siccoolum gulping hers like Maxxus did, and he refilled it and fried up the last batch for them. Working quick, he got the fixings from the cooler and using a large portion of his flour, made up four large loaves of sourdough bread and left them to raise by the stove's heat.

Seeing Maxxus eyeing them, he put down some scrapings that were left and the dog gulped them down. Then he sat down himself and took on some hot coffee. He wasn't really hungry, just had a coffee craving and while he satisfied that, he thought of what he should do next.

Three men were lying dead out there in the snow and he could imagine what the survivor was saying by now in the camp. It was likely he'd be facing a lynch mob soon. Better to go in and face the music. The Miners Committee was made up of good men and he thought he might have their regard for what had gone on last summer. They'd at least listen to him, maybe even believe him.

Image courtesy of Bob Cherry

Chapter 4

He'd arrived at the mining camp the year before like many others, too late for the best claims to be had. Camped up off the creek, whose stream bed was filled with frantically working men, he had let his three horses recover from the headlong rush to get over the mountains and give himself some time to see just what opportunities might be available.

Every camp had a place that functioned as a message center and place for advertising. This one's board was on the wall outside the Miner's Saloon, a log edifice that also boasted a dance floor. Hite found it and perused it intently. Lige Randall, the Miner's Committee chairman, was advertising there for a post rider to take mail to the other camps at a rate of 15 cents a mile. The mileage for each of the camps was listed and Ben, reading it, decided that it might be something to try for a time, maybe through the fall, anyway, to make a stake.

His wallet was thin and he had the horses so he looked up Randall, who'd asked him some pointed questions.

"Ben Hite. Any kin to the Hite clan in Missouri?"

"Yes. They's kin o' mine but I don't claim 'em. I fought fer the Blue. Berdan's Regiment." He grinned.

"Guess they don't claim me neither."

Randall smiled. The war was just over but the scars remained. As it happened, the Miners Committee was composed of Union men, most of them men who'd served under General Sheridan and his answer had been the right one. Outwardly, there was no overt discrimination against Confederates but it was there, just the same, and there was constant friction between the two parties.

After he had been approved by the Committee, he had begun making a weekly trip to Bannack, Nevada City, Virginia City, Silver Star, Jefferson City and back to Sheridan. The circle took him two and a half days and he made twenty some dollars each time. Then, he would let his horses rest for the rest of the week. He was punctual and his reliability soon had all the camps using his services to send other things back and forth, finally causing him to use his second pack horse on the trip.

In July, Randall had come to him and asked him to carry some secret dispatches from the camp's Committee to the other camp committees.

"We don't want <u>certain</u> parties to know our business, Hite, so guard the letters close."

Ben knew the dispatches had to do with future gold shipments out of the territory, a concern of every miner and information that thieves would be glad to get their hands on.

"I'll take 'em, but if ye expect me to fight fer 'em, it's goin' to cost ye extra every time."

Randall agreed that the Committee would pay another 15 cents a mile whenever he carried messages for them.

* * *

That month he had no trouble, but the second week in August he was riding up to a ford he used on the Madison River and three men stepped from the willows to confront him. He didn't wait to see their intentions, just hauled back on his pack horses and kicking Flint, his saddle horse, into a run, got the hell away. Shots were fired after him and since he had not seen any rifles, he pulled up a couple hundred yards away and unlimbered his Sharps. His first shot had downed one of the men and the others had dived into the brush, where they returned fire, the bullets skipping around him.

Ben had turned and making a long circle, had gone back to his route. That month two more attempts to take him were made, each time when he was carrying messages from the Committee, which had made both he and the Committee suspicious. He'd shot his way clear each time. The attackers had grown wary of his skill with a rifle and tried some other tricks, trying to sneak up on his camp in the dark once, and again shooting from above him on a ridge as he trotted down the valley in the open. That was close, as he felt the whisper of the bullet by his head. He ran his horses until he was out of range and out of sight, then picketed the horses and circled back to set up an ambush himself. He was mad clear through at his narrow escape, getting damn tired of their antics and determined to make them pay.

He watched and waited patiently and after a time, two men came riding along on his trail. He had a good rest over a rock and when they came in range, took his shot. The lead man flipped backward off his horse, causing it to start into a run, dragging his rider by a stirrup. The other man was undecided as to his course of action: should he fight, charge after his partner and try to rescue him from being dragged over the rocky country, or should he instead try to run away and save himself?

While he was working all this out, Ben had reloaded and taking dead aim, shot him out of his saddle. Walking up to him, his horse grazing peacefully by the body, Ben turned him over and was glad he didn't recognize him. Going through his pockets, he found $200 in gold eagles and some change. He carefully replaced it. He caught the horse and with difficulty, loaded the corpse on and tied it securely. He looked for and found the rifle the man had been carrying: a beat-up Sharps carbine. That went in a scabbard on the saddle. Then he put a big rock on the reins to anchor the animal.

Following up the other, he caught the skittery animal after some difficulty and got the dead man untangled from the stirrup. Looking at him, it was impossible to say whether he knew him. The head was too battered from being hammered on the rocks. Like the other, though, the corpse had $200 in gold in his pockets. He loaded it up and proceeded on his way.

The procession caused a stir on the street at Bannack when he arrived. A man stepped out from the crowd standing in front of the Crystal Saloon and waited for him to come up. Ben saw it was Ike Corley, a deputy sheriff he'd seen around the camps. The man seemed pretty proud of his badge and Ben had made a point of staying away from him when he could. Corley thought he was a man of humor.

"Howdy there, Ben. Who's that follering ye? "

"Don't reckon I know either one of 'em. They tried to kill me over by Beaver Crick and I got 'em, instead."

He dismounted and untied the reins of the dead men's horses. Handing them over, he said, "Likely they was after the mail. Strange, though, there ain't no money in it."

The deputy averted his eyes.

"Yeah? Didn't hev some grudge against ye, did they?"

"Don't believe so."

Men came up and helped Corley get the men to the ground and Ben remounted and made his way to the Assayer's office, where he turned over his mail and the dispatches from the Committee. Then he saw to his horses and later made his way to the Crystal. There, he saw Corley engaged in conversation with a group of men. Seeing Ben come in, he separated from them and came to where Hite was just seating himself. The Crystal functioned as a restaurant, too, and Ben usually ate his supper there on his way through. At five dollars a night, it was too expensive for him to stay at the Gauge Hotel, so he took his horses and slept out on the trail after his meal. The waiter brought him his usual coffee and he ordered while Corley fidgeted.

"Well, you want ta know who it was ye killed? John Lester and Joseph Blackburn. One of the Virginia City boys knew 'em. He says they was workin' over there as carpenters for Jay Gilbert. Don't know what a couple hammer heads would be doing, setting up to be road pirates. I'll have to send over to Sheriff Plummer and have him talk to ye about it. Guess you can carry the letter?"

"Fine by me. I'm leavin' in an hour or so."

"Ye'll have to wait until I git it writ."

"All right. I never searched 'em, Ike. Did they have anything on 'em? Money or such?"

Corley turned away. "Nope. Pockets just had a little change in 'em. One had a cheap watch."

Hite knew he was lying but decided to let it go. Later, though, when he mentioned the money to Lige Randall, Randall had warned him to keep that to himself. When Plummer had come from Virginia City to talk to him about the ambush, he'd not told him about the $400 in gold. Plummer was mystified as to why he was being targeted for ambush and wanted Hite to elaborate on the subject but Ben said he didn't have a notion why, refusing to mention that he thought they might be after the Committee's dispatches.

* * *

He'd carried Randall's warning with him in his mind on another trip then made the decision, when he'd heard that the two Wisconsin Creek claims were for sale, to go into the mining game. He'd traded two of his horses and six hundred dollars for the claims, keeping Flint, his grulla saddle horse. Later, though he hated to do it, he'd sold the horse for more than enough to get his cabin built and buy the stove. He'd put the ad on the message board for a two week auction and Plummer had been high bidder. He'd joked about the horse 'being faster than a bullet—just the kind he needed.' Hite wondered later if he maybe had a premonition.

* * *

He worked his two claims and like he'd figured, the gold was there. A ten foot sluice box cost him $20 and he made it back in one day, even though he was a novice at its use. He kept at it, even when Randall came and offered him double pay to resume his mail route. He felt the job would only lead to his death. It wasn't worth it and that idea was vindicated when Jude Nelson, who'd taken over, was ambushed at Point of Rocks and killed in October. His death and the loss of his mail and dispatches resulted in two gold shipments out of the gold country being intercepted by masked robbers. Now men were being killed almost weekly and unless a miner joined a strong party who was alert and ready for action, it was foolhardy to try to get through the web of thieves watching all the time. Who were they? Evidently, Randall and the Miners Committee had a pretty good idea but they were being close mouthed so far.

Point of Rocks stage station, built 1862

Chapter 5

Hite pondered his move while he watched Siccoolum caring for the babies. Her little one was maybe a month older than Katy, a chunky little warrior whose round face peered from out of a peculiar kind of laced cradle board that she typically carried on her back. Right now she was feeding them both, the two suckling greedily, the other kids watching her curiously. She seemed oblivious to their attention. He drank his second cup and got up.

"Moira, we got trouble yet, with those men dead out there. I got to go in to town and get together with the Miners Committee, tell them just what happened here. The one who run is likely there right now tellin' lies about it. If I wait an' they come out here, it could be bad."

"You have to? You goin' to leave us with an Indian?"

"I got to. She won't hurt ye. Here's the shotgun. I loaded it again. Keep it handy, along with my pistol, like before."

She heaved a sigh. "All right, I guess. Hurry back, will you, Mr. Hite?" She looked at him. "Quick!"

He nodded and went to stand over Siccoolum.

"I got to go into town. You—he pointed at her—stay here with the kids." She merely looked at him and he was uncertain as to whether he had gotten through to her. Taking up his rifle, he went out.

He made good time and entered the little community just at dusk. Encountering a man he knew hurrying along, he asked, "Seen Lige Randall?"

"They's all over at the Miner's Saloon." He looked at Hite and said, "Talkin' about you, Ben. Did you really shoot those men down in cold blood?"

'You know me better'n that, Buck. They was tryin' to break in my cabin and rob me. When I come up, they started shootin'. I shot back."

Buck peered nearsightedly at Ben's rifle, nestled in the crook of his arm. "That woulda been like committin' suicide, Ben. You're deadly with that Sharps. Is it true you was in Berdan's Sharpshooter regiment? They says you was one of their best."

"Wal, this rifle was in a lot of battles—with me behint it. Talk to ye later, Buck."

"Good luck, Ben. Hope ye git 'em all!"

Ben walked on to the Miners Saloon and went up the steps and in. Immediately, he was struck by the smoky, smelly interior. The place reeked of tobacco, cheap whiskey, men who never bathed, and something else: a palpable tension you could cut with a knife. At the bar was a tall figure who cut his tirade short as Hite entered. He looked familiar, was likely the man who'd got away. He faced Ben defiantly, then pointed at him.

"That there's the man, boys, who killed Pete, Reese, and my brother, Tom! Gunned 'em down when all we was tryin' to do was git some help with our rocker up the crick."

All the eyes turned to Ben Hite. He set his rifle butt down on the floor and looked leisurely around the big room. To an onlooker, he seemed cool and collected.

"And just how did I do that, Mister?''

"Shot the poor boys down with that there Sharps! Yeah! That one! A goddam cannon. If I hadn'a run, he'da got me, too!"

"Shot 'em all, did I?" Ben grinned. "Seem's you fergot the first one—the one the little Gurl killed with my ten gauge 'cause he was breakin' in the winder. Blew his head near off. Easy to tell just what kilt him! An' it sure wasn't my Sharps." He turned and addressed the room.

"What they bin doin' was spying on me. They saw me leave an' was tryin' to break in and steal my poke.

Didn't know I left some guards in there—a dog an' a bunch of kids."

At the mention of gold, and an attempted break-in, the atmosphere changed. All knew that there was a faction in the camp involved in robbery and murder of miners for their gold. Some right there in the room had been victims.

Now Randall came forward. "All right, men. I'm callin' a meeting of the Committee right now. Southby, you and Ward hold this man, Hamden, you said your name was. Paige, you, Healy and McPhee go on out to Hite's and bring in those dead men. Look around some, too. Better all take lanterns." He looked at Hite, who said,

"Go ahead out there. You'll find one dead man behind the cabin. He was trying to smoke the kids out. Shot him off the roof. You can see how he slid off. The others I pulled into the trees to keep the kids from seein' 'em. You kin see all that, too." He smiled and looked for a chair.

"Be a mite careful about tryin' to get in the cabin, though. The Gurl is in there with the ten gauge and a big ole Pit Bull dog a' theirs. He's mighty protective of those kids an' I am, too. I don't want 'em bothered. You want me to, I can come along an' you can talk to 'em."

Randall considered, then said, "No, Ben. You better stay." He turned to the men as they were about to leave. "Now, you heard Ben. Leave the cabin alone for now."

Ben took his ease with a beer offered him and the room's noise level picked up, with men at the bar and the card games resuming.

An hour later, the men returned, dragging the dead bodies right into the bar, leaving a slimy blood trail, to the objections of Ancelle Atkins, the owner.

"Now, goddam it! Someone's gotta clean all that mess up!"

Randall took charge again. "Be still, Ancelle. We'll see it's cleaned for you. Now, let's see those wounds."

Everyone in the room crowded around the bodies, with the exception of Ben, who'd already seen them and had no curiosity.

Paige pointed, "Sure as hell, Lige, that one there was lying back of the cabin, just as Ben said. You could see where he slid on off it, spouting' blood as he came. Right through the heart with that .52 caliber. His smoky coat was still layin' there, all sooty from him tryin' to stop up the chimney. Now, this one here, his head is near off. Ten gauge for sure, right in the face. There's still some glass from the winder bottles stuck in his head. Third one here is Hite's again, another dead center shot." He turned to Ben. "Good shootin', Ben!"

Ben nodded his head graciously. "Were the kids all right?"

"Heard 'em stirrin' in there and told 'em what we was up to." Paige chuckled. "Didn't want that lil' Gurl bustin' me with that big shotgun." The bar crowd laughed.

* * *

The Committee meeting convened swiftly and the verdict was justifiable self-defense. Hite was escorted to the bar and urged to quaff several congratulatory drinks, which he did, ordering beer. Then someone saw Hamden trying to sneak out the door while his guards were bellying up to the bar. He was mobbed and hammered to the floor by some exuberant miners, then held up bleeding and half-conscious.

"Hey, boys, what should we do this sonofabitch?"

"String 'im up! Give 'im a necktie party!"

A rope was called for but Randall held up his hands. "No, boys. We'll blacksnake 'im and run him out of the territory. We don't want to be judged as killers."

The idea didn't meet with universal approval, especially with those who advocated the rope. However, the Committee prevailed and the others gave in graciously, as a whipping was good entertainment, too. Hamden was stripped near naked and hanging by his tied wrists from a rafter right there in the bar, was given thirty

34

six lashes by one of the freighters in the crowd, who laid it on, raising welts and leaving bloody stripes. Then he was rolled out in the snow and booted on down the road. Later, some travelers found his frozen corpse less than a mile from the saloon. Hite bought a round, then left as soon as he could get away, pleading the kids needing him.

Chapter 6

The kids were ecstatic to see him return unharmed. Moira opened the door right away and began chattering as soon as he appeared. He grinned. Even the dog seemed glad to see him, wagging his tail. And he saw Siccoolum sitting on her robe, feeding the babies again, a cocked pistol in her hand.

"We heard something going on out there, Mr. Hite, then some men yelled to us, askin' us what happened. They said they was friends of yours. I talked to them but I did what you said, I never opened the door. We was scared but she—Moira pointed to Siccoolum—she made us sit down. She took the pistol up and shushed us so she could hear what they was up to. They tramped around the cabin some, then took off. Will they be back?"

Hite turned to Siccoolum and cautiously, oh, so cautiously, took the cocked pistol from her yielding hand. He put the hammer back down and set it on the table. A look passed between them. Ben turned to Moira.

"No, Gurl, ever'thing's fine. They believed me when I told 'em what happened. I brought back some more grub. Open the cooler fer me."

He deposited his purchases, made when they were waiting for Paige's crew to return. Now their supplies should hold them for another week or so. He wondered if he could get some hunting done, maybe get another elk. Even a deer or two would be a help. Growing kids needed food. Meantime, he needed to do some serious scouting. He wanted to see if he could spot the watchers, and if so, follow them up and get a handle on who was involved in all the thievery going on. For the meantime, he sipped on a fresh cup of Arbuckles and cleaned the guns.

* * *

Two days later

Baby Katy was much better. She would perhaps lose a toe, maybe even two or three, but not her feet or her hands. Putting them in the mouth and sucking them gently to get the circulation going again was doing the trick, it seemed. Privately, Hite wondered if the same method wouldn't have spared the other kids from losing theirs, but they seemed to be healing fine and with Siccoolum's missing fingers, the whole mutilated bunch seemed to mesh together and become almost a family. Moira was a great help with the babies and the cooking. Siccoolum insisted on coming out and helping him gather wood and water. The dog followed them and kept watch.

* * *

The weather warmed and spring, it seemed, was just around the corner. Soon, with the creek open, Ben would be mining again. He wasn't looking forward to it. Towards the last of the open water last fall, it seemed the gold was diminishing. Creek mining was an iffy thing, with pockets here and there and the gold in streaks along the bottom. Maybe it was time to sell out and either find some other claims or go do something else. He had a yen to go on the road again and was thinking hard about freighting. He liked being around horses and going places, not stuck wading in freezing water all day. Death by pneumonia was common in the camps.

He considered the approximate cost of an outfit which would get him started. It wouldn't do to buy around the gold camps. Wagons and harness were too pricey. And horses were too high, especially big freight horses, which had been mostly eaten in the last months of winter. They just couldn't exist like the Indian horses did, chewing bark and eating willows. They needed to be grained and fed hay. He thought of the Bannack herd. His discerning eye, even as distracted as he was at the time,

37

had noticed some good looking animals in the big bunch. There were a few there which would make light draft horses, capable of pulling a wagon if it wasn't loaded too heavy.

Or he could pull out of the country. He had the gut feeling he was a marked man here. He'd killed too many, and if they really were organized, as he knew Randall and the Committee felt they were, he was nothing more than a target they would eventually strike. The thought of the kids being orphans again made him gloomy. The mood carried him into town the next day to post an ad on the board.

FOR SALE
2 producing claims
Located on Wisconsin Ck.
$1000 each
Cabin with good stove included
Ben Hite

* * *

Moira had helped him write it and correct his spelling. Their father, she said, had been an educated man. The next day, the cabin had several visitors, among them Lige Randall and a member of the Committee. Hite took them in and made them acquainted with the kids and Siccoolum, who looked at them from her robe, her dress down unconcernedly as she fed the two babies. Both men gawked at her, embarrassing Ben. Since the cabin was so crowded, he seated them outside on a log bench and Moira brought them coffee from the big pot.

"Things getting too hot fer you, Ben?"

Randall looked at him over his cup. Hite gathered he was referring to his putting his claims up for sale. He nodded matter-of-factly.

"No sense denyin' it. They've got me in their sights and I'm a dead man sooner or late. It could have happened yesterday easy as not."

"Maybe not, if you hang in here. The camp Committees are getting set to move. We want you with us when we do. That rifle of yours would come in mighty handy." Moira came out and refilled their cups.

"Don't you think I killed enough of 'em fer ye, already?"

"There's a sight more that need it. Startin' with—." Eli Giles began excitedly. His arm was jogged by Randall, who gave him a warning look. "Let's make sure of our suspicions before we start throwing out names, Eli."

They sipped their coffee and watched the two younger kids pitching snowballs at each other, the dog joining in. The day was warm and the sky a bright blue. Snow fell in the trees and it seemed the creek was starting to flow some water. Randall pulled a small flask from his coat pocket and poured a dollop in each of their cups. Ben, never a drinker, let him, though he liked his coffee strong and pure.

"Nice lookin' dog—Pit Bull. Looks like he's been fought some. Wonder how the kids came by him." Randall commented. By now, they knew the general story of the orphans and Siccoolum.

"Moira tells me that their father got him from a man for a debt he owed him. Said he'd never been beaten in the pit. Gettin' a few years on 'im, now, though. Reckon he's earned the right to a good old age. He saved the kids by taking care of them when their folks died."

"Reminds me of my old dog, Shep. He was a great stock dog, could put a flock of sheep in a pen quicker'n you could blink an eye." Giles reminisced. The one eyed old timer, like Randall, was a Union man out of the same regiment, the 10th Wisconsin, and had been one of the first rushers who made the strike just up the creek from where they sat. One reason so many Union men had congregated there was because the men involved had pledged themselves to secrecy until word had gotten back to their Union compatriots. Ben felt he owed them an explanation.

"Wal, I mebbe won't go too far. Bin thinkin' about gettin' into freightin'. Sellin' the claims should give me enough to get an outfit together. This mornin', just before you and Eli showed up, had a couple men offer me a pretty good deal—eighteen hundred dollars fer the claims along with a big wagon and tack they had. No horses. They're down on the crick right now, lookin' at the color." He chuckled. "Hev to take an ax and chop a hole in the ice to find any."

Randall, who owned the mercantile, chuckled likewise.

"Yes, once the gold fever bites, the poor wretches will spend their health, their all, to follow their dream of El Dorado."

He was an educated man who'd attended Yale and had a literary background he liked to plumb at times. Their backgrounds were dissimilar but Hite liked him in spite of it.

* * *

Ben had come off a backwoods farm in northern Missouri and spent his early years hunting, caring for stock and farming. HIs family had an unsavory reputation, with many renegades and cutthroats in their family tree. Some were slave owners. When war had threatened, the family had to a man gone for the South. His four brothers had ended up in Quantrill's infamous band of cutthroats who had and still were, terrorizing Missouri.

The lone exception was Ben. Serious, God fearing and deep thinking, though largely illiterate, he had searched his conscience deeply and reluctantly. Knowing it would cost him the love and regard of his family, he had wrapped up his meager belongings in a threadbare blanket, left in the night as he heard his mother sobbing and made the long hike to St. Louis. There he had found a Union recruiter working the streets and he had enlisted in Grant's Army of the West, which was preparing to move down the river.

* * *

Within three months, he had participated in three battles: Fort Henry, Fort Donelson and bloody Shiloh. He had made an almost instant transformation from a callow youth to a combat hardened veteran. After Shiloh, he had heard of Colonel Berdan's call for outstanding riflemen to assemble a sharpshooter regiment. Having made some notable shots during the battles he'd participated in, and being recommended by his colonel, he'd tried out and beaten the other candidates in a hotly contested shooting match that was watched by most of the Western army. The top twenty men of Grant's army were sent east to Colonel Berdan.

* * *

Berdan had been made a colonel of volunteers when he'd managed to interest the Secretary of War in his scheme to raise two regiments of excellent marksmen to use as snipers and skirmishers. These men would be the eyes and ears of the Union armies, advancing out ahead and scouting the enemy. For putting themselves square in the sights of the enemy, they received no extra pay, no extra privileges or benefits, just better equipment and some extra ammunition. And the respect and admiration of the Union Armies.

* * *

Berdan had been the top shot in the country for over fifteen years before the war, taking on all comers in highly publicized shoots and so his fame was considerable and his ideas on the subject carried considerable weight. He wanted to combine the best rifleman with the most accurate and reliable weapon of the time and his past experience was that that weapon was the breech loading Sharps rifle. In the frantic beginning of the war, though, with all the Union regiments desperate for armed soldiers, a Sharps with its rifled barrel cost three times that of a smooth barreled Springfield musket. Generals like Winfield Scott, though sympathetic to the idea, opted for quantity and numbers over quality. Never mind the fact that a rifled barrel was three times more accurate, they could field and equip three times more soldiers for the cost. To Berdan's frustration, the arms order was stalled in the Requisitions Department.

It took Lincoln's Presidential decree to bust the money loose to fund the purchase of two thousand Sharps made to Berdan's specifications.These specifications were for a .52 caliber double set trigger breechloader which weighed eight pounds, 12 ounces with a 30 inch barrel length. This shot a 350 grain conical paper patched bullet in front of 64 grains of black powder wrapped in a paper cartridge. The 1859 Sharps, with bayonet and sling, cost $45.00.

The order was finally approved by the penurious Quartermaster but the Sharps factory would need four months to produce them. In the meantime, anxious to get into the fighting, Berdan had promised that if a man passed his test, he would buy the personal rifle he used to pass the test into service at fifty dollars. Most of the men who could shoot well enough to win a place in the regiments used special made target rifles such as the one that Ben Hite had brought from home and later sold, a Fish-made turkey shoot gun that tipped the scales at twenty four pounds. These guns were hand made in a bewildering variety of calibers and weights, some as much as fifty pounds, and had to be carried in a wagon. Ammunition was a constant problem. Added to this was the fact that usually several men used the same weapon to qualify, which meant that, except for the owner, they were unarmed and had to fall back on the hated, much vilified, inaccurate muskets the army gleefully supplied them.

Colonel Berdan had devised a simple test to weed out the best riflemen: keep ten shots in a ten inch ring at 200 yards, any position, then another ten shots in a ten inch ring from a standing position. Seeing the tight groups that Ben shot convinced Berdan quickly that he had a gifted marksman in the young man from Missouri. He was accepted and assigned to Company 'C' of the 2nd Regiment.

* * *

Being from New York, Berdan's call had been answered by his state right away, and so the 1st regiment was chiefly made up of New York recruits and those of the surrounding states: four 75 man companies from New York, three from Michigan, and one each from Vermont, New Hampshire and Wisconsin. The second regiment was more eclectic: two of its companies were from New Hampshire, two from Vermont, and the others a mixed batch from Minnesota, Michigan, Pennsylvania, Maine and all the other states. A few were from as far away as California or other parts of the west.

It was one of these who was to become its most celebrated marksman: Truman Head, the one the men called "California Joe." This man was one of those from that state but where the "Joe" came from, not even he knew. Written up in various tabloids for his notable exploits on the battlefield, he was a deadly shot who could "out-Injun an Injun," according to the many scribes who delighted in scribbling about his exploits, true or not. Certainly, though, there were others, such as Hugh Johnson, Hank Givens, Stephen Flick, Will Kernzy, Ben Hite and "Parson" Barber who, though not as famous or perhaps as colorful, were as deadly and collected as many or more "kills."

* * *

At a time when the world was used to the traditional battlefield tactics and movements of armies such as those formulated at the turn of the century by Napoleon and Wellington, where whole divisions formed squares, marched and counter-marched and volley fired, Berdan emphasized war by the individual, as learned through fighting Indians in the big woods of the east. This was an unprecedented concept to the era's most prominent military minds.

It was Lieutenant Colonel Frederick Mears, Berdan's able subordinate and an old Indian fighter himself, who was tasked with training the regiments in "practical warfare" which meant essentially the men were taught how to load while prone or in just about any position, use cover for concealment, how to judge the wind and distance, always using their ammunition sparingly. He and Berdan dressed the men in green and tans to better aid them in blending in with the backgrounds they fought in and the regiments came to be known in the Northern Army as the "Green coats." One reporter, seeing them in bivouac, likened them to "Robin Hood's merry men."

Maybe they resembled the merry men in costume, but at war's end, after 65 engagements and separate larger battles, including such as Petersburg, Antietam, Chancellorsville, South Mountain, Gettysberg and both sieges of Vicksburg, the death loss was 40% of the men and 50% of the officers, a terrific toll. However, the two regiments, chopped up by companies and scattered throughout the whole theater of operations, as they were, still killed more Rebels than any other two regiments in the Union army. Those who survived to the end of the war were
hardened veterans who'd seen it all. When the end came, the units were disbanded and the men allowed to keep their weapons.

Above: *California Joe in April 1862 with the Sharps rifle that he had privately purchased year earlier. It is thought that the regimental armorer must have refitted his rifle with double-set triggers and a new lever*

"The Army of the Potomac - A Sharp-Shooter On Picket Duty"
A detail of Winslow Homer's painting published in 1862

Chapter 7

Ben's two claim buyers came back from their sojourn at the creek, ebullient because they'd recovered a small nugget and some solid color where they'd been panning.

Over coffee and some lunch, a bowl of stew and some sourdough bread, a deal was concluded and the two handed over eighteen hundred in gold, carefully weighed on Ben's scales after they had checked it with their own scales they had brought along. At Ben's request, Moira wrote them a receipt and a bill of sale. The wagon they would deliver the next day, using a borrowed team. They could stay in the cabin for a week before they would have to move out. Moira was distraught.

"Now where we going to go, Mr. Hite? This cabin is the warmest place we been since last summer."

"We need to leave here before we all git killed, Gurl. An' I got me an idea. I'll need yore help, though."

The next day, the two new owners came out with the big freight wagon pulled with a struggle by a team of gaunt horses. Moira, Siccoolum and Ben made short work of gathering the cabin's contents and stowing them in the wagon. Then, as Ben had already worked out with the men, Frank Harbo and George Clay, they split up, Frank staying with the cabin, George driving the team down the valley to the Bannack camp, with Ben riding the seat holding Katy and the kids and Siccoolum in the back. As before, Lame Wolf and his braves met them and Ben had to show them the hands and feet of the baby, which was getting better by the day. Then he showed off the rest of his crew, including the glowering Siccoolum, who was clearly not happy to be returning to her tormenters. As the Indians gathered about, George unhitched and started off on their back trail at a high lope with the team. Indians gave him the shivers.

As Ben got down, he gave Moira the shotgun and whispered, "Guard the wagon but don't shoot anybody. Just fire in the air if things get touchy. I'll come runnin'."

Behind a smoky cloud back in Lame Wolf's lodge, he made a deal for six horses, his pick, and a small tipi, for a quantity of flour, sugar, and coffee, the rest of his winter's supply. To the band, horses were a flexible commodity, here today, gone tomorrow. More could be stolen, perhaps even the ones they would trade today. The tipi could always be replaced.

The herd was rounded up out of the willows and Ben went through them with a practiced eye. Among them was a pair of grays that he'd noticed and matched up well, ten year olds by their mouths and accepting of the harness he cautiously threw on them. Another pair he was able to match were two bigger sorrels that looked to have some draft horse in them. Those picks were more than favorable to the band, who were used to choosing horses for speed and good looks, not strength and size. However, when he topped the herd with his next picks, looking at last for a couple good saddle horses and choosing a tough looking buckskin and a racy bay, the band's faces turned to scowls. For a while, Ben thought the deal was off, but Lame Wolf prevailed and Ben threw in the very last of his tobacco to seal the horse deal. The smoke-filled tipi became congenial.

* * *

On the trail back to Sheridan behind the grays, which evidently were well broken to harness and pulled the near-empty wagon with a will, Ben looked back and relished the sight of the horses following them, Siccoolum riding the buckskin and leading the others by neck ropes. She rode astride on his saddle, her deerskin skirt hiked up her long legs. Her baby, whose name Ben still had not gotten his tongue around, but which sounded like "Waddawheela" to him, was in its usual spot, on her back out of the way. She seemed happy to be horseback again and headed away from the camp. He saw she was an expert with the horses.

In town, Ben tied off at Randall's Mercantile and told the kids and Siccoolum to "wait thar!" Going in, he bought supplies enough to replenish his traded goods, carrying them out to the wagon. Randall wasn't there and his assistant, Saul Augustine, a one armed vet with a limp, waited on him.

"Seen Lee Selman today?" Ben asked.

"Over at the Crystal, I reckon."

Paying out of a poke made heavier by the recent sale, he loaded all his purchases in, then handed up some candy he'd gotten to the kids looking over the high sides of the wagon. Going to Siccoolum, who stood beside the buckskin, still holding to the ropes of the other horses, he handed her a couple pieces. She looked at them and he took a last piece and stuck it in his mouth, saying, "Eat, eat. You like."

She licked them. Then, her eyes widening with the sweet taste, popped them in her mouth and savored them. He thought it likely she had never tasted sugar or anything sweet before. Most Indians he'd met had a taste for white man's food and drink, though they weren't high on salt or pepper or some of the other spices, preferring their own native herbs.

Going over to the saloon, he stepped in and glimpsed Selman sitting in his usual daily poker game. He got a beer from the bar and walked over. When Selman finished the hand, he asked, 'Say, Lee, you still got that wagon for sale?"

Selman perked up. The cards had not been favorable to him lately.

"Sure have, Hite. You want it?"

"Might take it, if you throw in the harness."

"That'd have to cost you extra. It's near new."

"You said you wanted $75?"

"Yeah, but for a hundred, you can have it and the harness, too."

"Soon's you're done mebbe we could go look at it."

Shortly, the two were standing by a stout freight wagon tarped over and covered with snow. They worked it out and throwing the tarp back, exposed the harness, greased and in excellent shape. The deal was made and Hite walked back to get his outfit. There was a small group surrounding the wagon and as he approached, he heard Moira yell, "Now keep away!"

One of the men said something that Hite didn't catch, but which made the others laugh uproariously. Ben waded through them and swinging up on the wagon, seated himself and shaking out the lines, slapped the team on the rump. They started and the men jumped out of the way.

Siccoolum followed the wagon and one of the men, a burly miner named Saul Williams, reached up and felt of her leg as she passed, saying,

"Hey, boys, Hite found him some prime Red stuff, all right!"

Ben had just turned back to see if the other horses were with them and saw it happen. He stopped the team and jumped back down. For some reason, he was mad clear through. Striding up to Williams, he gave the man a brutal shove and the man staggered. Then as he came back up, a knife in his right hand, Ben saw in his eyes that the encounter had been planned. Williams grinned.

"Pushed the wrong man, Hite! Lester and Blackburn were friends of mine and now you're gonna git carved!"

He leaped at Ben and the knife came streaking towards his stomach as time seemed to slow. Ben had been in many actions over the war years and a number of them had gone finally hand-to-hand. He swatted the arm to the side as he turned and left-handed, drew his own blade from behind him, a trimmed down version of the bayonet favored by the Army of the Potomac. It came in and down and sliced a deep gash across Williams' back, right through the man's coat and heavy shirt. The man howled and swung back with his right arm, his knife searching for Ben. Instead of stepping away, Hite went in, grabbing the wrist with his own right hand and bringing him in as he buried the knife deep in the struggling man's side, then ripped across. Williams sagged and his weapon dropped to the frozen ground. He fell and as he laid there, blood pumping from the torn heart, Ben bent down and calmly wiped his blade clean on the man's clothes. His gaze swept the crowd.

"You men all saw him pull on me first. I'da made it a knuckle dance, if he'da let me. Too bad."

He reached back and replaced the knife in its scabbard. He saw no threat in the rest, only awe at the sudden action and the unlikely outcome. Williams had a reputation as a brawler who was good with a cutter and clearly had done some talking before he'd braced Ben. Glancing up, he saw Siccoolum looking at him. He stooped, and picking up the dead man's blade, handed it up to her. Deep in her dark eyes, he saw a glint. She nodded her dark, braided head.

Moira's eyes were wide. "He was going to kill you, Mr. Hite!"

"He tried, Gurl, but he was clumsy. Sorry you kids seen it."

* * *

At the wagon he'd just bought, he unloaded the harness and beckoning the Indian woman to bring up the sorrels, he fitted them and hitched them up. Then, driving the team back and forth, he showed Moira how to work the lines and the brake. As he'd thought, she had driven before at times on the way out to the gold fields and could handle a team pretty well. The sorrels were a little antsy and he shifted her to drive the grays, who were steady.

"Foller me out, Gurl, and we'll be on our way."

They passed the scene of the incident and the dead man was still lying on the frozen littered street where he'd died. A few men were still standing around, but the majority had gone on their business. He hupped to the team and they headed out of town, Moira and Siccoolum following him.

Image courtesy of Bob Cherry

Chapter 8

A couple miles out there was an open bench that butted up to the river. Ben stopped there for the night and they pulled the two wagons close and spread the tarp across them to make a shelter that would hold in the warmth of the fire Ben started with wood that Siccoolum gathered. Then Moira got the coffee on and a pan heating for the two jack rabbits Ben had shot as they bumped along. Both times, they had nearly had a runway but the horses were not fresh any longer and all had some experience with gunfire. Ben figured it was as good a time as any to get them used to it.

He was gutting one of the rabbits when Siccoolum came up and took it from his hands and finished the job, using the knife he'd given her. Clearly, it was woman's work and she didn't want him doing it. Then, as they settled themselves in, he sitting in his chair he'd brought along, Moira brought him a steaming cup of hot coffee. He was being pampered and he wasn't used to that.

The sun was an hour from setting and he watched as the woman and the girl expertly meshed on the cooking chores. Since it was late winter, no potatoes were to be had but Ben had bought some canned beans and fruit at a high cost and with the breaded rabbit cooked in bacon grease, a good meal was eaten as the sun dipped below the horizon.

* * *

Hite looked around him and estimated the lay of the land with a practiced eye. He intended to stand guard

53

all night, then doze during the day as they went on their way. Point of Rocks was their destination and once there, they would hold up until the Committee's dispatches to all the camps resulted in a gathering of miners who together would make the journey back down to Salt Lake. This would likely take a month or more, and by that time, spring would hopefully clear the route. Once through the mountains, it was a matter of following the trail to Salt Lake City. A week, maybe two, should see the danger past.

That night, he and Maxxus sat watching out from the camp where the fire wouldn't wreck his night vision. It was late and he was a little sleepy when he heard a rustle and a soft whisper. Turning, he found Siccoolum just sitting down beside him on a blanket she'd brought out. For a while, they sat companionably, then she peeled off her dress and laying down, beckoned him. The stars twinkled and the moon shone down upon their love making. Maxxus, more mindful of his duty, remained on guard.

* * *

At Point of Rocks, he looked for and found an open area that satisfied him. The river willows were a little closer than he liked, and if anyone chose to attempt an ambush, it likely would come from there. However, the distance was over three hundred yards and he thought it unlikely they would try him at that range, knowing his skill with the rifle. While the others made camp, he went for tipi poles, cutting and dragging them out in a loose bundle with the gray team. Siccoolum directed the raising of the tipi and she was particular about the poles, rejecting a few he brought her, making them firewood. He placed the wagons between the willows and the tipi, making it harder for any shooter to see his target, and they settled in for a stay.

There were deer along the river and he bagged two that afternoon, gutting them and dragging them into camp with the buckskin, the bigger of the two saddle horses and used to a white man's saddle and a rope. Once there, Siccoolum took over the skinning and butchering. He marveled at her use of the knife he'd given her.

The tipi up, he took the buckskin along the river and brought up some loads of driftwood, which he piled in heaps on either side of the tipi and against the wagons for a buttress against an attack. He intended to add to the barrier as the days went by, the camp assuming the character of a small fort.

* * *

Three days later, the sun well up, he was just settling comfortably into his chair by the fire with a cup of coffee, when a volley of fire boomed out from the willows. In the tipi, he heard Betty scream. The firewood soaked up the bullets as the shots threw chips and splinters in the air. Ben grabbed his Sharps as he hit the ground, then crawled to a firing position behind a stump he already had selected as a spot to return fire. A quick glimpse over the solid wood and he had one spotted, like him, lying prone in the brush there. Previously, he had deliberately paced off the distances of some possible firing positions and now he set his sight for 320 yards and taking a deliberate aim, touched off his shot. The figure out there jerked his head, then dropped it to the ground. One gone.

A trio of shots came back at him, one thudding into the stump directly in front of him, one screaming over. Someone out there could shoot, too. He reloaded swiftly and then wiggled his way to another position. He poked the rifle through a firing slot and watched as a man rose to his knee to take aim, and taking a quick sight himself, both pulled trigger at the same time. Ben heard the bullet whap into wood by him as the shooter spun down to the ground. Two away.

He changed positions three times as the rifle duel drew to its conclusion, killing another two men before those left started to retreat through the brush behind them. He watched, changing his sight as the three men still alive climbed the far river bank at a distance of over six hundred yards, then took dead aim and touched off a deliberate shot. Out there, one of the men fell forward on his face and lay still. One of the other men started to turn back, then scrambled away and disappeared over the rim.

Hite called, "Anybody hurt?"

Moira yelled, "Betty fell in the fire when they shot first and she's burned her hands. We're fixin' her up. Are they gone?"

"Yeah. Those who could leave."

He waited and watched for another half hour, wishing he still had his Signal Corps field-glasses that he'd used so often in the war. They had been stolen from him just before Antietam and he'd never replaced them. Now he wished mightily that he had. Finally, he got up and running in a zig-zag, made it to the willows where the first man lay. He'd taken the bullet in the collar bone just to the right of the neck and it had gone the length of his body, nearly. He picked up the rifle the shooter had used, a Sharps nearly the twin of his own. Hite grunted with pleasure, another great weapon! This one he'd keep. To have two Sharps of such quality was a blessing. Going through the man's pockets, he found as he thought he might, $260 in gold eagles and some change. Evidently, his death was worth more than it had been.

The man, a red haired and bearded individual Hite didn't know, also had a knife and a Remington revolver. He took both and the rifle back to the camp. Two more trips were made to the willows and he returned each time with rifles and pistols. By the time he had retrieved the weapons of the last man on the far bank, he had a sizable weapons collection. The last man had carried a well-used but serviceable Sharps carbine. Sorting them out, he decided he'd give the carbine to Siccoolum and show her how to use it. Moira would get the little Colt pocket pistol, which like Siccoolum, he would teach her to shoot. He had plenty of ammunition now and it would pass the days to teach them to be proficient with rifle and pistol.

The bodies he dragged into a leaning cut and covered by caving the bank over them. The others, like the first, had considerable gold in their pockets. It bothered him not at all to take it or the weapons. The men were trying to kill him. He said a few muttered words over them and strode back to camp.

* * *

Betty's hands had been badly burned and Siccoolum's treatments and Hite's salve helped them heal but she had to be fed and clothed and Ben took it on himself to do the most for her, as Siccoolum had her hands pretty full of babies and Moira was tasked with most of the cooking and cleanup. The little girl came to depend on the gentle man's ministrations and a great bond developed between them, which made Freddy jealous. He pestered Ben until the man taught him to shoot the only pistol that fit his small hands, the little Colt .31 pocket model revolver Moira had been given. He banged away with it until it was empty, then Hite watched, helping as needed, as he awkwardly recharged the cylinder and reprimed it. Later, he showed them all how to clean and care for their guns, just as he did his.

One of the dead men had carried a nice Bacon Excelsior revolver with a curious etched cylinder in .32 caliber, complete with a mold and some bullets and he traded that to Moira in exchange for the Colt, which Freddy had begun claiming as his own. He presented Siccoolum with another, a Confederate made Dance Brothers pistol in .36 caliber, a crude clone of the Colt. She looked her satisfaction at her new arsenal and he taught her to load the Sharps and the pistol and to sight properly. He was extremely patient with them all and soon they were, if not expert shooters, at least competent. It made him happy to see how both the boy and the Indian woman, lacking fingers, still developed a dexterity and certain skill. Moira, though, still had a tendency to shut her eyes when she pulled the trigger and they worked on that.

* * *

They were left alone now and in another week, miners began drifting in. He directed them to camp along the river up and down from him, showing each of them where the ambush had taken place and warning them against setting up too close to the river where they might get overrun. His reputation had preceded him and he was listened to intently. They followed his directions implicitly. Soon the encampment had collected nearly a hundred men. Hite had found among them three men he knew were solid, with notes from Randall who vouched for them, and these screened the newcomers. They turned away several who attempted to enter the camp who were on the list as being suspected members of the organized band of thieves. Each of the Miners Committees had sent along quantities of gold from the various members to be deposited in Salt Lake for them. He had Moira write receipts to each of them and stowed the gold carefully in the second wagon.

* * *

Four weeks to the day, they pulled out on the trail, Ben's wagons heading up the convoy, one of which was driven by Bless Ketchum, a cranky old crippled teamster who had freighted through the war, the other by Ansel Kittledge, a little wizened prune of a man who laughed continually at anything and everything and loved to make the little ones laugh, too. Betty's hands were much improved and she and Freddy rode with him, their laughter trilling above his raucous cackle as they went. It made Ben grin himself as he heard them. His horses looked good and were shod, one of the miners having been a blacksmith who'd kept his tools with him when he'd come to the mining camps.

He was riding Monte, his bay and Siccoolum, the buckskin. He had made her an indian saddle and though she rode astride, he'd had her make a split skirt that hung down to her stirrups, warmer and not so revealing. Waterwheel, her baby, rode in front of her and Katy rode in the cradle board at her back. She alternated between the two and Hite noticed the new beadwork along the top of the board, which served to shade the baby from the sun. Katy had taken to the carrier and seemed very content as she swayed to the horse's rhythm. One of the men from

Bannack had a small jar of trade beads and had given it to her for a haunch of venison. Hite had grinned when she came first and had asked hesitantly if it was all right. Deer were plentiful but some men were not hunters and poor shots. He laughingly gave his consent and soon beads were decorating everything.

Siccoolum had her Sharps dangling by a thong on her saddle and her pistol tucked in her waistband. Her black hair was in long braids that shone in the warm April sun and her beaded decorated dress fitted her long frame well.

He saw that she had finished her new moccasins and they looked good, beaded also and peeping from under her dress. She smiled brightly at him as she rode up alongside and he reflected with some surprise that he was a contented man as he smiled back and the two horses matched strides.

Monte was a good horse, with a reaching walking stride that ate the distance, but he still missed Flint. That horse had been his favorite among all the horses he'd owned. Maybe this one would take its place but he doubted it. He looked over at the buckskin. It was a horse with some excellent qualities, too, small black hooves, a pleasing head, alert eyes and a good disposition. But though he knew their reputation for toughness, he'd never cared for the color. Siccoolum seemed to like it, though, and so he considered it hers.

As word had spread through the camp of the encounter he'd had with Williams, men had tended to pay her more respect, as if he'd staked a claim and warned everyone else off. Whatever, she had not been molested since. It suited Ben. Some had even called her Mrs. Hite and he'd not bothered to correct them.

* * *

They had to wait eight days for the pass to clear enough to get through and the stock was weak, so they went slowly. Several times, the men had to go forward and shovel their way through big drifts, the wagons double-teamed. Once over, though, and down to a lower elevation, they hit some green grass and stopped to let the animals fill up and gain some strength. Some of the men wanted to go on ahead then, but Ben wouldn't let them. They didn't argue too much and he kept them all together right on down to Salt Lake City, where some split off to continue on east to St. Louis. He'd not lost a man and the men presented him with a collection they'd taken up to show their appreciation. It amounted to several hundred dollars and he hesitated to accept it, then decided '*what the hell, he'd use it to buy more supplies and another wagon and teams.*'

* * *

In two weeks' time, he was headed back, leading a group who wanted to get to the gold fields and feared highwaymen and Indians. He still had Kittledge and Ketchum working for him and had added two more wagons, all of them with four horse teams, along with the drivers to work them. These he'd found among the men who'd heard that he had just lately brought in a large group from the camps and were wanting him to guide them back. Like his other drivers, they were experienced older men. Ben had loaded the vehicles with the basic food stuffs that were easily freightable and valuable at the far end: flour, beans, coffee, sugar, dried apples and salt pork, plus one wagon, a full ton, of potatoes. He'd bought nearly a whole Mormon farmer's crop out in the valley.

A freight wagon which would stand up to the grueling rough trails of the Rocky Mountains, had to be reinforced, its wheels wide and iron rimmed, with a strong axle and tongue. That made it weigh about 750 pounds. Adding the weight of a driver and the harness, with a few other odds and ends, such as the man's kit and weapons, and the weight topped a half ton, which Ben figured equaled one horse pulling. That left three quarters of a ton, maybe a little more, for the load. If too much was added, the teams would struggle on the hills and steep grades. Belgians and Percherons were wonderful draft horses, but like all heavy horses, they needed grain to keep going. Ben had thought he might switch to oxen, which could pull more on less feed, but he was a horse man, and oxen were slow, so that meant carrying feed along, which cut the load's net value further.

His new teams were mostly quality road horses, leggy Percherons, which, though a couple hundred pounds lighter than the one ton Belgians, were taller and leaner and had a longer stride. They were freight horses more suited for the road than the Belgians, which were slower, steady horses suited to the plow. Unable to find all Percherons, he had reluctantly bought two teams of the heavy, stolid Belgians, the biggest he could find. These would pull the potato wagon.

The draft animals had all cost him dearly and his purse was about empty, but they were worth every penny, he figured. The harness was blacked and saddle soaped. The vehicles had been worked over by a blacksmith there who'd tightened felloes, replaced axles and greased hubs, then Ben had his crew paint them a bright sky blue. The word "Hite" was lettered in yellow script on their sides. Each of them had an extra wheel and grease buckets slung under them. One vehicle, Kittledge's, held their camp kit. Hite had traded the cumbersome tipi for a large canvas tent that was easy to set up and take down and much lighter. He'd added some other gear, too.

He'd fixed it to have the children stay behind in a boarding house in town. He had it all worked out in his mind: leave the kids there to be taken care of by a nice Mormon family he'd found where they could go to school. He could visit them when he got in after each trip.

However, that plan had run into a whirlwind of protest by them all—even Siccoolum.

"NO! We won't stay! We want to be with you!"

They begged him to take them, were scared to be alone again. Both Betty and Freddy had clung to his legs, sobbing uncontrollably. Moira was crying on Siccoolum's shoulder, with the Indian's dark eyes looking accusingly at him. The babies, too, had cried and added their fuss to the bedlam. After a stormy hour of it, he'd given in, and now the kids were bumping along happily with the laughing Kittledge and here was

Siccoolum riding, as usual, by his side. He scowled, still out of sorts.

'What had happened, he wondered, to his plan?' But despite himself, and his outwardly sour demeanor, he was happy inside at the outcome. He would have missed them. And with two more men and those following them, the trail should be safe enough. He'd made sure to arm his drivers well. Each carried one of the .52 Sharps he so loved. He had loaded up on the linen cartridges they required and he had bought molds, powder and lead for the pistols and other guns in a large quantity. He could always sell any or all at the gold camps.

'Gonna be an interestin' trip,' he thought, looking back over his shoulder complacently as the city faded from sight over the hills. Ben's little train was followed by the emigrants, another fifteen wagons and a variety of riders and assorted stock, including a small band of sheep.

"Pulling" image courtesy of Dan Rick

Chapter 9

He'd decided to take the Laramie Route. Not liking the heavy sustained pulls over the Continental Divide, he had opted to divert over to the Arkansas River, to the Republican River, on up to the North Platte to Fort Laramie and so on up the Bozeman Trail, which, though longer, was not nearly so hard on stock. High in the mountains, one contended with scant grass and grades which meant double teaming several times a day. Water was at times a problem. On the Laramie route, he could graze the stock on nutritious buffalo grass and following the Republican and the Platte and picking up the Powder River, be near water nearly all the way.

* * *

Though they encountered blow sand and some steep banked coulees, the little train worked its way on up the Arkansas and Smoky Hill river, then on over to the Republican on a well-marked trail that led through immense buffalo herds. He had made an early start and at the time, the route change made sense. Even the old freighters, Ketchum and Kittledge, had endorsed the plan. Later, he was to think it foolhardy, for he'd known it was hostile Indian country, though not that they were on the warpath. Red Cloud's warriors were allied with the Arapaho and Cheyenne to contest the way from Fort Laramie up to the gold fields, which crossed their best buffalo grounds and disrupted their hunting.

However, the trip's beginning was encouraging. Julesburg and the lightly garrisoned little stockade, Fort

Sedgwick, came and went without incident, though once they were threatened by the fringes of a buffalo stampede.

They corralled the wagons and shot until their guns were hot, building a wall about the train of dead buffalo, which diverted the thundering mass around them.

He got the first warning of real danger at Fort Laramie when he visited the fort. Coming up the south fork of the Platte to the imposing stockade, surrounded by tipis and the white canvassed prairie schooners, with herds of cattle, horses and even sheep and some rooting pigs making a confused dusty swirl of movement, they were all impressed at this key point of commerce and military might so far from civilization. Ben directed the wagons to a place away from all the hustle and bustle and jogged Monte on through the open gate.

The First Sergeant at the post office was a grizzled old timer who thought he knew Hite but could not place where they'd met. 'A 'Green Coat'! Let's see. Was it South Mountain? Maybe Gettysburg? Possibly Cold Harbor.' Hite tried to bring him back to the immediate issue: the route north.

"Well now, you heard jest about all the tribes are on the war path?"

"War path? Thought the Army had them pretty well under their thumb by now. Those outside the wall here don't seem so hostile."

"Not hardly. Those are Kiowa. Buncha lazy drunken sodomites. Red Cloud's Sioux, though, is hell on wheels an' causing a storm o' trouble all along the upper Platte an' all. You'd do better to turn around and go back up the North Trail like you shoulda. Keep yore skelps that way. Hey! I got it! Antietam. You an' yore 'Green Coats' was givin' Johnny Reb hell just to our front and we had to come up and pull yore chestnuts from the fire!. Some'a you boys came up to our line and thanked us."

To save time, Hite agreed. "Sure, I remember now. You 10th Wisconsin boys saved our bacon that day. Hood's Division had our company boxed up and was ready to kick our ass."

The old timer was delighted that Hite had remembered, finally. He offered his chew and Hite obligingly bite off a chunk. They chomped companionably.

"Course, you heard 'bout Fetterman and his troop? Crazy Horse and his skelping fiends ran over 'em this winter an' kilt him and eighty troopers—pulled one o' their slick ambushes." He spit a huge gob. "Oh, the Injuns are boilin' like a stirred up red ants hill up there. Red Cloud and his bunch got Fort Reno and Kearny besieged and, Hunckly, the CO here, ain't letting any small trains go through. He's bunchin' 'em into big ones to be sure they make it—if they do." He spit at a running spider and enveloped the insect completely with tobacco. It was information Ben hated to hear.

"Damn!" Going back to the train, Ben gathered the men and acquainted them with the situation.

"So, we wait here until the Gen'ral says the train is big enough to pass—about a hundred wagons and three hundred men—or turn around and head back."

Ketchum asked, "What do you think we should do, Ben?"

"Well," He looked at the kids sitting by the fire, Maxxus by their side. "Sure hate to risk gettin' us killed but I guess I'm inclined to keep goin'. I don't like the prospect of goin' the whole way back and around."

"How long you think until we can go forward?"

This from one of the men with the following wagons, their leader, Lakey Steele, a solid and intelligent man whom Ben respected. The feeling was mutual and they had worked well together the last three weeks.

"With our wagons to add to the ones waitin', it shouldn't be too long. You remember there was a couple trains behind us."

"Then, with a large group like that, we should be okay. Most of these freighters an' emigrants are war vets, even if they did wear gray, and a force of three hundred well-armed men should be able to cut through the Sioux like a knife through cheese." Steele commented. The others all nodded their heads. Ben was more leery.

"Maybe. Red Cloud is s'posed to be able to muster five thousand warriors. Plus they got the Arapaho and Cheyenne with 'em. That's damn stiff odds, if they all come at us at once."

One of the younger men, Johnny Curtis, a curly headed brash energetic, stocky teamster with Steele, shouted, "Hey!! We'll just need more ammunition! Come on, men! Let's not let a few mangy redskins stop us!"

His friend, Mark Evans, a follower in whatever mischief Johnny got into, echoed him. Hite and the older men merely looked at them. Steele, like Ben, was a veteran of many engagements, and he was not impressed, as he and some of the others had to break up a fight the two had gotten into at Julesburg, between them and some of the 10th Infantry. It had turned into a brawl and Steele's jaw was still sore. He thought he might have a cracked tooth.

"Damn   loudmouths,"   someone   muttered. Privately, Hite felt the same way, but he knew the young men had no malice in them, just high spirits. And they had no family or kin to worry about. Still, he was worried.

* * *

They were held up a week before the big train was assembled and allowed to head up the Platte. Part of the time was taken up getting the whole cavalcade across, with the use of Jim Bridger's cable ferry. The operation went well, with no accidents. Bridger's two ferrymen were expert by now at transporting wagons, people and stock from one side to the other. Hite paid and thanked them for their service. Seeing Bridger sitting by the cable post, he complimented him on the passage. The old man nodded.

"Went slick. Not like a month ago. Lost a family. Queer deal all around. Man had a team 'o crazy mules. One a' them took a notion to jump off the ferry and the whole wagon tipped off. Dumped the mother and two kids in the river an' the man, he jumped in arter 'em. Whole bunch drowned, includin' the mules." The old frontiersman shook his gray bearded head.

"Hate a mule, I do. Stubborn contrary bastids! Cain't trust 'em." Hite, who'd had some experience with the breed growing up in Missouri, privately disagreed with Bridger but just nodded, not up to arguing with the vociferous old character. He was more interested in getting his advice for the trail ahead.

"So what would you say to do, if'n you was us?"

"Don't be goin up thar!'" he cackled. "Jest stay raite 'chere 'til the Army gits done cleanin' up their damn mess! Gen'ral Connar stirred 'em up when he wiped out Black Bear's Arapaho village along the Tongue last year. Stupid bastid! I 'as along and tole 'im they was peaceful! But no! He says ter me, 'Well, they's redskins ain't they? We'll send 'em all a smoke signal when we set the village ablaze.'" He paused and took a chaw. "Wal, he did, but they near put us under when they came aroarin' back at us. If'n Connar didn't have his howitzers to pull our nuts outa the fire, they'd a killed us all!" He glared back at the fort.

"Now they want me to do some more scoutin' fer 'em but to hell with 'em! If they don't keer whether a Injun's peaceful 'er hostile, damn if I'll help 'em." He spit in the river. He put a shrewd eye on Ben, standing there.

"Nope, best idee is to stay raite 'chere. They's some good bottom land just over there in thet bend ye could plant yet thet'd bring ye a crop by next year. Sell grain ta the fort and vegetables, an' make yerself a good livin'! Do it myself but I'm not a farmer." Another gobbet of tobacco went in the water.

Ben said, "Me neither. Had enough of it when I'se a youngster back in Mizzouri, follerin' a team back 'n forth across a field. Least, freightin', I'm seein' some new country."

The old man's eyes unfocussed and his mind turned inward to some memory of his trapping days in the far mountains. "Know what ya mean, son, know what'cha mean, always fun to put a horse to a new trail." He shook himself like a dog. "Man's gotta live, though, an' the beaver's gone in the high country."

He looked at Hite, seeing a competent, well set up man with a direct look to his blue eyes and an open countenance, with something defining about him that engendered respect. "Ya shoulda bin with me! It ware a grand time!"

"Wish I had bin, old timer. Wal, gotta go."

They shook hands. The train was nearly out of sight over a hill.

"Good luck, son. God speed. Nice squaw ya got there. Bet she kin make 'em come with that there carbine."

"She gets by all right. Damn good with a knife, too."

The old man's eyes twinkled. "They all are, son! Watch yer hair, now."

"The Big Boys" image courtesy of Dan Rick

Chapter 10

The train wound its torturous way through sage brush covered flats and scrub cedar coulees and over rocky ridges, constantly shortening and elongating over its length.

The hundred plus wagons and bands of stock and out-riders stretched over a mile and dust hovered like a cloud over all. In the week of its being composed, the men met several times to elect a leader, finally selecting the wagonmaster of the largest group, just because of their majority vote. It happened that the man, whom they called 'Major', was Paul Simons, who'd risen to major of the 24th Georgia Regiment, a hard fighting Rebel unit, and many of the men in that train were either from that regiment or were Confederates of another brigade. Of course, that rubbed the Union men the wrong way. Ben liked what he'd seen of him, however, and certainly didn't resent his not being voted leader, though his name had been mentioned as a front runner.

He thought, taking stock overall, that the division of north and south in the train was about equal, and he guessed that things would heat up at some point. The old flame ran too deep and tempers flared when men were pushed to the limit. He thought, though, it might be averted if the Indians did attack, since it might bring the men together against the common enemy.

* * *

Johnny Curtis was the spark that brought on the first fight. It had been decided after some

71

experimentation, that the whole train was just too cumbersome for all the wagons to circle, so they would break into three interlocking ones of thirty plus wagons. It was natural that Rebels and Union men would clump together, but that meant that the one circle would be made up of both. Of course, Ben's group had to be in that division.

Nights around the mess fires in the circles after supper meant music, for many were good, even accomplished, musicians. The more portable instruments like the fiddle, the mouth harp and the banjo were popular in the train but they were usually accompanied by singing and that was where the friction started. Such songs popular to both sides like *'Annie Laurie,' 'There is a Happy Land',' I'm a Pilgrim,' 'Home, Sweet Home,'* and others were fine and all joined in. But Rebels voices and their musicians were silent when the Union people tuned up with *'Red, White and Blue,' 'Yankee Doodle Dandy,' 'Wait for the Wagon,'* and other Yankee songs. Then, Union voices and their musicians refused to play or sing,' *'My Old Kentucky Home,' 'Arkansas Traveler,' 'When Johhny Comes Marching Home,' 'Maryland, My Maryland', and 'Dixie,'* and other southern melodies.'

At such times the tension was high and on the fourth night, when the Union circle beside them on the left was booming out *'Tenting on the Old Campground'* and the Rebel circle to their right was softly singing *'Swanee River,''* a wife of one of the Rebel men said,

"Oh, I <u>do wish</u> those Yankees wouldn't shout so off-key! They're making it <u>impossible</u> to hear *'Swanee.'"* In the ensuing silence, Johnny Curtis was heard to sneer,

"Oh, why don't you blow it out yer ass!"

Shocked silence gripped the camp. Then the husband came at Johnny swinging and the young man met him with a roundhouse punch that felled the Rebel. It wasn't ended with that, as two other Rebel men came on the attack and this time, Mark Evans stood with his friend and they traded punches with the men until inevitably, it degenerated into a general melee, men fighting the War all over again. Ben saw no reason to get involved until one of the Rebels pulled a knife. At that, a Union man swung up a pistol. Then Ben's roar and the shot he fired into the air got the attention of them all.

"You men want to knuckle dance, you go on out of the circle. Usin' knives and pullin' guns is somethin' else! This ground inside the wagons has wimmen and kids and I'll not hev 'em hurt!"

His fierce manner and cocked pistol deflated the fighters and they separated reluctantly. It happened that Major Simon was visiting the circle just then and he came and sided with Ben. Steele strode up, along with Ketchum, Kittledge, Harver and Murchison, Ben's other drivers. Standing there resolute against the flicker of the fire, they made an imposing group.

Ben, seeing the fight was over, holstered his gun and grabbed Curtis by the neck in an iron grip and stood him up on his tiptoes.

"Now, you squirrely little peckerwood! March on over there and say your apologies to Mrs. Green 'er we'll throw you out of the train and you can head on back to Laramie!"

Shamed and with a surly manner, Curtis put the best face on it and did as he was bid. As he went, Ben strode over to Mr. Green, who was wavering yet from the powerful punch Curtis had delivered. He grasped him as he had Curtis, by the neck in a grip that made that worthy start to turn a deep shade of red.

"And you, sir! I am holdin' you responsible fer that gabby wife o' yers! She makes any more trouble like that with 'er mouth, I'm takin' it out on you!"

He spun him around and gave him a shove toward the offending woman, who let out a wide eyed gasp. Ben turned back to Simon, who gave him a tight grin.

"Well, boys, I guess we have our Master-at-Arms of the train, standing in front of us right now. Hite, I'm asking you, will you take the job on?"

A chorus of 'ayes' and 'damn right' came from both Union men and Rebels, who saw the justice in what Ben had just done. It had struck the right chord, something Simon was good at doing. Ben saw he had put himself in the way of a difficult job and only reluctantly agreed.

* * *

The next morning, as Ben went to check on the group's horse herd, he saw Ketchum harnessing the big Belgians. The huge horses were exceptional pullers and quickly had gained a reputation throughout the train as one of the teams to call on when some hard task of hauling was required. Ketchum would set them to the task, getting them ready by his voice, then hup them and they would set down in their harness and walk away with the load, be it a stuck wagon or a stump that needed to be taken from the roadbed. Ben, watching, was proud of them and steadily turned down some top offers. Kittledge's grays, too, were a good team, but just weren't in the same class as the Belgians. The train had a horse herd that numbered in the hundreds, and though many were draft horses like Hite's, there was excellent saddle stock among them, also, like his Monte horse.

Ben, knowing of the Indian's greed for horses, was adamant that the herd be well guarded. His idea of how many men it took to do the job and Simon's, who had never fought the red man back in Georgia, clashed right away. Simon said the men were tired from the day's drive and standing guard, too, every night, was too much to ask. Hite, said if the train was without horses, 'they'd get much tireder pullin' the wagons themselves.'

He lost the argument but persisted in bringing Monte into the circle with him and tying him at the wagon. Siccoolum did likewise with her buckskin, which upset some of the women. She had already come in for some heavy criticism, being an "Injun squaw." Presuming to bring her horse into the circle was just too much! She ignored the white tongue clackers and did it anyway.

* * *

Two weeks away from Laramie, the train had left Bannack country and was encroaching on the Sioux lands. Ben, with his sharpshooter eyes, had glimpsed dust and movement far off that he didn't think were buffalo, but he couldn't be sure. Several times, he had loped out beyond the out riders skirting the train and set himself to do some watching. He saw nothing moving each time except for the ever present antelope, deer and buffalo that dotted the plains, but his sense of unease persisted.

Again, he wished for his stolen pair of binoculars. He'd been so busy at Salt Lake that finding another pair had slipped his mind and he'd passed up his opportunity to replace them. At Fort Laramie, he had made an effort to find a pair and couldn't. Now he decided to see if the train might harbor some field glasses and put out the word through Kittledge, a great gossip and somewhat of a scrounger, that he was in the market for such an item.

Early one evening, just as he was coming back from quelling yet another North-South squabble, he was intercepted by an old woman carrying a package.

"Mr. Hite,?"

"Yes, ma'am, what kin I do fer ye?" He was hungry and Siccoolum's stew was beckoning. His temper was short and he had little time anyway, for the women of the train. Besides, he'd seen this silver haired old woman mingling in the group of Rebels and knew she was one of them.

"Mr. Hite, your driver, Mr. Kittledge, told us of your need for a good pair of binoculars. I just wanted to bring these to you. They were my Charlie's. He was a colonel in the war. Killed at Gettysburg. He had his best pair with him and of course, they were not recovered. These were at home when. . . " Her face crumpled with hidden grief that came to the surface. She pushed it back and resumed.

"When Sherman came through and his men burned our plantation, I was able to save them. It came to me today that they were doing me no good, so I brought them to you to have."

She handed the package over and Ben, feeling distinctly uncomfortable, unwrapped it. Inside was a pair of well made English field glasses, by far the finest that Ben had seen. "Well. . . Mrs. . . . ."

"McDowell. My husband's name was Charles Artemus McDowell. He was decorated by Lee himself for his regiment's action at Chancellorsville. . . .but I guess, you wouldn't be interested in that." She turned to go.

"Wait! Mrs. McDowell, these are beautiful, Ma'am. Too nice fer the likes of me. I cain't take 'em!" He looked down at them and coveted them intensely. . . . "Or, at least. . . let me pay you fer 'em."

She looked at him with a direct gaze that made him uncomfortable. He sensed that she was a woman of culture and refinement such as he'd seldom met.

"Mr. Kittledge says you are a good man, Mr. Hite. I heard about your little orphans, your succor of the Indian girl, who was a slave of the Bannacks, and the stand you made against the terrible criminal element of the gold camps. He said you could use those binoculars for the good of the train, maybe to save all our lives. My Artemus would not want me to take any pay for them. Just use them well."

"Ma'am." He stepped forward and took her hand. It was frail and thin in his big paws. "Thank you. I certainly will do my best."

She smiled at him and walked away.

Chapter 11

The train wound its way into the hill country at the head of the North Platte. The simmering North-South issue had finally come to an explosive head when Ike Ainsley, a Union man, caught Luke Winstead, a light fingered Southern youngster with a yen for sweets. Ainsley had several sacks of sugar in his wagon and Luke somehow had found out and managed to drill a small hole in the bottom of the heavy freight wagon with his father's auger. The hole went right up into one of the sacks and in the darkness, Luke would sneak under, pull the plug he had made and get a tobacco can full. The trouble came when the plug worked loose and Ainsley's wife, walking behind the wagon, saw a trail of sugar coming from it. Her squawk brought Ainsley.

Ike, crawling under, saw the bored hole and decided to set a trap for the culprit. He whittled another plug and stuck it in, then watched and waited. Two nights later, Luke came to fill his can and Ainsley grabbed him and was administering a well-deserved licking to the youngster when his dad came running, hearing his boy screaming. The resultant fight was another donnybrook, with Northern neighbor taking sides against Southern countryman.

Ben was out from the train using his new glasses when he glimpsed Siccoolum giving him a blanket wave, her signal to come quick. He put the binoculars in their case and made sure they were secure on his saddle before he jumped Monte out and headed back to the train. Steele met him and with several men he'd picked as steady, stout helpers, they headed for the back of the train, where the near riot had turned ugly. Fists had turned into clubs, which had progressed to knives and just as Ben arrived, a pistol went off. Ainsley, having taken a clubbing, had shot his assailant.

Ben and his men dived in and order was finally restored, though it was dark and hard to distinguish just who was fighting who. Both sides, of course, claimed the other had started it. Major Simon had come up, also. Simon was livid as he surveyed the broken heads, the slashed arms and the injured man, who lay moaning.

"This is getting damn tedious! And now, we got a gunshot man who'll be laid up for days, if not weeks. The bullet broke the leg and we'll be lucky if it heals. Ike, we could be trying you for murder, if he dies."

Ainsley was barely able to stand, with blood still running down his face and an ear that needed stitching. "And what the hell was I s'posed to do when he was bashin' me with an ax handle? Turn the other goddam cheek?"

He smeared the blood with a sodden sleeve. "No jury'd convict me —unless it was a damn bunch of Georgia Cracker sonsabitches!"

"Now, Ike. . . Now, just what started it this damn time?"

Hearing the story, Simon shook his head. "Yes, the boy needed a paddling all right, but you should have taken him to his father, and come to me or Hite, if you didn't get any satisfaction."

"Oh hell, what good would thata done! You'da just let it go, like you both do all the time! The boy needed his butt tanned and that's what I'sa doin'. He's a damn little thief!"

"Goddam you! Don't you call my boy a thief! You Bluecoat dog turd!" Ben stepped between them.

"All right! That's enough out of both of you! Shut the hell up and let the Major have a little time to think."

This from Ben effectively silenced them all. Three days before, they had watched him take on the biggest man in the train, a huge North Carolinian who had used a whip on a Northern wagonman's team. The Union man was unlucky enough to be in front of the Rebel and his gaunted team was slow on the grades, pulling a heavy, overloaded wagon. The train's rule was that each man worked his own stock and kept his whip off the other's stock unless there was an emergency. Leon Woodsock had watched their interval getting wider all the time and finally, after swearing and hollering had no desired effect, had taken his whip to the man's team and was threatening to do the same to the frightened owner, if he didn't lighten his load or double team to keep up. A crowd had gathered as the train came to a stop.

Hite had cantered up, swung down and, listening to the man rant a while, told him to settle down and keep his whip 'to home.' Leon, in a fury anyway, had welcomed the confrontation with the man who had the job he thought rightly should have gone to him. The swing he took at Ben would have broken bones—had it landed. Ben went under the blow and had come up with a punch to the throat that nearly killed Leon. As he was gagging and trying to get some breath, Ben measured him and threw another punch, a straight right that landed on Leon's big nose, breaking it and spreading the appendage all over his face. He went down like an axed ox, out. It took five minutes and a pail of water to wake him. He had a sore throat, two black eyes and a nose that was swollen like a blue egg for a week.

His face was a testament to Hite's authority and all the men walked softly around him, including Leon, who had stood watching the present set-to nervously. He said later that the reason he hadn't participated was that he saw the Major—and Hite coming. The biggest reason, of course, was that he couldn't stand the thought of another punch landing on his still swollen nose.

Major Simon thought and finally said, "Men, I can only think of one thing to do to solve this damn problem—split up! Split the train and let each wagon go with whichever part they want. We'll flip a coin for who goes first. The other waits a day or so, and follows."

The men around him were enthusiastic about the Major's solution. Each section would have their own people! They could sing their own songs! Play their own music, have their own religious ceremonies with their own ministers, Cook their own kind of food, make their own rules! All agreed. Sometimes the simple solutions were the best. Ben wasn't so sure, but being damn tired of settling altercations, decided to let it go.

* * *

It was easy enough to find a Rebel flag and a U.S. flag among the train's wagons. Simon found a wide flat nearby and had the Southerner hold up his "Stars and Bars" and a Union man wave the "Star and Stripes" some yards to the other side. Then he had the train drive toward him and peel off whichever way its driver wanted to align himself with. After the last wagon passed, Simon had counted sixty-three wagons in the Southern contingent and forty seven in the Union outfit. Looking the train's individual wagons over, though, he made the sober observation to Ben and Steele, standing by him, that it looked like the Northern train had by far the best equipped wagons and the better stock. This was to be expected, he supposed, 'since the Southerners had not been so well off at the start as the Northern people.'

Ben saw Mrs. McDowell riding in one of the Southern wagons and loping to her side, asked, "Want me to return the binoculars, Ma'am?"

"Not at all, Mr. Hite! I have a strong feeling there will come a time when you'll need them badly! Keep them!"

* * *

The Southern train, having won the toss, led off with the Rebel flag waving from the lead wagon. "Dixie" was being loudly sung by the whole train and it took a long while for the last refrain to fade in the breeze that was blowing over the sagebrush flat that held the Union camp. They had agreed to wait two days, since the next day was Sunday. While they waited the next day, the train first sung "Battle Hymn of the Republic", then listened to Reverend Morris, their elected minister, give a sermon on the "Parting of the Red Sea". After that they held a meeting and elected Ben Hite the train leader by acclamation.

Chapter 12

Ben lost no time in changing some rules. He doubled the horse guard, making sure that he had some old experienced veterans in each shift and explaining just how he wanted them to stand their watch. That caused some complaint but he silenced it by saying "You men elected me yore leader! Now, ye'll take my orders or I'll be doin' some talkin' with ye out in the sage brush!!"

By now, they all knew how Ben Hite talked. None wanted to be forced to listen.

The next rule change was outriders. "You outside guards bin ridin' too close to the train and doin' too much visitin'. Get on out thar about three hundred yards and stay even with us. No ridin' back fer drinks 'er a sandwich when ye're on duty. Eat breakfast and throw a pancake 'er two in yer saddlebag fer lunch 'er just go hungry and eat at supper. Won't hurt ye any. And keep a damn sharp watch! Ye see Injuns, why fire off yer gun and skeedaddle back to the train."

Then came the day's march. "Now, if'n ye take a gander at the stock, ye'll see thet we bin pushin' too hard. Now, I know thet ye are in a hurry to git up to the gold camps. So am I. But we plain won't git thar if our teams give out. So, we start early, like we bin, since it's cool then, take it easy on our stock, go on through the noon break, then stop mid-afternoon so's the horses kin graze and recover. We'll try to stay close to water, but it won't always be possible, so keep yer barrels filled. Then, after five days on the trail, we'll lay over Saturday and Sunday.

Saturday, we'll use to do the washin' and fix what needs fixin'."

"Next and last thing: Some of you need to lighten yer loads. Too much weight and you're wearin' yore stock plum out."

Some immediately objected to that, too, but the older heads sided with Ben. Kittledge, a popular figure in the bunch, spoke up. "You men take a look at Ainsley's team now. See what Ben means? It just <u>has</u> to be done, and better now, then when your team's down in the traces an' there's no gittin' 'em up!"

Ben felt that there were some other changes that needed to be made, but thought these bigger issues needed to be digested, first.

* * *

A pile of furniture and miscellaneous junk, some of it precious to those who'd reluctantly discarded it, lined either side of the train as they pulled out. Ben still had his sorrel team and he directed that Ainsley hitch them up in place of his worn down pair of bays. Then he went through and checked each wagon for filled water barrels and greased axles. Finding some negligent drivers, he spoke with each of them away from the train, out in the sagebrush. When the two came back, usually the one spoken to went right to correcting whatever it was Ben had pointed out. Few had to be told a second time.

* * *

Two days out from the split-up, Mark Evans, one of the outriders, spotted the train's first Indians and shooting off his weapon and yelling at the top of his lungs, he came spurring back to the wagons. Ben, seeing him come, signaled to Ketchum in the lead wagon to bend off to make a circle. He used his whip on the Belgians and Kittledge following, with the rest tailing behind, a nice, tight circle soon was made. Behind Evans, whipping their ponies, came a war party ki-yiing and screaming their war whoops. There were ten or eleven in the bunch and some of them had rifles or pistols, which they fired off. Mark spurred his horse and jumped it over a wagon tongue and into the circle as the Indians came whooping up, only to slide to a halt as a volley came blasting out at them. Two fell from their horses and the others, grabbing their friends up, retreated as fast as they came.

That began the first of frequent encounters with the wrath of the red man for invading his lands. Ben, remembering how it was on the trail when he had first come west, talked with Siccoolum of the wisdom of trying perhaps to attempt to negotiate a safe passage. She, getting more proficient with English all the time, said it was too late for that. The tribes were too angry and would rather kill the white invaders. They would have to fight their way through.

Shots from long distances were sent at the train, the outriders were ambushed, once one was pulled from his horse and tomahawked. Attempts were made to stampede the horse herd. Each day in early afternoon, the wagons were circled tightly and the horses and stock were carefully watched while they grazed at the buffalo grass and watered at creeks or often, the river, if it was nearby.

* * *

Now, they began passing piles of ransacked debris from earlier trains who had run into difficulty with worn-out teams, the stuff they had left behind gone through and some stolen, the rest either hacked or burned, some still smoldering. Clothing littered the prairie, the sagebrush beside the trail looking at times as if it was wearing the dresses, shirts, overalls and other items. Signs were posted that invited anyone passing to help themselves to what had been left. Some did, as they exchanged worn out boots that were usable, or shirts or overalls, but the heavy furniture was left to weather, beautiful tables, dressers, armoires, sofas and chairs. Some had been piled together and burned. Some were discarded with love, people's heirlooms. Ben passed by a Dwyer stove that he nearly retrieved, then, knowing his wagons were heavy enough as it was, he left it.

Now dead stock was passed, the gaunt ribs of abused horses and mules which had pulled their loads until they died in their harness. Graves began showing up, too, the causes of death sometimes written on the wooden head boards and crosses, sometimes not. Some were gruesome, as the dead were not always interred in graves deep enough to keep out the wolves, who tore the corpses apart and left bones and scattered pieces of body parts about the site.

* * *

Ten days out from the split-up, Ketchum signaled for Ben to come up. He was back talking with Steele about a sick horse. He loped Monte forward to the lead wagon and started to ask Bless what was the matter, when Ketchum held up his hand for quiet. "Shhh, Ben! Now! Ye hear that?"

Ben listened and far off, he heard the sound of firing, unmistakable to a veteran.

"Sounds like the Johnny Rebs hez run into trouble." Ketchum grinned. He spat.

Like so many other Union men, he harbored a deep, abiding hatred of Rebels and all the Confederacy had stood for. Too many accounts of horror and atrocity, many of them true, haunted the memories of every man who had fought, be they blue or gray. One persistent story of the Rebels bayonetting the wounded after Chicamauga had gone the rounds of the Union camps. Another tale of a Northern regiment poisoning wells in Georgia and North Carolina had circulated through the Rebel encampments. Stories of mistreatment of wounded were most common and some, perhaps, were true. The prison camps of both sides were hideous examples of man's inhumanity to his fellow man. Certain it was, that as the war progressed, collective hatred rose higher and more misdeeds were perpetrated on the helpless enemy. Leaving the Union wounded in front of the Rebel trenches to suffer in the blazing sun at Vicksburg for two agonizing days was just one of the many occurrences, but it happened that Bless Ketchum had been one of them and the memory burned.

Ben had seen enough of it himself to know that neither side was lily-white. He looked at Ketchum and said,

"Pull over thar in thet big meadow. Make'er tight, Bless."

"Yessir." He hupped the team and started off. Ben rode down the line gathering men as he went.

"Each man with his rifle and a pistol and forty rounds for each. Rest stay here and fort up. No! You stay here, too!"

This was directed at Siccoolum, who had handed off Waterwheel and Katy to Moira and had just settled into her saddle. She sat back and watched as the mob of men pounded off, then kicked her horse into a lope and followed them. Behind her, the wagon circle had grown and dust billowed up as the stock was run in and it came together on the ends.

* * *

Topping a rise two miles from his circled train, Ben got down from his horse and taking his glasses, focussed them on the action below. The Rebel train had only gotten partially circled and fighting was going on, even in the circle, Ben could see. Off to the north, Ben saw the last of the train's horse herd just going over a low hill, Indians running them hard. Though he hadn't time to estimate, Ben guessed that there was five hundred Indians working the train over, with even some hand-to-hand fighting going on.

"My God! There's too many!" Someone exclaimed behind him, with a tremble in his voice. Ben ignored it and yelled back to the men as they came up.

"We'll head on down there, then pull up and give them a volley. Stay together! Follow me and pile off your horse when I do!"

He remounted and spurred Monte into a run down off the hill. The Indians were intent on overrunning the train and Ben's fifty men came up swiftly, dismounted when Ben did and fired off a ragged volley that got their attention. Some, a sizable group, started in their direction and Ben hollered,

"Reload! Let 'em bunch up and we'll give 'em another one! Hold yer fire now!"

One or two nervous shots were banged off as the Indians came on the run, a hundred or more. Ben waited until they were in good range, about a hundred yards, and yelled, "Fire, boys!"

The rifles roared and Indians fell, though some stayed on their horse, wounded, and cantered off to the side before the rider slipped to the ground. Those left surged around the kneeling riflemen.

"Load! Give 'em another! Pick a target either side."

He led a striped brave with a streaming war bonnet aboard a swift pinto and touching off, knocked the rider off his horse. Guns went off around him and more braves fell. A third volley was better aimed as the men, mostly veterans, steadied up and took a careful sighting.

"Now, boys! Remount and we'll go on in! Stay together! Don't leave anybody back!"

Ben remounted and kicked Monte into a run that brought him into the partial circle the wagons had made. The fighting there had degenerated into clumps of men swirling back and forth and Ben fired his pistol at a big brave about to club a man he was holding on the ground, the one below trying to use his knife. The warrior slumped. Around him now, his men had come up and he gathered them about him and directed their fire as they fought to clear the wagons of the red horde. With no direction on the warriors part, the aimed volleys had deadly effect and the Indians, faced with directed fire that was killing them in too great a number, were pushed back and soon on the run.

Simon came up, his face bloody from a knife cut that cleaved his right cheek to the bone and said, "Hite! Thank God! We were about to be massacred! Hundreds of the red devils! What . . .what about. . . ?"

He fell and Ben saw that he had been clubbed, his head dripping blood. All about him, men were coming up to thank them, women crying hysterically, children screaming and downed horses neighing, the din deafening. He looked around, trying to concentrate on the Indians and saw that most of them, those still alive, were streaming off to the north, following the horse herd. Some were still to their front, however, either helping their wounded to clear the field or gathering perhaps, for another charge. He bellowed to his men.

"Reload yer rifles. Follow me!" As he swung aboard Monte, he saw Siccoolum with her carbine at the ready, and a wagon man about to shoot her.

'HEY! She's my wife! DON'T SHOOT!"

Amazingly, the man heard him and dropped his hammer. He rode to her and gripped her arm.

"Damn you! I said, Stay back! They don't know you from a hostile! Now, keep close to me 'er ye'll likely get shot!" They rode out and faced about a hundred Indians who were grouping for another attack. Ben swung down and got his men in a rough disordered line.

"Hold fire 'til I give the word, then pour it to 'em!"

The Indians came on, walking their horses to get their own line straightened, then whipped their ponies into a screaming charge that threatened to overrun the little party of white men. "Steady, boys. Steady! Fire!"

The volley was devastating. Horses somersaulted, Indians were blasted from their mounts and those who could, kicked their ponies into a hard run to the north, leaving their dead and wounded where they lay.

"Once more as they run, men!" A ragged fire dumped some more of the retreating warriors, not many as the distance had increased. They were gone.

Johnny Curtis, with Mark Evans right behind him, went whooping out from the party then, and together, the two men rounded up several of the battlefield's loose horses. Ben, seeing that was a good idea, directed some others to do so, and he watched as Siccoolum herself went out and captured a white horse that was standing by a dead brave. She cut the tie rope from his wrist, then bent down and picked up his rifle and took his knife from his belt. As she grabbed his hair to scalp him, Ben yelled at her. Regretfully, she dropped the dead brave's head and just cut off his braids and ears, instead. She grinned.

"Damn bloodthirsty hellcat," he muttered, then turned back to the train. She hopped nimbly on her horse and followed him.

Chapter 13

"Eleven dead. Sixteen wounded or so. Would have been all of us if you hadn't showed up, Hite! We're forever obliged! We've got men who'll die if they don't get treated. Woodsock has an arrow clear through him. Auburn was tomahawked but he's still breathing. Liza Criswell was scalped and her husband found her headpiece but it needs stitching back on. Mrs. McDowell was shot and scalped, but she's still alive. Some others. . . . We need a doctor but ours has been killed. Could you bring Doc Clarence up quick?" Simon was close to fainting again but held himself up by a wheel as he talked.

"You need some attention yerself, Major." Ben turned and yelled,

"Steele, take ten men and go get the Doctor. Come right back. We need to have a powwow about that stolen herd."

Steele and his men took off as Ben directed the train's men to gather up teams and help get the wagons into a tight circle. "And men, you need to chain those wagons together when you get 'em lined up, so the circle cain't be broke."

That done, he had time to ask,

"Mrs. McDowell, is she gonna make it?"

"She'll die, I'm afraid. Shot in the chest."

"She's a grand lady. Hope he kin save her."

"She surely is. Her husband and her son were killed in the war and she was burned out of her home, so she came out with her sister's family."

Simon looked around, visibly about to collapse.

"Damn it all, Hite! We should have listened to you. Elected you leader! I don't know what we're going to do now, with most of our stock gone. We're stuck here."

Steele's men pounded up in a little while, the doctor with them. Simon went off with him to show him the wounded, who were gathered under a spread tarp for shade. Ben beckoned to Steele.

"Siccoolum says it's Sioux, all right. Crazy Horse's bunch. They got nearly all their loose stock and killed some of their using teams. I'm thinkin' about goin' after them and hittin' them back tonight. I doubt they'd be expectin' it. They know they hurt the train bad. Mebbe we kin git some of their stock back."

Steele's face took on a grave demeanor. "Hells Bells, Ben! That's sure askin' fer trouble." He looked at Hite. "Guess I'm game, though, if you call fer volunteers."

"I'm callin' and I'd like you with me."

"Then I'm your man, Ben Hite."

"Damn good. Knew I could count on you." He slapped Steele's shoulder.

He turned and said, "All right, Major, listen up. Tonight, I aim to take a strong party an' try to get yore horses back if we kin. Even if we cain't, we're goin' to try an' give 'em a lesson they'll remember. We'll need to eat and load up on ammo. And I want some volunteers. I have fifty men here with me but I need another fifty of yours. We'll pull out when it gets dark."

* * *

Night came and Ben waited until it got pitch black before he led the men, dismounted, from out of the circle and along the trail cut by the running horse herd. Out a ways from the train, he mounted and walked his horse. Before leaving, he had passed the word that he wanted them to follow silently in single file behind him. His eyes were excellent and he had little trouble keeping to the path churned by the hundreds of hooves. The worked earth made for silent passage and he could barely hear the men coming behind him.

They traveled several hours and then he smelled smoke. He stopped and let the men gather quietly about him, making sure he had them all.

"All right, come close. Kin ye hear me?" Assured they could, he said, "All right. Stay right here 'til I git back. I'm goin' to scout their camp and git the lay of the land. Steele, don't let them make any noise 'er smoke. We need surprise 'er we 'might's well go on back."

He disappeared in the dark and they waited, most lying down or sitting. A few times, Curtis or some other chatterbox wanted to talk, but Steele kept them quiet. A half hour went by, then another fifteen minutes. The men were getting restless. At times, some thought they could hear drumming. Then Ben reappeared.

"They're down by the river. Several hundred of 'em. Doin' their scalp dancin' and looks like they got a prisoner. Torturin' somebody, fer I could hear him screamin'. Looks like the herd is bein' held off to the right a ways. Now here's what we'll do." He whispered his instructions and the men listened intently.

* * *

Crazy Horse was leading his warriors in the dance of the scalps, of which there was nine. One was silver haired, another was red. One was a bald fringe. The others were shades of brown and black. It didn't matter, for they were all from the heads of the hated yellow eyes. The braves gyrated and screamed and voiced their finest yells as they circled the pole on which the scalps were tied. There was a whiskey keg a brave had looted from a wagon and many of them had drank from it, so that some braves staggered and fell as they tried to keep the tempo the others were stomping out. Most all were deep in the music of the drums, acting out their participation in the day's fight.

The prisoner they had captured, a young white boy, was quiet now, his mind gone from his fear and from the pain of the fire. Crazy Horse snorted. They had built the big scalp dance fire and taken the boy and thrown him in. It had made the warriors laugh to see him hop right back out, so they had done it again . . . and again.

In the late night, as the dance drew to its close, they would bind him and throw him in for the last time. His screams would help assuage the anger that enveloped the brooding chief as he thought of the near victory that had been snatched from them by the white men who had come from the other train. There should have been many more palefaces to torture. The drums were inside his head and he winced at their throbbing. His head was hurting yet from the graze that had cut a furrow along the left side of his skull. His medicine had averted the bullet and saved his life, he thought thankfully.

The noise of the drums and the yells of the dancing men masked the advance of the attacking party as they came forward. Ben, running bent over, formed them up at less than fifty yards distance from the edge of the huge fire and the Indians milling around it in drunken disorder. The drums drowned out the clicking of ninety rifles as the men behind them readied themselves. Then, Ben shouted,

"Fire! Fire! Give' em hell, men!"

A tremendous volley crashed out and pandemonium reigned about the fire, as warriors fell and other warriors staggered away, some shot multiple times, as heavy bullets at that range ripped through more than one body. The mass at the fire melted away as the sustained firing took its deadly toll, with warriors yet alive stumbling over dead ones to get away in the night.

"Now at 'em, boys! Use yer pistols and bayonets!"

The whites advanced and the melee became a blood bath, with warriors running into the dark, into the river, anywhere to get away from the white devils who came screaming out of the night, many with bayonets fixed on their war rifles.

Ben had advanced with the rest and suddenly he heard, over the firing and hoarse yells of his men, the screams of a youngster. "Mr. Hite! Save me! Mr. Hite!"

Peering in the darkness, he glimpsed the forlorn figure of the boy tied at the post. He grabbed up a loose blanket and cutting him free, wrapped the little figure in it and carried him along on his shoulder. He emptied his Colt, then used his foghorn voice to bid the men to regroup. Most heard and he directed the old vets to gather those who had let their blood lust carry them too far into the night. Their shouts brought the others to their senses and they reformed and made it back to their horses. Unwrapping the child, he set the boy on his horse and mounted behind him. Then he hurriedly had the men count off.

Ben swore when he saw that, as usual, Johnny Curtis and his buddy Evans were among the five men absent. Then Steele came running out of the dark with the missing men, Curtis by the arm, Evans following.

"We're here, Ben! Just had to catch up to these damn kids! They 'bout run me out of breath! Now, Goddammit, let's get the hell out of here! We damn sure gave 'em hell that time!"

* * *

They caught up to the horse herd and Ben sent men off to either side to keep it closed up. Two hours later, just as dawn was lightening the sky a rose red, they came in sight of the train and responded to the questioning shouts with exultant yells of their own. The camp had been awake, worrying and wondering.

* * *

Ben gave his burden over to the boy's parents and they wept when they saw his condition. Mrs. McDowell, had died in the night. The next morning, as they were eating a gloomy breakfast, Doc Clarence came from tending to Woodsock and shaking his head, said that he taken the arrow out but didn't think the big man would live. So his grave was dug beside the others. Then, as Ben readied to make his weary way back to the Union train, Major Simon stopped him and said,

"Ben, we talked it over while you were gone and decided it was best if we asked you if we could rejoin your train. And we want you as the wagon master. We're all ready to take your orders, Ben. Will you ask them for us?"

"Well, you hold up here and we'll catch up. I think it's best, too, if we all stay together. There's just too many Injuns out there fer us to divide up agin 'em."

* * *

When the Union train heard what had occurred and listened to their exhausted men tell of the big swarm of Sioux they had seen and fought, the unanimous consensus was to rejoin. That occurred by midmorning and it was heartening to hear the cheers of the Rebel contingent, who had feared that the Union outfit would not elect to join forces. It was uplifting to Ben to see the outpouring of sympathy given to those families who had lost their men or some relative, and to watch as help was freely given those unfortunates who had been injured.

"Guess some good has come out of this set-to, after all." He remarked to Major Simon, who stood watching as the women of both trains comforted each other, then busied themselves getting together a good supper.

"Yes, human nature rises to a new level when adversity strikes. Differences are forgotten—for a time, at least."

Kittledge was telling some of the Union trainmen of the surgery done by Doc Clarence, who had been the head surgeon for the state of Michigan's 2nd Medical Corp. and had seen it all through the entire war. Like many surgeons who came out of the conflict, he was an addict, though not of whiskey. His failing was laudanum and he worked hard to keep the dosage below 500 drops a day. He was slight of stature, like Kittledge, and his hair was a solid white, though he was only in his early forties. Along with the hair, he had a facial tic and a tremor in his hands, the result of three days and three nights of continuous operating table work during the Gettysburg Battle. He dosed with a stiff shot of whiskey before going to work each day, saving the laudanum for early evening, so he could sleep.

"So the doc sez ter me, 'Kittledge, I hear you were a medical attendant in the war. Which I was, when they pressed me into it, at the Battle of the Wilderness and Cold Harbor. 'You will assist me,' he sez. 'All right,' sez I.

And we go take a look at Woodsock, alying there in his bed. He couldn't lay on his back, ye see, since the arrer had gone clear through and was stickin' out.

'All right then,' sez the Doc, 'Whiskey!'" "He 'uz used to hevin' three or four assistants helpin' him, ye see, and orderin' 'em around. I goes out and finds some whiskey and brings it back and gives it to 'im, thinkin' he's needin' a snort. So did I, seein' the arrer. Well, he pours it on the ends of the arrer stickin' out, then sure enuff, he takes a pull o' the bottle and hands it ter me. Well, I niver turn down a drink, so I upend the bottle.

'Quit yer drinkin!' he sez, 'That's needed fer medicine! Hoof trimmer!"

"Well, I goes out and finds him a hoof trimmer, wonderin' if he's fixin' to trim pore Woodsock's toenails." The men listening laughed.

"Well, he takes the trimmer and snips off the end of the arrer with the feathers on it. 'Are ye ready, Mr. Woodsock?' he sez. 'Ready fer what, Doc?' sez Woodsock, alying there all weak an' tremblin'.

'This!!' Doc sez, and he pulls the arrer on through. Pore old Woodsock passes out cold. I ast Doc why he didn't pull it out as it went in, from in front, like, and he sez,

'Cause the lay of the tissue in the wound channel is pushing forward in the direction of the arrow,' says he. 'Therefore, we must not disrupt that tissue further, or more hemorrhaging' will result. Elementary, says he!'

And he takes a pull of the bottle and hands it ter me. I takes a pull and he sez,

'No! dammit!, Use it to soak a pad fer either side and apply a bandage wrap!' To which I sez, 'And how do

I do that, yer Honor, when he's as big as a damn ox?"
There was laughter.

"Well, we got it done, finally , and laid him back, and mebbe he might live yet. But twarn't nothing to be done fer pore Mrs. McDowell, other than give 'er some laudanum. to ease her passin,' pore soul."

* * *

The doctor also treated little Luke Winstead, whose hands and feet were badly burned, as was some other parts of his body. He was in a partial coma, the doc told the apprehensive parents, likely induced by the shock, pain and fear. With some good care and tenderness, he should come around, though privately, the doctor had his doubts.

* * *

The division of the Indian ponies captured in the horse herd, which numbered well over a hundred was left to Hite. Ben solved that problem by letting each man who had participated in the raid draw a number, then going out and with Betty and Freddy, having them call out a number at random when a horse was brought up to them. Then it was matched with the man who'd drawn the number of that horse. Most were happy with their draw, as the horses ridden by the warriors to battle were always good ones. Those left over, he spread around the train, and a few he kept. Siccoolum garnered another horse, too, and her draw was a good one, a speedy black with three white stocking feet and a blazed face. Its glossy coat and good looking head made a picture as she rode it up and down the train and of course, gave the women tongue-clackers something to talk about.

* * *

The train's new rules as listed by Ben were endorsed by the Rebels, who were ready to accept his leadership now without question. He limited the song sessions to no more than an hour and banned any music which was considered pro-Rebel or Union. As he had done with the Union train, he laid down the law as to weight and went through the Rebel wagons as he had the other train. He doubled the herd guards, saying that the Indians would surely attempt to regain their mounts. He gave the outriders their instructions and shortened the day's march. They agreed to all he ordered without any backtalk, which privately amazed him.

In any event, the train was at a stand until their wounded were able to travel. In Woodsock's case, that might be some time. For two days, he was at death's door, and it took all Doc Clarence's skill to keep him with the living. Then, he turned some corner and started to get well, which amazed the whole train.

'Shot through and through with an arrow, likely poisoned, and still among the living!'

The grave they had dug for him was used for another, a woman who had been shot in the leg, which had turned gangrenous. Her death was a hard one for them all to bear, as she had three little children who badly needed their mother. Their father had been killed by the Sioux attack and she did her best to cling to life for them. But it was not to be. It took a week, a fretful, fearful week, before the train could move. In that time, though, the stock was rested, and the people had found a way to overcome their differences and work together.

Image courtesy of Bob Cherry

Image courtesy of Bob Cherry

Chapter 14

Reno Cantonment came up, with its puny garrison. Captain Tyson, who commanded the 18th Infantry detachment there, came out to meet them and was devastated when he found out that there were no U.S. Army wagons with the train. He had expected to be resupplied and reinforced. His men were fearful that the fort would be overrun, as they had seen Indians in force frequently. With the small unit he commanded, he could mount no patrols, and hunting was out of the question, so he and his men subsisted on government rations, which meant hardtack and rancid bacon, mostly. They were out of coffee, sugar, flour, all the necessities, and he almost begged the train for relief. He had lost another man just that week to suicide, making three out of sixty so far.

"Was me, I'd come along with us, right up to Fort Kearny." Ben told him.

"I'd give anything to do that, but Colonel Carrington would have me cashiered. He told me to remain here and I can't disobey him."

The train members left some staples for him and he responded with some government script, to be redeemed at the fort. Some of his men, watching them pass, had tears running down their faces. Clearly, they thought they had been abandoned there to die.

The train had been left alone after the battle and Ben had worked hard to keep the outfit on an alert footing. It had helped to have Luke Winstead come out from the Winstead wagon and start riding in the seat, still festooned with bandages and a wan look. Seeing him, and his condition, and remembering what had occurred all over again, made people keep their eyes open without being continually reminded. Luke was continually on the lookout for Ben, and when he saw him, he begged to ride with him. Ben, for his part, was patient with the boy and when he could spare the time, took him in front of him and let him ride along. Doc Clarence thought the boy was making progress and would recover well physically, if not mentally.

Several times, Ben had stopped in to visit with Woodsock, who was doing as well as could be expected, bumping along in the back of his wagon. He, for one, was extremely grateful for the early stops.

"I'll be up and around, Ben, pretty soon! Then, we'll shoe them big Belgians again." Leon was the best horseshoer in the train and loved to work with the teams of Belgians. The huge horses, which stood nineteen hands at the shoulder and weighed more than Hite's prized Percherons, seemed always in need of new shoes or those they had being reset. All the teams, even the Rebels mules, needed constant shoeing because of the rocky country and the hard use.

* * *

And now, the Sioux paid them some attention again. The horse herd was their main focus, and every night there was an alarm, gunshots and sometimes a turnout of the men to come running, weapons in hand. But no large force came against them, partly because Ben approached each possible ambush site very cautiously, scouting it in force, and keeping it secure as the train came through. Ben promised himself that if and when he made another trip up the trail, he would try to bring along a field gun. A cannon would have been a blessing, two a veritable godsend.

* * *

Finally, they came over a last ridge and saw the fort. Fort Kearny had been built between the two creeks:

Big Piney and Little Piney. It was shaped like a long egg, of ten foot logs set in the ground for the walls and ringed with firing platforms. At intervals around the walls, there were bastions and larger blockhouses, with log barracks, storerooms and officers' quarters positioned in its walls. Three hundred men of the 18th were besieged inside, in conditions similar to those being borne by those poor souls in the Reno Cantonment.

Colonel Carrington, a pompous, inflated ass, in Hite's private opinion, commanded. Of course, Ben had a jaundiced eye against officers, especially those who made their promotions on the backs and shoulders of their men. The fact that Captain Tyson had been threatened with cashiering if he abandoned a post that was dangerously untenable made Ben think the colonel was a misfit in uniform. The man had even seen fit to bring his wife and family to the fort! And his officers had been encouraged to do the same, so that his family wouldn't be lonely! Obviously, the post's commander had no idea of the enormity of the danger facing them until Fetterman's debacle the last winter. Now, though, he could see the fear in back of the facade the man portrayed.

This fort, situated as it was in the heart of Indian country, was helpless to do what it was supposed to do: protect the travelers on the road to the gold camps and keep the Indians tribes under control of the Army. Any patrols sent out came under immediate attack and scurried back in. Wood was a scarce commodity, hunting was impossible as the Sioux had run all the game off from the vicinity of the fort. Supply trains from Fort Laramie were turned back under attack. Now the man was forced to beg or requisition the post's needs from those trains strong enough to make it up the trail.

* * *

Carrington wanted to give them Army scrip for some of their staples—just enough to tide them over until the expected supply train arrived, he said. The trainmen demurred, they could get better prices at the gold camps. Carrington insisted, finally grew angry and said he would take the supplies, anyway, and they would, by God, take the scrip! With bad feeling all around, the trade was made. It was decided that those who had commercial stock, such as Ben, would contribute a share, as little as possible, to supply the fort's needs. The scrip would be redeemed at Fort Ellis, the colonel said. Then reluctantly, Carrington let the train go on, evidently hoping that it would lure the bulk of the Indians away from the fort.

Above Fort Kearny, the trail wound through the wooded foothills of the southwestern end of the Bighorn Mountains, and ambush sites became frequent. Some of the train members urged speed, to get through quickly, but Ben kept to a steady pace and continued his cautious way of scouting ahead. Though Indians were sighted every day, and they experienced some random shooting into the train or the horse herd, the Sioux refrained from attacking in force, preferring to continue their siege of the fort.

* * *

Two weeks later, they came off the bluffs over the Yellowstone and into the wide valley. Water had grown scarce and tempers had shortened but with the last leg of the journey one that followed the Yellowstone, then up and over a low pass and on into Bozeman, it seemed that their hard times were over. There had been no Indian trouble now for several days. Water was at hand. The trail had gotten easier as it wound through the Cottonwoods of the lush valley. Game was plentiful again and the train, which had also been conserving their food, could enjoy some rich feasts in the evenings, replete with buffalo steaks and roasts, venison and small game as side dishes. One of the New England contingent had a seine along and seining the river brought a full net of catfish, sturgeon and a few trout, which were a welcome change to the menu. Spirits raised in proportion to full stomachs and the wounded, including Woodsock, regained their strength on the nutritious soups and stews the women concocted.

* * *

There were no ferries on the Yellowstone and the river had to be crossed several times at fords that were sometimes treacherous. By now, the train had come to work like a well-greased machine, though, and these crossings were taken in stride, with no mishaps. Here, Hite's Belgians did excellent work, as they were double-teamed with the other wagon's horses. The big horses were a sight to behold as they threw their enormous power into the pull.

A large village of peaceful Crows, their tipis lining the north bank of the river at a place of high sandstone rim rocks, came in sight, their braves riding out to meet the train with upraised arms. Siccoolum was expert at sign language and rode out with Ben and Major Simon to talk with them. Ben was favorably impressed with their looks. The men were tall and well formed, with some proud dignity in their demeanor. Chief Tall Bull, an older man with streaks of gray in long braids, looked at the men attentively as she translated.

"River Crows." she reported. "They hate the Sioux and Cheyenne. They say we are safe now. Their enemies won't be down in the valley here. They will protect us, they say. They want sugar and coffee for their protection."

"You tell them that we have been protecting ourselves. That we killed many of their enemies for them. That we will give them some sugar and coffee because we are friends." Ben said. He nodded at the chief, who looked at him and nodded back. He seemed interested in Siccoolum's black horse and made some swift talk to the other braves in Crow.

Then he threw some sign at her, looking for the first time, directly at the woman. She turned to Ben.

"'Do we want to trade horses,' he asks. He sees that some we have are Sioux war ponies. He recognizes them. He asks how we got them. I will tell him."

More sign flew from her hands and the faces of the Crows, despite themselves, grew astonished. They looked at the white men with more respect. These men had come through the country of the Sioux, Cheyenne and Arapahoe seemingly unscathed, and they had managed to capture a large number of their enemy's war horses along the way! How did they do such a thing?

They wanted to hear of the exploit in greater detail and nothing would do but that the white men come to a feast in their honor that night. Then, waving, the Crows galloped back to their village. Soon, the men heard guns banging and whooping going on, which alarmed the train until the men returned and told them all what it was all about.

The village harbored some whites, one of which Ben was sure was a deserter from Fort Kearny who had somehow made it to the Crows. These men, another of them an old voyageur from the keelboat days who had lived with the Crows for thirty years, a mulatto named Jim Beckworth, listened avidly as Major Simon related the happenings of the train as it had passed through the country of their enemies and fluently translated it to the listening Crows.

The meal had been recognizably buffalo, with strange herbs and some unknown tubular vegetables that tasted somewhat like potato. The men had eaten their fill, then smoked with the chief and his friends, who had gradually filled the extra-large tipi to overflowing as the 'White Crows" began questioning the train men about the trip. When the story came to the scalp dance fight, the whole tipi rocked with their war whoops and yells of exultation at the slaughter of their enemies. They, were, however, dismayed that the white men hadn't done any scalping. Where were their proofs of the deaths of their foes?

For answer, Simon said to go among the horse herd and see the war ponies they had brought back. Huu! Huu! This had been done and the warriors had recognized some of the horses as those which had been prized war horses of their antagonists. The Sioux would never trade or let them go willingly. It was all true and they marveled.

Instead of demanding passage fees in the form of white man's staples, coffee, sugar and flour, they ended doing their best to trade the train out of some horses, particularly Siccoolum's black one. The train deferred to Hite, who reluctantly parted with some of his stock just to satisfy the village, though he let her keep her black. At the time, he thought little of the items he received: robes, war shirts, shields, lances, bows, and in some cases, other horses. Later, the items were traded or sold for as much or more than the value of the horses he had let go.

The whole Crow village turned out to wave goodbye as the train went on. Some of the men rode with them and followed for miles as they traveled north, riding with the column and being friendly. Siccoolum, wise in her people's ways, told Ben that more likely they were waiting to see where the train stopped and the horse herd was being held, then, they would attempt to steal some. She herself, brought her two horses and Ben's Monte to the wagon and kept them close tied that evening. Maxxus was stationed under the wagon to guard them.

Hite agreed and that night, he tripled the guard, to the dismay of the encroaching Crows who had worked hard to get within their circle and escape with a coveted animal. Ben had said it might be better to shoot to scare, not kill, as they wanted to preserve some semblance of friendliness with the tribe. Shots were fired but no Crow was killed, at least to Ben's knowledge. And no horses were lost.

Chapter 15

Bozeman was finally reached. All afternoon, they had been passing scattered shacks and cabins on the outskirts of the town, a rapidly growing camp in a scenic setting of the Gallatin valley, protected by Fort Ellis. Now, on a sparkling little creek, they found a large meadow and circled the wagons for perhaps the last time. A stock raiser came out from a nearby cabin and blustered that they were camping on his grazing ground. The trainmen, backed by Hite, disputed the claim and he left, saying that he was going to the post to make a formal complaint against them with Colonel Hale.

They looked at each other and laughed. After meeting all the Sioux could throw at them and the other hardships of the trail, a mere threat to go tell the Army, who couldn't give them any help all the long way, had begged them for help, held no terrors. They stayed where they were for a week and he never returned.

* * *

That Sunday, the whole train came together for a last church service, the ceremony shared by both the train's Baptist and Lutheran ministers, and the hymns soared into the bright blue sky of the Rocky Mountains.

After the service, Major Simon came forward and spoke feelingly of their deliverance from the "hardships of the trail and the clutches of the bloodthirsty savages." The train, like Moses parting the waters of the Red Sea, had been saved by the "Hand of the Lord and His able servant, Ben Hite."

His speech recapped the highlights of the trip, dwelling particularly on that terrible day the Rebel train had nearly been overrun by the Sioux. When it seemed all was lost, Ben and the Union men had suddenly appeared "like avenging angels to save them." Some of the women wept, reliving the loss of their loved ones all over again. Woodsock was there, sitting on a stool his wife had carried out for him. He had lost a third of his weight, Ben guessed. His gaunt face looked haunted and he nodded solemnly. The boy, Luke, clung to his mother and kept his gaze on Ben, smiling when he saw Ben's eyes meet his.

The feeling of gratitude which emanated from the assembly embarrassed Ben and he squirmed, hoping that he wouldn't be asked to say anything. A vain hope, for at the conclusion of Simon's laudatory speech, he presented Ben with a new rifle from the assemblage: a Henry repeater that looked as if it had just come from the factory. Ben wondered where the train had come by it. It was a beautiful weapon. Then Simon asked him to speak a few words. Ben got up, cleared his throat a few times, and said,

"Folks, I just did what needed to be done. We all did. Sure glad it worked out. . . and thanks for the gun! Guess that's all. . . except I hope the best fer you folks in the future. I'll likely be around the camps if'n ye need me."

He waved the Henry above his head and there was thunderous applause as he was surrounded by the train members, all who wanted to shake his hand and tell him how good a job he'd done to get them through. He saw Siccoolum and the children all clapping, delighted that "Father Ben" was being so honored.

* * *

As he returned to his wagons, he saw Maxxus sitting there on the seat of Kittledge's, panting in the heat of an early July day. He reflected that the train had very few dogs left from the many he'd remembered at Salt Lake. Ainsley's collie had been bitten by a rattlesnake and had died before Julesburg. Harver's shepherd dog had followed under his wagon for most of the journey, even beyond Fort Kearny, only to disappear one night. Ben had heard wolves howling, he remembered, and thought that one had lured the dog out from the train and then killed it. He'd heard of it happening before. Woodsock's big coon hound, Skeeter, had fought over his master's body until he'd been tomahawked by the Sioux. The fight the dog had made had perhaps saved his life. Hite remembered that the man had cried like a baby when he'd heard the dog was dead. Winstead's dog had died trying to protect the boy when the Sioux had taken him. Many of the Rebel dogs had died that day, fighting for their families. But here was Maxxus, the grinning old devil, still alive and doing his duty, protecting the wagons and his extended family. The kids loved him, particularly Betty, and Hite, not a dog man really, had come to be fond of him, too.

* * *

The next day, Ben rode in to visit with Abe Kahn, the Miners Committee chairman there at Bozeman. He found him sitting in his restaurant which was located on the dusty rutted main street. Several coffee coolers were lounging at their ease about the large table towards the back. The men were sipping their drink and watched as he approached. Then one got up and stuck out his hand,

"Hello, Ben Hite! I thought you were dead! We'd heard that you took the Kearny route around, and the Sioux been masacreeing a slew of travelers along there. Guess you made it though, after all! Good to see you." They shook hands.

Looking at the man, Hite remembered him. Buck Epson, from Sheridan. The man was wearing a pair of glasses that made his eyes appear large behind them.

"See you got yerself some eye glasses, Buck. Must help. You knew it was me, right off."

The man laughed. "Sure did! And they give me a new lease on life. I kin see agin. Well, you likely want to talk to Abe here. I gotta go. See you, Ben—and I will, too!"

The others shook his hand and introduced themselves, merchants on the one main street, then left also, leaving the two men alone.

"Sit down, Hite. We heard you got in, finally. Long trip! Bet you won't take that route again, huh?"

"Damn straight you are. Too many redskins fer me."

"Coffee?" Kahn signaled and a waiter came over, a cup in one hand and a blackened pot in another. He set the cup down, filled it and headed back to the kitchen. Kahn leaned forward and spoke in a near whisper. "I'll tell you now what you may not have heard. Plummer was the brains behind the bunch of cutthroats that were doin' all the mischief. The damn sheriff! Yer tip was a good one." He stopped and took a drink of coffee, then added some milk from a small pitcher on the table.

"We rounded him up and twenty-one of his goddam murderin' sonsabitches and hung 'em all! Some got away, though, and the roads aren't completely safe yet, but they's a damn sight better'n they was. Most of the bastids skipped the country, if they had any sense. I can tell you that it looked for a while as if it started as a Confederate plot to help them finance their cause. Randall still thinks so. But, with the war ended an' all, the rest of us don't go along with that. Mebbe we'll never know for sure. Anyway, the word I was s'posed to pass on to you is that you aren't a marked man any more. That nest of snakes is wiped out."

He sipped his coffee and his shrewd eyes twinkled. "I wouldn't let down your guard just yet, though, Hite, was I you. From what I heard, you killed quite a bunch of them yourself and they could always have friends or relatives—Williams, for instance."

He signaled and the waiter came and refilled their cups again. "So, what are you freighting?"

"Food stuff, mostly. Flour, sugar and coffee. I got one wagon full to the brim of potatoes."

Kahn's eyebrows raised. "A whole wagon full? The valley farmers are just getting started. Most of them are putting in grain and hay. Those who mess with garden stuff like potatoes plant just enough for their families. A whole wagon load. . . Hmmm. Tell you, Hite, I'll give you fifty cents a pound fer 'em, if there's no spoilage. I got a root cellar I just had dug back of the restaurant here that'll hold the whole shebang. What'll the load weigh?"

"Sixteen hundred, less two hundred used on the trail. Call it fourteen hundred, but I don't like to take first bid, so I guess I'll poke around a little, first. Maybe take 'em to Virginia City. Well, thanks fer the coffee." He got up to go.

Kahn put a hand on his arm. "Wait a bit! Have another cup. Coffee's on me. Hite, I kin use those spuds. You said you never took first bid. Here's a fair second. Seventy-five cents. You could maybe get a little more at Bannack or Sheridan or the other camps, but why not off-load them with me at a good price and take a load of grain over from the valley here? You'll make that much more, that way."

Before Ben left, the man had offered eighty-two cents and Ben had accepted it. Going back to the wagon, he told Harver to hitch up and take the spud load in to Kahn's restaurant. Then he rounded up the freighters who had supplied Fort Kearny and they headed for Fort Ellis.

Colonel Hale refused to honor the Army scrip right away, saying he was strapped for cash right then, so would pay them as soon as the expected supply train arrived. They left his office in an angry mood. The man had given them scant courtesy. Steele, particularly, was upset.

"It's always the _expected_ Army supply train! If you ask me, we'll be waiting a hell of long time afore we git our money. Red Cloud's outfit is goin' to keep the road sealed tighter'n a tick." The others agreed. All that could be said was that the loss was spread between them.

The train quickly disintegrated, as some settled in, farmers who liked the looks of the land in the valley, some went on to Virginia City and Nevada City with gold on their minds, or took the trail on over to Bannack or some of the other little camps. Hite and Steele took time to rest their stock and themselves, then followed the others to Virginia City.

Chapter 16

Sheridan came up first. The little mining community was about the same, and almost the first person he saw was Lige Randall, standing on the steps in front of his store. He yelled, "Ben Hite! By the Lord!" His handshake was firm and he was clearly glad to see him. Ben rummaged in his saddle bags and came up with the receipts for the gold that he had transported to Salt Lake the year before. It seemed like a lifetime. He handed them over to Randall, who took them appreciatively.

"You're a sight fer sore eyes, man! And so's this! I can use this money right now. Things bin tight here, with Red Cloud closin' the road east on the Kearny Trail. The route south to Salt Lake through the mountains has bin tough. Snow up high hez kept the passes closed fer months. What you got in yer wagons? I kin damn sure take anything you got, at a premium price!"

"Wal, I had a wagon load of spuds but Kahn talked me out of 'em in Bozeman."

"That sharper! What'd he pay you fer 'em?"

"Eighty-two cents a pound."

"Damn! He git the whole load?"

"'Fraid so."

"Hate to tell you—I'da give a dollar!"

Ben cussed. He'd lost some money there. "Knew I should have come on to the other camps. Just got to feelin' I needed to git my purse filled up agin."

In truth, his men had needed to be paid and he hadn't the money to do it.

"Guess you heard about Plummer? Strung 'em up, Ben. Helm, Plummer, his deputies and as many others as we could round up. You should sleep a little better now, by God! Come on in. Let's have a snort."

They went in to the store, the shelves looking bare, all right, as they passed down its length. Hite obligingly sat down and took a drink with the storeowner, sensing that they would likely make a deal for the other merchandise he had brought.

"You know, Ben, your idea about Plummer and his deputies was on the money. Guess when you told us about Corley, it made some sense and then, when we got to watchin' it all came out." He upended his drink and poured them both another. Ben was not a drinker but it had been a long road and he had a worked up a month's long thirst, so the whiskey, good stuff actually, went down pretty well.

"Yeah, Lige, when Kahn told me, it was good news, fer sure. Just wish I'd bin here to pull on a rope. Those bastards killed some friends and near done fer me."

Randall took his foodstuffs, all three wagons, paying him a price that took Ben's breath. And after supervising the unloading, Randall paid him with a check on Salt Lake. Now he'd gotten proof of the deposit in hand, the new bank there at Sheridan would cash it for him, Lige said. Since the amount was large, he walked with Ben to the recently built establishment and they completed their business. With gold and a roll of greenbacks in his pocket, Ben calculated that he was close to paying for his outfit. Another trip would see him clear and make him a hefty profit.

He found a vacant meadow down by the river, a mile from where the Bannack village had been. They were gone, evidently out on the buffalo grounds, making their yearly hunt. The site was littered with excrement from the time the village had been there and the grass had been grazed down to bare ground. Additionally, as with most winter camps, there was no available firewood left.

They went a mile away, to a little bench that was, to Ben's expert eye, an even better site to defend. Ben and

116

Siccoolum picked a spot for their tent and she and the drivers, with the kids helping, began making a permanent camp.

* * *

While that was being done, Ben decided he would take a ride to Virginia City to see about some loads back to Salt Lake City and maybe find out if the Southern route was usable yet.

The town had grown some, the shacks and cabins dotting the hills on either side of Alder Creek and up onto the ridges above. A cemetery had been started on the south hill and it looked to Ben that there were quite a few new graves. One of them would be Plummer's, he guessed. Boone Helm, who he'd had a near fatal run-in with, would be another.

The big man was a killer from California who had barely escaped a noose there. Boone had bumped into him deliberately on the boardwalk and both men had drawn their knives. Helm, seeing his antagonist armed and ready to fight, had growled, "Another time, ya bastid!"

Hite had smiled. "Any time, Helm!"

Both had stood and measured each other. Then Helm had turned and walked away. That had been Hite's first intimation that he might be marked for death by the organization called, Randall had told him, "The Innocents." Now, as he entered the teeming street, his senses were heightened, though he knew that the outlaw element had largely been erased.

He became aware that a figure was running beside Monte, and looking down, saw it was the Winstead boy, Luke, just as he'd done when the train was on the move. He reached down, and with a strong arm, swung the boy up and onto the front of his saddle, like he'd done so many times. The youngster wanted to tell him something and he bent down to listen.

"Mr. Hite! I heard 'em! They said they was gonna kill you when you came to town!" He looked around, like a gopher peering from its hole.

"Now, son. Where'd you hear that?" At first, Ben was skeptical of anything the boy might make up. He was always full of all kinds of disjointed stories on the trip, after his mind had been injured, as the Doc had said.

"I was playin' in the livery and I heard 'em talkin' about you. They said, "We'll wait 'til you call him out and when Hite steps out, we'll blast him from either side." The boy looked up, seeing the doubt in the face of the man he adored. "It's true! I heard 'em."

"Know who they were, son?"

"No. I was up in the loft playing and listened to 'em when they came in the livery. I hid. I never seen 'im. Just heard your name, is all."

"They see you?"

"Nope. Pretty soon, they saddled up and left. I never come down 'til dark. I was skeered."

So he was still a marked man. The boy had heard it just as he said. It was unlikely he would have made the whole story up.

"Listen, son, you run on back to yore folks. Don't say anything about this. It's between you and me, Luke."

"Yessir. Bye, Mr. Hite." He got down and scampered off.

Ben looked around. He saw no one that might be a threat. That meant nothing, though. Most of the men he'd killed the year before had been strangers. These men would be, too, most likely. He thought it through. According to the boy, he was going to be called out. That meant someone would brace him and there would be an altercation which they hoped would cause him to respond to a challenge and obligingly step out in the street to settle it. A calculated ambush. So he would have to be watchful for it to happen and make a move they didn't expect. That might let him live to get out of town.

* * *

He rode on up the street, trying to act casual and keep loose. Unobtrusively, he shifted his Colt to an easy position for a quicker draw. Three blocks up, he came to the Bale of Hay Saloon and stopping, dismounted and

118

tied Monte to the hitch rail. Then he stepped up on the boardwalk and parting the bat wing door, walked into the dim interior. The interior was crowded and he did see a couple miners he knew.

He walked to the bar and ordered a beer. The bartender brought it and he sipped it, watching the crowd in the dirty mirror in the back of the bar. A man detached from those standing watching the play at the poker table and came next to him as he stood there, the beer in his left hand, his right ready to draw his gun.

"You're Ben Hite, is that right?" The man said, a half filled beer in his hand, his right hand, Ben saw. Ben turned a little. The man could be either handed, as he was, or left handed. He watched him for a quick move and tried at the same time, to scan the crowd.

"Yes, that's right. Who's askin'?" He tried to make it as casual question but it came out a little sharp.

The man, a young slender individual with a sparse blonde beard, put his beer down and held out his right hand.

"Kermit Hart..man. He slipped a little on his utterance of the last name and Ben thought, '*I wonder...*' This man had a resemblance to the one who'd tried to sway the Sheridan crowd that Ben was a murderer. Ben put his beer down. What <u>was</u> the man's name? Then, it came to him.

"Hartman? Or maybe. . . Hamden. The man was your brother, wasn't he?" Ben grated. The other turned white and snarled,

"Yes, damn you! He was. My older brother, and you got him killed! Now, I'm callin' you for the sonovabitch you are! Come on out and we'll settle it now!"

He swung away and started to go out the door but Ben grabbed him and whirling him around, pulled the gun from the man's belt, then slammed him with a heavy fist, and as he started down, gave him a tremendous kick. Hamden went hurtling through the door, slamming the bat wings back and quieting the crowd.

"Not right now, son, I'm busy havin' a drink!"

He placed the gun on the bar and picking up his mug, took a pull on it. "Let's have another beer, barkeep."

The man brought it and took his money, showing by his bored look that altercations in the place were an everyday occurrence.

"Any law in this town yet?" Ben asked.

"Nope. They hung the last sheriff and all his deputies. Nearest law is over in Idaho. Some town constables around the territory but none here—less you count the Committee."

"Thet'd be Eustice Bayles? His crew?"

The man, a dumpy fat individual with a bald head and a handlebar mustache, took another look at Ben. Then his eyes showed some awareness.

"That's right. And you'd be. . . . Hite?"

They shook hands. "I'm Quayles, partner of Eustice's in the saloon here. On the Committee, too. Here, have this one on me. Sorry I didn't recognize you."

The man slapped his money back down and refused to take it. Hite raised his mug and drank, then said,

"The man who just left by way of my foot was the brother of a man who tried to kill me in Sheridan last year. I think he's got some friends hidin' out around town to take some pot shots at me when I come out to meet him. They hoped to get me to step into the street agin him and get a cross-fire. Friend of mine tipped me off."

"Well. Guess we'll see about that! I'll go get Eustice."

He left and presently came back with another man, who Ben recognized. The men shook. Bayles was beaming. "Sure happy to see you again, Ben. We'd heard that you were dead. You got somethin' fer me, I hope?"

Ben pulled Virginia City's gold receipts from his pocket and handed them over. The gross total he had carried to Salt Lake for the VC Committee totaled more than a quarter million dollars. Bayles sighed with satisfaction when he saw the deposit slips. With Hite rumored to be dead, more than thirty miners had been sobbing in their beer because they thought that their hard earned gold was gone.

* * *

Hamden rubbed his gut where Ben had kicked him. It felt like he'd been busted by a mule.

"He grabbed my gun, but I got another. We'll still do the job. I'll step up to him when he comes out to his horse and you both shoot then."

The two other men, both seedy looking nondescripts who were carrying rifles in the crooks of their arms, looked at Hamden. The taller man said, "This's startin' to have a bad feel to it. You said it'd be simple to get 'im out in the street. Now you say we shoot 'im before he draws on you?"

"That's right. Do what I paid you to. . . .Shhh!"

Bayles came into view, with three men behind him. All had their pistols leveled at the surprised ambushers.

"I think we heard enough, boys. Now!"

One had started to raise his weapon and Bayles drew a warning bead on him. "Just put those rifles down easy. Keep your hands quiet and Wylie, you go relieve 'em of their hardware."

"Who are you men? What do you want with us?" Hamden quavered. This whole deal was going wrong, and his gut was aching badly. It was soon to be his neck. Life was cheap on the frontier and the Vigilance Committee had gotten their fill of ambushers and outlaw scum. Especially those who were trying to kill their upstanding citizens.

* * *

"How'd it go in VC, Boss?" Kittledge asked when he rode up that evening.

"Oh, fine. Had me a couple beers in the Bale of Hay. Saw a few people I knew. By the way, we got some people want to go back with us when we head for Salt Lake. Miners, most of 'em, who made their poke and want to go stateside. We'll haul their gear and let 'em ride. Won't be as good as a stagecoach, but we'll charge a fare to haul 'em and make a fair bit of change. Better'n running empty. 'Course, there <u>might</u> be a fair amount of another item."

The drivers all knew that Hite had made some secret compartments in the bottom of their wagons and by now, knew exactly what they would be carrying. Each of the Miners Committees were using them to send out their gold.

Chapter 17

And now as they repaired wagons and harness for their return trip, Ben had some time for his family. He looked at the kids and was amazed at how they'd all grown. Freddy had sprouted out of his pants and Ben was sorry that he hadn't thought to buy them all some extra clothes when they'd been in Salt Lake. He'd been so busy with his own business that he hadn't thought of their needs. He made a resolution to do that thing as soon as they pulled in to the city.

The boy was a horse lover and the Belgians were his pets. To get on them, he'd grab their tails and pull himself aboard right over their rumps. The huge horses stood steady through it, merely looking back at him until he hupped, then they walked off. He rode them everywhere as they grazed, and often as they worked, like a bird on their broad backs.

Betty was a quiet one, content merely to ride between Moira and Kittledge, giggling when he laughed at one of his own anecdotes, always with a smile on her face, though her hands and feet caused her constant pain. She could do for herself, making her mutilated hands do what was needed, though Kittledge, who doted on her, wanted to do it all for her. Moira and Siccoolum, more practical, knew that she had to learn to get things done herself and encouraged her to be self-sufficient. So the little girl, not babied by the others, didn't baby herself.

Waterwheel and Katy were inseparable. The little girl's feet and hands had healed and even seemed to be regrowing some of the toenails and fingernails she had lost, to Ben's wonder. The little boy was walking now and would be a strong youngster.

The two little ones were still suckling Siccoolum, who followed Indian custom of letting their babies suck up into the second year or farther, until their teeth were in and they could eat regular food. It was a frequent sight to see them toddle to her and demand a meal. She would pick them up and opening her dress, allow them to suck even as she rode or worked. Ben, knowing it bothered the drivers, had a talk with her, but it didn't do much good. She continued the practice. It was in her motherly nature to put her children first.

Moira was turning into a fetching young lady, though Ben felt she should be in a school there in Salt Lake so that she might acquire some schooling. As it was, she seemed content also, to just ride with Kittledge and little Betty. She could turn her hand to everything around the camp now, even to using an ax, and worked right alongside of Siccoolum when they stopped, to put out meals that all of them looked forward to.

Siccoolum herself, was content to ride beside the wagons, take care of the children, cook, wash their clothes, and sleep with her man. What else was there in life but that for a woman? She never told Ben, but he knew she wanted a child by him and the two worked at making her dream a reality, if good sex between two people who liked and loved each other could ever be called work. He was good to her, never beat her, seldom even raised his voice, yet she knew he was the man of the tipi. And she was his woman. For her, life was good.

* * *

A month later, they were back in Salt Lake. Ben had carried returning miners and secretly transported another large gold shipment back to the city. He'd had no trouble this trip, though his vigilance was ever-present and he took no chances. The gold was their primary freight but it was masked by the transportation of those heading back to the 'States.' As usual, the train went at the speed of the slowest teams: the Belgians. To those passengers who complained at his slowness, Ben always made the same rejoinder: "Get off and walk, then."

Some did, but they were usually ready to ride again at the next rest stop. As before, he felt relieved when he carried the gold in to the bank and got his receipts for the valuable cargo. Then, he went as he had intended, back to the wagons and gathering the children, took them to the stores and bought them clothes. Siccoolum, too, got some new dresses and white women's 'doin's' though Ben privately thought she was just fine in her buckskins. Why was it Indian women looked out of place in white women's clothing? Still, he felt good, indulging her.

* * *

Using some of the money filling out his bulging account, he found a farmer in the valley out far enough from Salt Lake towards the Rocky Mountains at a small town the residents were calling Ogden who sold him a half section of pasture and some good bottom ground. The Mormon also agreed to put in oats and enough potatoes for another wagon load or two. The oats would be rolled and sacked for horse feed. Part of the deal was a trade for the Belgians and Freddy's heart was broken—until Ben gave him his very own pony, complete with a new saddle and tack. Then he was able to leave his big friends to their work in the new owner's fields. Ben filled their place with Percherons.

Scouring the valley, he had found a reputable breeder and bought a stallion that topped 19.5 hands at the shoulder and weighed over a ton. The huge dappled gray featured the strong, heavy shoulders and broad back coupled with the good looking head of the breed. While a stud, he was intelligent, good tempered and easily handled, like most of the draft horse breeds. Ben bought Atlas, as he named him, and three mares that took his eye, and trotted them over to his new place, with intentions of buying more when he could find or afford them. He watched the balanced gait they displayed as they went along and saw the hint of Arabian in them that the breeder said was in their background. Freddy, on his new pony, helped bring them to their new home.

* * *

Through the bank, he found a contractor, a Mormon named Torry Owens, who had just finished a job and with his good advice, they worked over a set of plans he had drawn out on some wrapping paper. The two story house had a bedroom for each of the kids and the usual rooms, plus an extra-large pantry and a root cellar underneath it. Ben also had him build a large bunkhouse for the men, who would be glad to have a more permanent place to stow their gear and live at their ease in the winter, for Ben intended to spend the winter months there, where prices were cheaper, pasture was available and the climate was milder.

The place was out along the river and secluded enough that neighbors wouldn't intrude on their privacy. It wasn't that he was ashamed of having an Indian wife, he thought, it was more for Siccoolum's sake. And the fact that he'd be living in Mormon country made it more sense to isolate themselves, since he was, in their eyes, a Gentile. He was in a quandary, though, about schooling the kids.

Finally, a solution came without him having to do anything. A man came to see him about being transported to the mining camps. His name was Miles Troyer and he was a teacher from Chicago. When he found out the passes were closed for the winter and the Kearny route impassable because of the Sioux, he confided to Ben that he had expected to make it up to the camps and find work before snow fell. Being a Gentile, he couldn't find any work in the city or the surrounding area. The Mormons refused to hire him. Might Ben know where he could find employment for the winter? Ben liked the young man's looks and asked him if he would consider tutoring the kids for room and board until such time as the passes were open and they'd leave for the Territory. He hinted that if Miles succeeded with the children, he might give him free passage to the camps. Troyer readily agreed and became one of the family as they camped on the property, watching their new home being built.

The children took to Troyer, to Ben's relief, and so did Siccoolum, who sat in on most of the lessons. Troyer was a good, patient teacher who had a way of instructing that inspired his pupils to learn. "He pulls, rather than pushes us," Freddy said.

The house done, and furniture bought and delivered, they started to move in. Ben was troubled when he saw Siccoolum standing in the front yard, looking up at the two story newly painted edifice. For the first time since he'd known her, he could have sworn she had tears in her eyes.

"What's wrong, luv?" he queried?

"Nothing—my warrior has a big tipi! He must be a chief!"

Despite that, she seemed ill at ease in the new place and it took her weeks to learn to use the big new kitchen stove properly.

Image courtesy of Mary Ann Cherry

Chapter 18

The trip up that spring went well. There was the usual horde of gold seekers on their way to find their fortune. By now, the trail was starting to take on the look of a road, with coulees and washes worked over by continual usage so that the wagons could make it through them easily, and the grades well enough known by now that they could be double-teamed at the right times. Each campsite was familiar to them, and each turn of the route predictable. So it was perhaps inevitable that Ben and the others might let their guard down a little on the trip.

Just after they had topped the pass that signaled they had crossed the Continental Divide and were headed down, their stop was by a sparkling spring that Moira had named the "Crystal Campsite." As was usual after the horses had been cared for and the evening meal eaten, the travelers gathered around the fire, listening to stories, even sometimes doing a little singing, if they had a passenger along who was so inclined. All the children, especially little Betty, enjoyed the songs.

Sometimes a bottle was passed, but Ben kept that to a minimum. He'd given obstreperous riders the choice of pouring their whiskey out or walking several times and since Ketchum was a binge drinker who didn't quit until the bottom of the bottle, he didn't like to tempt him. Coffee cups were in every hand, though, even the kids'.

Kittledge came into his own then, for his gift, so he thought (and most who heard him concurred) was to be an entertainer and he had an endless variety of jokes, stories and anecdotes that kept the group laughing. He was telling his listeners about a mule he once had which was the most stubborn animal he'd ever seen when suddenly, from the darkness, came a stern,

"HANDS UP!"

Everyone was taken by surprise, even old Maxxus, who was snoozing under the wagon, close to Betty and Freddy. Ben cussed himself for letting his vigilance lapse. Now, who knew what they had let themselves in for? His rifle and pistol were in the wagon.

A man, a scruffy figure, stepped into view, a little revolver in his hand. He looked around and said,

"You!" pointing at Siccoolum with the gun.

"Come pour me some o' that coffee and then go bring me a plate of food. Lots of it, now!"

He sat down on a stump and waved his tiny pistol at them. "The rest of you, keep your hands where I kin see 'em! I don't want your money, just somethin' to eat an' a horse. Bin starving an' I hurt my foot, so I cain't walk, an' no one would help me or give me a ride. Here, let me have that!"

He took the cup that Siccoolum handed him and gulped a drink. The coffee was hot and he burned his mouth on the tin. For an instant, his guard was down, and Siccoolum threw the whole pot of near boiling coffee in his face, making him rare back and fall off the stump, the hot liquid steaming off his clothes as he squalled at the pain.

As he started to get up, Freddy came from behind and gave him a thumping whack over the head with a piece of firewood. Maxxus, no doubt feeling guilty at not doing his duty, came charging at the man, too, and savaged his leg. He went down again.

The thief was nearly out and Ben was sure he was going to shoot either a child or Maxxus, waving the gun as he was, but he was too far away to act. Then Moira got into action and hammered the man with a pan. Ben decided they had things under control as Siccoolum snatched the tiny weapon from his hand. Kittledge and one of the passengers jumped on him and with a piece of rope, soon had him tied securely.

Ben, looking at him, almost felt pity. What were they going to do with him? String him up? If they took him all the way to Bannack, the Committee there, feeling that Virginia City had gotten too much of the action, would be glad to hang him. The poor man was just hungry and needed some help. The camp settled down again, the would-be robber coming to and squirming miserably in his wet clothes. Moira went to make a new pot of coffee.

Siccoolum brought the gun to Ben and he looked at it. A rusted little pin fire piece that likely wouldn't even fire. He pointed it in the air, pulled the trigger and it went off, scaring them all. He unloaded it and stuck it in his coat.

"See if he has any other little surprises fer us." He directed. Kittledge, still upset at his being interrupted, turned out his pockets and found little but some coins and a little bible, the *New Testament*. The man's head came up as Ben said, "You a preacher?"

"That's so—a poor one who has no flock." He snuffled.

"What the hell you doin' on the trail with nothin'? A man needs some gear to tackle the mountains."

"I heard the gold camps were heathen Sodom and Gomorra's and felt I had a call to bring some heavenly light to those miners' sinful lives."

Ben laughed, "By being a road agent?"

"NO! No, I had a goodly amount of food, blankets and camp equipment for the trip, even some money, but it was all stolen from me by some cowardly thieves who laughed when they led my horses away!"

A sob came out from the scraggly beard and he began to weep.

Ben walked over and cut his ropes. The man wiped his face with his dirty hands. "You had come to our camp peaceful, we would have helped you without being threatened. Where'd you come up with the little peashooter?"

"I found it in the litter on the trail. Someone had tossed it away. It wouldn't fire and I fiddled with it 'til I got it to shoot."

Ben let him ride until they reached Bannack, the first camp on the trail. As they came down the little main street, crowded as usual, with miners, gold seekers and the detritus of the camp: gaunt dogs, Indians, black frocked gamblers from the saloons and horses everywhere, the would-be thief, Pastor Byrd, as he'd asked to be called, suddenly called out, "There's one of my horses! That white one over at the rail there."

He tried to hop out of the back of Kittledge's wagon and promptly fell, hurting his foot again. He yelped and Ben hearing him, stopped the little caravan and they listened as the Parson limped to the horse and looking around, identified the other pack horse he had lost on the way. Both horses were as he had described them to the group before, even to the one black foreleg of the white one, and Ben was just asking a man he recognized if he knew where one of the Committee was, when the saloon door swung wide and a big individual came storming out.

"I hear someone's messin' with my horses!"

He came straight to the Parson and shoved him, making the injured man fall, then drew back a foot to kick him. Ben, just behind him, kicked it up and upended him. The man's hand went under his coat as he started up and Ben, caught a little off-guard, had begun to reach for his Colt, knowing with a sick feeling that he was maybe too late, when a shot slammed out. The man laid back with a groan, the gun falling from his hand. Siccoolum, from the back of her buckskin, had used her Sharps carbine. Ben knelt down at the man's side. He was dead.

Now, the street was for the moment still, then, from the saloon, another man came shooting from the door. Ben, his gun finally out, fired back and the man toppled on his face, shot at the base of the throat. At that, Mapes, the Committee chairman, came on the run from the hotel cafe, a big Dragoon pistol in his skinny hand.

He skidded to a stop when he saw Ben. "Hite! What the hell's goin' on?" Ben gestured with his gun.

"These two men robbed Parson Byrd back there on the trail. We give 'im a ride in. The Parson here saw his horses when we come to town and then here comes this gent, who was about to shoot me, an' Siccoolum puts a bullet in him. His pal came shootin' out of the saloon and I had to put him down. Lively town you got here, Mapes."

"Yes." He mopped his brow. "Gets more lively every day, seems like. You got my receipts?"

"Sure thing, in my saddle bags. Just give me a minute. What'll we do with these two?" He indicated the dead men.

"Oh, Coroner Phelps will come and clean up fer us. He'll charge you $10 fer diggin' the holes, though."

"Holes are gettin' expensive. Any money they got in their pockets belongs to the Parson here."

"I'll tell him. Here he comes now. Musta smelled the dead bodies. He's got a goin' business lately. Now, did I hear you say the squaw shot him?"

He looked around at the crowd that was starting to gather. "That's bad business, Ben! An Injun shootin' a white man. The Committee might not stand fer it."

Ben, feeling his temper rising, lifted his pistol and put a bullet in the dead body. "Just tell 'em I shot 'im, Mapes. Which I just did."

He gave the Committee chairman a level stare.

Mapes mopped his head again and said, "Oh Hell, that's all right, then. Ben. Now. About those receipts?"

Parson Byrd waved until they were out of sight when they pulled out for Sheridan.

Colt Dragoon Pistol

PART II

Chapter 19

<u>1876 Four years later</u>

"Guess you heard about Custer and his 7th Cavalry, Ben? Hell to pay up in the Territory, for sure. The damn Sioux have finally gone too far! I hear Gen'ral Sheridan gave Miles orders to conduct a winter campaign against them. Damn Injuns! Should just <u>kill 'em all</u>."

The man realized who he was talking to and said,

"Of course, I meant the hostiles, Ben. Not those who have shown to be friends of the white man!" He had just remembered that Ben lived with a squaw.

"Sure, Elias, I knew what you meant. A winter campaign now, that would likely break the hold the tribes hez got on the Territory, fer sure."

Ben Hite shook hands with Banker Rawls, the Mormon of the ridiculous looking side burns that curled out from his fat jowls. Ben, however, needing the loan for the new wagons, would never say anything about the man's comments to Siccoolum, who wouldn't understand, anyway. Maybe to Miles, though, if he got a private word with him. He pocketed the account receipt in his new vest and getting up from his chair somewhat awkwardly, because of the leg that still bothered him, he left the man's office and proceeded, limping a little, down the crowded street to the Benson Brothers Wagon Yard, where his fifteen new wagons would be built. Like Rawls, they were Mormons also, but good workers who made stout, reliable wagons.

He would have them painted with the yellow Hite sign on either side, with the addition, "and Sons." Miles, he thought, would surely be pleased with that recognition of his hard work. The youngster had come far in his own schooling to become a freighter and besides being a quick learner, he handled men well. If he didn't have quite the sand in his craw that Ben privately thought he should have, still, he seemed to please Moira, and that was of prime importance. The couple had been married now for nine months and she was showing the last stage of pregnancy.

The two had hit it off from the first and as time went on, Troyer had forgotten about his big plans to get rich in the gold fields and accepted the freighting job that Hite offered him, as his business grew larger. He still tutored the kids on the side, and the two had seen enough of each other to fall in love.

Ben had insisted that they wait until she was seventeen and so, on her birthday, they'd tied the knot. Siccoolum had helped make her dress and watched the ceremony from a curtained side room of the church, where the few Indians, Mexicans and other people of color attended. The church was full and Father Marquis had done a good job of tying the knot, Ben felt. Moira had wanted a Catholic wedding. Afterwards, the reception fed more than a hundred and fifty people and Ben was complimented many times on the beauty of the bride and her gown. He relayed that to Siccoolum and she beamed with satisfaction and reflected pride.

Now, the newlyweds lived in the house he had built for them as a wedding present, on the half section that adjoined his back horse pasture, and the other kids were constantly going to and fro. Siccoolum, though, he saw, stayed pretty much to home. Ben had hired a Mexican woman to help her with the washing and the housework, and taken her husband on as a grounds man. Their two teenaged kids helped with the stable work in the long eighty horse stalled stable he had Owens, the contractor he always used, build him on the property.

Now, with the new wagons, he would fill those stalls with Percherons from his two farms. His new stud, although not the great horse Atlas had been, was doing its job well enough.

* * *

Hite wagons could be seen on every road around Salt Lake and its environs. Ketchum ran this leg of the enterprise from his office in town, with Troyer as his assistant, taking loads, dispatching drivers, sending wagons as far east as head of track, hauling from the railroad as it came towards Salt Lake, and as far south as Phoenix. The northern and western region, Ben handled himself, particularly the gold shipments. And that was a major problem right now.

The transportation of valuable shipments of the heavy metal from the camps was still an integral part of Ben's enterprise, for he had proven to be completely reliable and the miners Committees had trusted no one else with the job. He, in turn, charged two percent of the total value to carry the gold from the camps to the banks at Salt Lake. It had been that way for four years now and was still an extremely lucrative business but times had changed.

Shallow draft steamboats had made travel to and from the camps much easier, as they made their way inexorably up the Missouri and finally to the head of navigation at Fort Benton. Some had even gone as far up the Yellowstone as Pompey's Pillar and a little above that, even, in their quest for a shorter route to the gold camps. But those attempts were usually ill fated and at least with the Yellowstone, could be done only during the June raise, at high water. Then, too, the Yellowstone country was still hostile territory. The Missouri flowed more water, and Fort Benton or at the least, Cow Island, was achievable, 2600 miles up from the Mississippi. Then, offloaded, the freight went overland on the Carroll Trail another 170 miles or so, to end finally at the camps.

Hite wagons had pulled their loads nearly from the beginning of that route and now, Committees wanted him to take gold back over it to the boats, for speedier delivery to the banks. The boats, with a good run, could make it in three weeks or even less, while it took his wagons more than double, even triple, that.

He had resisted so far, saying what everyone knew, that the boats had a poor record of keeping afloat, that for every one that made it up and down the river, one went down. The Missouri just had too many snags and hidden bars, which ripped the bottoms right out of the hulls, all the way down, right to its mouth into the Mississippi. He knew it took longer, but damn it, by wagon was still the safest mode of travel for shipping their precious cargoes. And except for the time he'd broken his leg and been laid up, he'd accompanied all the large shipments over the mountains. Just the one trip he'd been absent, the Committees had seen fit to try the boats and the steamer, *Luella*, had made, of course, a near record run straight down to the bank at St. Louis. That one run had convinced some of them they needed to turn the transportation over to the boats. And the boat captain, Grant Marsh, dammit to hell, had charged one and a half per cent, undercutting Ben. That had not been lost on the Committees, either.

* * *

The night Ben had broken his leg, Freddy had been in the stable. Somehow, the lantern had been bumped over and a fire started. Kittledge came shouting into the house, yelling "Fire! Fire! <u>The stable's burnin'!</u>"

They all had run out to the building that housed nearly forty of the business's teams. By risking life and limb, they got thirty of them out, sixty horses in all. Ben had gotten his leg broken when one of the mares, badly burned, terror-stricken, had torn loose from Moira and run over him. Atlas had died, along with forty-four of his mares and colts. Reliving that night over and over, Ben still couldn't get it out of his mind. The screams of the horses, the pandemonium, the broken leg, the screams of the kids. It all ran together in his memory and he had to shy away from thinking of it. Then, Freddy had gone missing.

From his bed, Ben had directed the search. The men even went through the burned stable, looking for his corpse. Nothing was found. He was missing and an extensive search that widened through the valley, turned up nothing. His horse had been in the stable, too, but Ketchum, looking hard, said it appeared his tack was not burned, nor was the body of the horse there, for sure. There was such a blackened, smelly mess, it was hard to tell. Ben's enterprise ground to an instant halt, with no teams to pull his wagons in the Salt Lake area.

Clearing the debris, replacing teams, rebuilding the stable, replacing tack and Atlas, the sire and mainstay of his breeding program, had taken all his money and then some. He did it, but not with the enthusiasm he had at the beginning. It had become a job, a business execution that gave him no pleasure. And Freddy was missing, with his Henry. Had he started the fire and run away? Most everyone thought so. Ben didn't know. But he was heartsick and those who knew him well, could see the difference.

The Steamer Luella

Maxxus

Chapter 20

Ben had gone to the bank and gotten the money easily. They knew of his affiliation with the Territorial mining Committees and had seen the large influx of money in his account at various times. They were glad to oblige such a prestigious customer and gave him an extremely low interest rate, one reserved for Mormons.

He used the same contractor as he had in the past: Torry Owens, and, with his brother, they built his new stables, only this time, he had learned the lesson of the fire and built four small ones, well apart, and of brick, rather than wood. They were more expensive but much less flammable. He also took precautions in each of them, with fire barrels situated at each end of the structures.

Replacing his teams was a different matter and he had trouble just getting enough Percherons. He had to settle for more common draft horses to fill his needs. And replacing Atlas, his beloved stud, was another matter. None came up to his high standards. It took a trip east to Illinois, finally, to come up with one that satisfied him. He named it Nemesis, for no good reason. It was a large black stud, neither as intelligent nor as good looking as Atlas had been, but a tremendous horse, just the same, and a willing sire which threw exceptional foals. Ben could work up no love for him, though Ketchum made much of him.

* * *

Ben was still talking with Nate Benson about the new wagons when Katy came hurrying to find him. She waved a paper.

"Father! Ben! A letter from Freddy!" She put it in his hand and he opened it with a trembling hand and as Nate turned away to give him some privacy, read,

Yleta, Arizona

Dear Father Ben and Family:

My best regards to you all. I don't know how to write this. How sorry I am of the fire which began because of my carelessness! I knocked the lantern over when I was pitching some straw into Kitty's stall for her. The fire spread so fast, and when I called for help, no one heard me. I nearly didn't get out myself and my hand and arm are still badly burned and make it hard to do my work here at Mr. Parker's ranch where I am employed. He is kind to me and I am breaking horses for him, a job of work that I enjoy.

I can never make up for what you lost in that fire, father, and am so sorry I get sick when I think of it. I just couldn't face you so left without telling anyone, which I know now was wrong of me to do. I took Penny who was in the pasture, my saddle, your Henry rifle and just went south, down the road. I made it to Yleta, where I found work with Mr. Parker, a rancher who has a large holding along the Virgin River here. Please don't come looking for me, as I could not face you. Especially you, Father Ben, who loved your horses as much as I did. I think of you all with love. I will send money for the rifle when I get paid, Father.

Much Love,

Freddy

HE WAS ALIVE! That was the main thing, Ben decided. And the fire had been an accident! Of course, Ben knew that all along. Freddy loved horses, especially Atlas, and would never have done such a terrible thing on purpose. He would write and tell him that straight away.

142

And the boy should come home, not be living with strangers. Suddenly, Ben had a new lease on life. His boy was alive! He left Benson's yard with a smile and putting his arm around young Katy, they headed for home.

* * *

They all sent letters to Freddy, telling him of their love and affection and that they, of course, knew he had not started the fire on purpose. Accidents happen. Ben sent money for his trip back home, but time passed and though Freddy sent another letter or two, he failed to come. Then, a telegram from a Jefferson Parker arrived over the new wire. Freddy had been wounded by Paiute who had raided along the river. By the time this reached them, the boy might well be dead. If they could, they should come down.

* * *

Fearing what he would find, Ben nonetheless immediately took the road south with his two saddle horses, Monte and Spur, a grulla he had found while he was searching for draft horses. Armed and taking only Siccoolum along, with her buckskin, her black, and a pack horse, he set a hard pace and they made the trip in three days. They traveled at night and twice they narrowly escaped war parties who had been raiding all through the area.

Near Mesquite, following the Virgin River down, they came upon a small wagon train of Arkansas travelers, a whole small town who had uprooted themselves and headed out on the trail to go west, the magnetic draw of fresh new land and perhaps gold, prying them from their humdrum existence at home to start a new life together in California.

Ben noted the fine stock they had, the new wagons, the better dress of the people and thought it one of the finest trains he'd seen on the move. He and Siccoolum stopped with them for a while and the men were friendly but ignorant about safety on the trail, Ben thought. They had not made a circle of the wagons, nor had they sufficient guards out. Ben, trying to be helpful, had told them of this and they had laughed at him.

"We're in the hands of the Lord, Mister Hite. And the Indians are largely pacified. Were we down along the Rio Grande, though, where the Apaches hold sway, or up in the Dakota Territory, where the Sioux are, we would be more considerate of our defenses." Doctor Perkins, who was leading the party remarked. The others nodded.

"Thet carriage you got along is sure a fine machine!" Ben referred to a well-appointed, richly fashioned conveyance pulled by a smart team of Standardbred bays that had taken his eye.

"Yes, I plan to make use of it in California, making my rounds."

The doctor, a man educated past the point of common sense, Ben privately thought, grasped his arm and said, "Come, let me show you my stud."

Together, they walked out to the horses and he whistled a couple shrill notes. From out of the herd came a fine Standardbred bay stallion, nodding his head and trotting right up to the doctor, who fished an apple from his pocket and gave it to him. The horse nuzzled him and Ben could see the love between the two. The doctor, a fattish, well-dressed man, smiled at Ben. Evidently, he loved to show his pride and joy.

"My pet. Fastest horse in Arkansas and the surrounding states. A great begetter of wonderful foals. Line bred back to Savant and Leo Decour. His stud service makes me more than my work as a physician."

"That's a fine horse, Doctor. Hope you kin keep him out here. Lots of men would kill to own him."

"I pay for an extra guard to stand watch. We'll not let someone steal him."

* * *

Ben and Siccoolum left after the supper meal, continuing to travel by night. In the small dusty town of Yleta, they asked for directions at the single mercantile and a fat Mexican there told them in broken English to head on the trail south east until they sighted a set of twin buttes, then turn a little south along a dry riverbed. A few miles along, it would run into the Virgin River and they would come to Parker's ranch. Buying some supplies to replenish their pack, they rode into the desert.

Parker's ranch was a collection of dusty adobe buildings, the largest of which was the main ranch house, built like a fortress. Nearly empty corrals were grouped around a large burned out barn. The place had been hit hard by the Paiute, it looked like, and as they rode in, armed men began appearing, watching them come. As they rode forward, rifles came up and he shouted, "Don't shoot! We're comin' in to see about our boy!"

The Mexicans and cowboys heard the English, the guns were lowered and a tall lean man with a sweeping mustache stepped through the door, packing a mug of coffee. Ben swung off at the step. The man, who Ben took to be Parker, drawled,

"I'd say Freddy's dad and mom come to pay us a visit."

"That's right, sir. You'd be Parker?"

The heavily mustached individual took a swig of coffee and drawled, "Yes, that's me. Ben Hite?"

Ben stepped up and they shook. Parker narrowed his eyes at Siccoolum. "Yer squaw housebroke?"

Ben looked at him. "Yes. And she speaks English. Her name is Siccoolum. Luv, this is Mr. Parker."

Siccoolum inclined her head and got off her horse in a graceful motion. Ben saw Parker take in her female attributes, which were still considerable, and he turned, saying, "Come on in, then, and we'll hev some coffee."

Ben and Siccoolum followed him into the large adobe house, its walls thick and pocked with bullet holes, its windows more gun ports than apertures for letting in light. Inside, rifles leaned against each wall, and a large table in the center was covered with ammunition and pistols. A couple water barrels were stationed in the corner and Ben saw bloodstains not completely erased, there on the tiled floor. There had been a siege, a desperate fight, and the evidence was still visible.

Parker called, and a Mexican woman's voice, answered. Parker found them chairs and as they seated themselves, two women came carrying cups and a large coffee pot. She poured and offered them each one, though Ben noticed she looked hard at Siccoolum.

"Is he. . . did he. . . ?" Ben choked a little.

Parker answered. "He's alive. Bin holdin' on. I think he knew that you'd come. He's in the back where it's quiet and we'll head in there presently. He's sleepin' right now."

Like many desert people, his internal clock seemed to run slower and time was not important.

"Where'd he get hit?"

"He was shot in the leg, up high. Near bled to death afore we could stop the bleeding. Had to do thet with dirt and now it's infected." Parker grimaced, the lean leathered face taking on the look of a reptile

"Wanted to cut it off but he wouldn't let us. He's a horseman, you know, and said if he couldn't ride, he didn't want to live. And, damn it, I don't blame him."

He had fought from the barn, Parker said, to try to keep the savages from getting their horses. Put up a good fight there with that repeater of his. He'd been hit late in the battle and was at death's door.

Siccoolum got up and said, "I want to see him."

Parker looked at her and said, "All right. Come on back."

They trooped through the house, Ben seeing that the whole place was built for defense and had been used for that, perhaps several times. Toward the rear, they entered an arched door and into a large room with six beds. Three were occupied and Ben realized that Freddy hadn't been the only one who had been wounded in the recent affair.

Freddy was lying in the far one and Siccoolum bent down to take in his feverish, white face, so thin and pain stricken. He was in a laudanum induced trancelike sleep.

Parker, standing there, said, "We did all we could to clean the wound. Bullet went on through. Bin usin' laudanum fer his pain." His voice was apologetic. "The nearest doc is in Las Vegas, a hundred miles away, and he ain't worth a shit. Maria here is a good nurse and says, if his fever could break, he might make it. Is yer squaw got any leanin' that way?"

"She knows some. Both of us seen a lot of bullet wounds. Let's see the leg."

Pulling the blanket back, Ben wasn't surprised at what he viewed. The limb was swollen with blood poison and the smell told him gangrene had begun. However, in the war, a doctor had saved his own leg by a method he told Ben later he'd learned from an old grandmother.

He had taken flour and yeast, mixed it with water and let it sit in the sun until a mold had taken over, then after cutting the length of the leg, smeared the mess on it and covered it with a wet bandage. The concoction had drawn the poison out and somehow given the leg new life to fight off the infection.

The flour and yeast poultice had become fairly common practice in the later years of the war and many lives and limbs were saved. Now, if it could be used here, the leg might be rescued, but it was late, and he could see the red threads running up and down the bluish tinged extremity. Ben covered the leg and turned to Parker.

"Wal, we'll try somethin' I learned in the war. Hev yore wimmen some flour and yeast handy? I'd need about. . . two pounds of flour and a cup of yeast."

Parker was mystified. "Sure thing! MARIA!"

He threw some Spanish at her and she yelled back, then brought the flour and the yeast. Ben mixed it in a big bowl she brought, then after putting in enough water to get it working, covered it with a cloth and they put it out in the sun to work.

Meanwhile, Siccoolum was working on Freddy, stripping him and washing his wasted body with water and soap the Mexican women had brought her. With every move of his body, the boy moaned with pain.

The two men lying in the other beds had likewise been treated by Parker with laudanum. It eased their suffering some but one was near death and in fact, did die later that night. The cowboy had been shot in the stomach and Parker, not knowing what else to do, had administered the one medicine he had: laudanum he'd bought in Phoenix by the gallon. He'd had it used on him when he'd been shot in a set-to with Mexican stock thieves.

The wound this one had was such that he likely wouldn't have survived anyway, even given the best medical attention of the day. The other, tomahawked and stabbed multiple times, was a tough old Mexican who had killed his attacker and crawled to the house, then helped beat back an attack before collapsing. He had head wound which Parker had stitched up and his stab wounds were treated with Tequila and bandaged. He was drunk and wanted to sing but Maria, his wife, managed to keep him quiet most of the time.

While the mold was working in the sun, Parker took them out and showed Ben the results of the raid. The big barn had been completely burned, as were some of the nearer corrals posts and pole cross members. Horse hay stacks at the one end were still smoldering.

"How'd Freddy and the ones in the barn get out?" queried Ben.

"Wal, me n' the boys in the house made a charge out with our pistols goin' and grabbed 'em up afore the Paiute knew what was happenin.' Got 'em all back in the house an' the bastids ran away with all our horses but what we had hid out in a far arroyo a mile er so from the ranch. Sure glad I had the sense to do that or we'da bin plumb afoot."

He spit and offered Ben a chew, which he took, working the wad of tobacco back in his mouth. Together, they walked out to the ranch's grave yard, where three fresh graves laid by seven other older ones, sunken in from time. Parker gestured at the older ones.

"My wife and child. Died in childbirth. Wonderful woman. Buried 'em in one grave."

He pointed at another two, "My foreman, 'Jingle Bob' Brown and 'Heavenly' Peterson, two of my men from when I started the ranch here. One got throwed from a horse and broke his fool neck. The other had a little rope accident." Then he swept a hand toward the others. "Died by Paiute raids, Mexican bandits, 'er sickness."

He rubbed his face with a gnarled leathered hand. "How long you expect afore we kin use that medicine you worked up?"

"Well, in this hot sun, I'd say tomorrow afternoon. Have to see how it looks. The mold needs to be pretty well covering the mess to work well. Then, we'll have to cut the leg and work it in good. That may kill him, right there. You still have some laudanum?"

"Yep. Bought aplenty. Knew I could always use it."

* * *

The next evening, with Freddy delirious and in a coma, they operated on the leg, cutting it carefully its length in two long lines from his crotch to well below the knee. Ben, sweating profusely not just from the heat, had steeled himself and carried through on it, glad that the boy was largely out from the laudanum. They let it bleed and drain, the blood coursing out thick and dark, then Ben took up the mold goop and smeared it in the cuts their length, working it well into the wound and the incisions. Then, with Siccoolum helping, they wrapped it in damp bandages and left it to work.

* * *

The boy came close to death that night, but his strong constitution carried him through to morning. Late in the afternoon, his fever broke and he came to briefly, seeing Siccoolum and Ben sitting by his bed, she wiping his face tenderly with a damp rag.

"Father Ben. . . .Siccoolum, knew you would come." He whispered. Then, he closed his eyes and dropped into a deep sleep with a smile on his lips.

"Wolf" courtesy of Dan Rick

Chapter 21

It was two weeks before Freddy could be settled into the back of a light wagon and the trio started on the way back home. Ben took it easy and the journey went slowly. As before, they traveled by night. Close to Cedar City, in Utah, they reached their expected camping place, a high mountain spring early in the morning, where they would lie quiet for the day. The night was dark and wolves seemed to be all about. They heard them howling and snarling over something until dawn tinted the tips of the mountains about them a rose red.

Ben had stayed on guard and now, as the light increased, he looked around and the hair on the back of his neck seemed to raise. Once before, circumstances similar to what he felt had occurred—a late night crawl to get into position for an early morning shot or two into a Rebel company's bivouac had happened to put him into the midst of a corpse ridden battlefield, fought over two days before. The wounded in the field had been removed finally, but the dead lay where they had fallen. He had felt that something was wrong but hadn't pinpointed it until the sun had come up and the light had shown dead men all about him. He had turned and retreated from the field, leaving the dead to their final rest.

Now, looking about him, he saw corpses, many of them, torn by wolves so that there were limbs missing, and most of the bodies with the flesh stripped from them. And it wasn't just men. There were women, with their hair tangled in the brush there, children with their throats cut, some with their heads missing. Men with similar wounds or worse. Most of the bodies were naked. Their eyes had been eaten out by magpies and ravens.

Ben roamed the little dell and found where the recent remains had been originally buried in three shallow mass graves, all which had been dug up and scattered by the wolves.

He woke Siccoolum and together they looked the place over. It had been the site of a massacre, and not one in which the men had fought with guns or knives to save their kin, but one which the men were defenseless and all had been killed. Ben's expert eye told him that the place had been a perfect spot for an ambush. Looking on either side of the trail, they found evidence that men, some moccasined but also ones wearing boots, had hidden themselves to fall on the group of people, who had been walking down the path, likely headed for Cedar City.

They saddled the horses, loaded up Freddy and followed the trail back, where they found the wagon train had been. Evidently, the fight had gone on for some time, the attackers keeping the wagon people from water. A rough trench had been dug about the spring and on the hills above the site where the train had been sieged, and there were some rock parapets with holes from which to shoot. The rocks still had bullet marks from the shots the train people had made, trying to hit their enemies hiding behind them. These fortifications had effectively kept the train from the water.

Then, the train had somehow been talked into surrendering and giving up their weapons, thinking they could then go on their way. After they did, the attackers fell on them and slaughtered them piecemeal, even down to the young children. A few had gotten away and Siccoolum following a trail, found the remains of three little girls who had likewise been chased and wantonly killed.

They talked as they left the ghastly place and decided that it had to be the work of Indians, likely Paiute, but with the help of a number of white men. Indians would not bother trying to bury the remains of their victims. Indians would not be wearing boots. And who were the white men? Why would they do it?

Ben thought back to the Perkins train they had spent some time with on the way down. The train had some fine stock, new wagons and a beautiful stud horse which its owner delighted in showing off. The people were well dressed, evidently they had money along. Could the train have tempted the wrong people? It was incredible that white men would do such a savage thing.

Whatever the answer, they couldn't bury such a number by themselves. And, it was possible that they might bring the attackers down on them just by being there and seeing what had transpired. So they went on, Ben in a quandary about the terrible tragedy, Siccoolum more fatalistic. Ben had tried to shield Freddy from such a horrific sight but despite that, he had glimpsed enough to know what had taken place.

* * *

Four days went by and in that time, as the boy became stronger with Siccoolum's cooking and the short stages of each day, he grew ever more talkative. Finally, on the day before they were to reach home, he broached the topic they had all been skirting. Sitting by the fire, his face in shadow, he was silent for a time, then choked out,

"Dad, I. . . am sorry about the fire! Atlas, all the other fine horses. . . So sorry!" Ben came to him and held him in a gentle hug. The boy sobbed in the big man's chest and Ben smoothed his hair and shushed him, a well of love for the youngster choking him up.

"Son. It's behind us. Yes, I don't deny it was a hell of a blow, but not as bad as losing you was! You're my son, Fred, and we all knew it had to be an accident."

The boy gave a heave and said, "It wasn't an accident, Dad. And I didn't set it. The truth is, I was in the barn, messing with the horses, when Torry Owens and and his brother came in carrying some coal oil and poured it around, then they threw a match to it. I couldn't believe it! I came boiling out of where I was hiding, and tried to put it out and they grabbed me. I thought for a while they

153

was goin' to kill me or throw me in the flames, but then Torry said we'll just kill your family if you don't run off and make yourself scarce. We need someone to blame it on. You'll do. Get outa here!"

He snuffled and wiped his eyes. "I was petrified of what they'd do to you and the girls and so I left."

He looked up and Ben could see the resolve in him that would get stronger as he grew older.

"But I couldn't just leave you without letting you know I was all right. So that's when I wrote the letter. I still couldn't decide whether to come home or not, to let you know that there were men who hated you. Then the Paiute hit us at Parker's."

He buried his face against Ben again.

"Oh Dad, what're we goin' to do? The Mormons killed all those people!"

* * *

"Sure not the Ben we used to know." Kittledge remarked. "He works, he talks to you, but it's like he ain't really there. I thought gettin' Freddy back again and seein' him walkin' on thet leg, he'd be happy. Wisht I knew some way to get him to smile agin."

Moira poured another cup for him. "Maybe a baby would help." she said with a coy smile.

"Hey, Gurl! You tellin' me you're expectin'?" Kittledge exploded. "Well! That might do the trick, fer sure! When you goin' to tell him?"

"I've been waiting for the right time. Whenever that'll be."

* * *

The news that he was going to be a granddaddy did make Ben happy for a short time, but then the cloud descended again. Watching with a new perspective, he began to see just how all-powerful the Mormons were in Utah Territory. It came down from the top: Brigham Young, the Head of the Church, was also the Governor. Each and every head of affairs under him was a Mormon. The law was dispensed by Mormons, with the sheriffs and the judges all in the church. The banks were all controlled by Mormons. Most of the businesses were run by Mormons.

Now, he began to see with newly opened eyes just how they really thought about Gentiles like himself, so called, because they were not Mormon. Here in Utah, the Church had reversed the scorn its members had suffered in the states they had come from.

Illinois, he knew, had imprisoned and finally killed Joshua Smith, his brother and some of his devout followers, because of their practice of polygamy and some criminal acts attributed to them. So the growing cult had migrated to Jackson County, Missouri, where they had again been persecuted and ridiculed for their beliefs, again charged with crimes they may or may not have done, and finally driven from the state. More recently, a popular bishop had been shot and killed in Arkansas, by an irate husband who resented the attentions the Mormon was paying his wife.

Coming from that background out west to the lawless frontier, where every man had to be a force unto themselves, and Might, if it didn't make Right, certainly prevailed, the Church had become a mighty force to protect and further advance its members. They certainly resented the persecution of their faith, they had certainly suffered and endured the travail. It was likely, Ben thought, that there would be those of the Church who would not have any qualms about serving Gentiles back some of their own medicine, especially if they happened to be from Missouri or Arkansas. With the Indians masking their activities, who knew what other killings of luckless travelers had been perpetrated? Kill, then blame it on the Indians, who likely were willing participants, anyway, in some cases such as the Perkins train.

He somehow had to find a way to bring it to a stop, but taking it to the sheriff or even a judge here in Salt Lake would merely alert the Church. Then, not just his property might be on the line, but life and the lives of his family. So what should he do?

Colt Dragoon

Chapter 22

After three days of wrestling with the problem, he decided to call the family together and talk it out. He dismissed the Mexican servants and walked the grounds. All was quiet but he was so keyed up, he went to the closet and got out his old Sharps and his Colt and loaded them. Then, coming into the large parlor where his family, and Kittledge, had gathered, got their immediate attention as they saw him armed.

"I want to talk to you all. I bin mighty worried lately." Then he told them what had transpired on the trip home and just what he had come to realize about the Mormons who surrounded them. Their shocked faces and dawning comprehension of their danger showed on all their faces, except that of Siccoolum and Freddy, who nodded. Kittledge was silent, which was proof of how serious it was.

"So, what're we goin' do about it?" Moira, ever practical, asked.

"First, we need to somehow get away from Utah. Go where we know the Church has no power or influence. The question is, do we go east or west?" Ben responded.

Miles spoke up. "I'd say go east, then find a judge with some power with the government who can get us in touch with federal people who can do something."

"We kin do that. We could go back east. We have a route that hooks up with the railroad there already. But we couldn't take the horses."

"Or we could go with our wagons up north to Montana. We got a train about ready to travel just now, right, Kittledge? We could hook up with it, claiming thet we need to make some changes up there. Find some new routes, build some new headquarters along the Helena Trail. Our business is up there, not in the east. Once we get there, we get our school teacher to write some powerful letters to whoever we can think of who might take some action. And we need to do it right away, or all the evidence of the massacre will be gone for no one to find."

Miles said, "What about our homes, our furniture, the property here? You just got done rebuilding the stables! You just put in an order for more wagons. We got a baby coming, too. Moira shouldn't be traveling."

Moira shushed him.

"I'm fit for traveling! Lots of babies have been born on the trail. I'll be fine, just so we get out of Utah and away from these terrible people!"

"What about the horses?" Freddy asked.

"We'll take 'em. I'm not goin' to let the damn Mormons have 'em, if we can help it." Ben stated. The thought of the burning stable intruded for a moment and he thought of one other thing: revenge. This he would take care of himself. But not now. First, he must get his family away.

The meeting lasted into the night.

* * *

Carefully, cautiously, they began making their plans. Kittledge would bring the fourteen wagons as usual to the Mercantile warehouse to be loaded. Then, again as usual, he would head to the farm. The trip always started from there when the sun came up. Kittledge himself would bring one of the wagons up to the house after dismissing the drivers for the night. They would load what they could in it after unloading his freight, which he would specify to be flour. Most of the drivers were Mormons and therefore, any could be spies. Probably they all were. That meant the normal procedure would be followed and Kittledge would head the wagon train out at daylight.

Ben and the rest would follow on horseback the next night, herding the remaining eighty horses along with them. Everything would have to be left but what they could pack in the one wagon. When they caught up to the train, Ben would send the Mormon drivers back and the family would take their places as drivers. They would tell them they were taking the horses up to the gold fields to open another route there and the family wanted to come along to see the sights of the mining camps. Then, they would hurry on, hoping trouble didn't follow them. Freddy would trail the horses. Ben would try to cover their back trail. It was a poor plan, but Ben was convinced that their lives were forfeit if they didn't act right away.

* * *

He was overseeing the loading at the warehouse when he had a visitor: Hank Givens. The sight of his once familiar face astounded Ben.

Hank was a tall sandy haired, freckled man with a long nose, a blondish mustache and a piercing set of light gray eyes flashing under a large hat. He grabbed Ben and gave him a hug, which Ben willingly gave back in double measure, the back slapping raising dust off Hank. Then the two stepped back and took in the changes in the other.

"Been a peck of years, Ben, and words can't say how glad I am to see you fit and hale! I asked at the Merc and they said you were likely out here watching them load yer wagons. So I thought I'd come out and give you a surprise."

"You did that, Hank! I'm damn glad to see your ugly, freckled face! How've you been?"

* * *

Hank Givens was from Kansas and had been one of Ben's particular friends in the company during the war. They had always had a running argument going as to who was the best shot. They had fought together in twenty-seven engagements before Ben had been wounded at Mine Run, in Virginia, where Lieutenant Colonel Trepp, their beloved CO, had been killed. That was in 1864. Hank had gone on and fought another year, through until the end, then been mustered out and returned home. The two hadn't seen each other since Mine Run.

Life there in settled Kansas was damn dull.

"About all there was to see," he said, was "the south end of a team of horses goin' north. So, finally, I ups and sells out and headed west to go out to California—or wherever I might end up." He laughed. "My old lady left me for a shoe salesman and the kids are up and grown and gone so I got the idea to see some country."

"How'd you find me?"

"Not too hard to do. You leave a wide trail, Ben. Capt'n Albers lives in Leavenworth and I stopped to have a gab with him. He told me you had gone out to the gold fields and was doin' some mining. I saw Sergeant Tolliver in Omaha and he said he heard you were taking freight up to Montana. Then, when I was talkin' with Kernzy in Denver, he mentioned he'd heard you were running a big freight outfit in Salt Lake, so I thought, what the hell, we're going through anyway, why not see if we could look you up? So we did, and here we are, by God. Damn! Good to see you!"

"Will Kernzy! Is he here, too?"

"Sure. He came along, too. He's downtown lookin' fer a saloon to wash down the trail dust. He wants to see you. Claims you owe him some money!" He grinned. "'Course, we know who owes who."

"Ha! He'll play hell findin' a saloon in Salt Lake. It's dry as an old bone." Ben looked around "We got to talk. Serious. And what I'm hopin' right now is that you two might like to make a trip up to Montana with me."

Hank laughed. "That's what we came to talk to you about! We was hopin' to hitch a ride with you or one of your trains on up to the Territory."

"My friend, that would be a damn good idea for us both! But we do need to have that talk. In private. Come on. Let's go gather Will up!

Chapter 23

Ben had talked with Hank and Will, another old friend from Company 'C', for a long time. They at first were incredulous at what he told them. Then it sunk in. They remembered the Mormon troubles in the states east. They were Gentiles who had some possessions along. Each had a wagon, a good team and some stock, along with money and goods to sell later in the Territory. Each could be in jeopardy and it made even more sense to join up with Ben.

"Still got your Sharps rifles?" Ben asked.

"Damn right." each replied. "A Sharpshooter doesn't sell his rifle." Hank said. "Especially one he beat Ben Hite with at every prize shoot the Company put on."

"You always was a bullshitter, Hank," Ben said with a grin.

Will Kernzy laughed. He was a man of medium height, but with a tremendously wide set of shoulders, which gave some indication of his great strength. Few men bested him in an arm or leg wrassle, though Ben had done it. He was another veteran who had been wounded, like Ben, in the leg, and invalided out just before the end. The knee wound pained him and he was an alcoholic largely because of it. His red rimmed eyes could still focus well on a gun's sights, though.

"All right. the plan is that we act as rear guard fer the wagons and the stock. It'll be us three against quite a few, likely. I have an idea they'll send what they call their Mormon Militia: probably twenty men or so. If we can get far enough ahead of them, then take care of that bunch when they catch up, hopefully we can get free without a second fight."

"Three against twenty: sounds like the war, all right. The Sharpshooters against the Confederate Army. Oh, what the hell! It's bin a good life." Will said. Hank agreed.

* * *

It was not uncommon for other travelers to attach themselves to Hite's train and the drivers took little notice of the two wagons driven by Hite's friends. The cavalcade started at 7:00 o' clock: sixteen wagons with goods destined for the mining communities in the newly formed Territory that was being called "Montana, as it was broken off from the previous Dakota Territory, then the Idaho Territory."

That evening before, he gathered the workers, the gardeners, the cooks, the washing staff and the stable hands and told them the next day was a memorial day to him: the day he had been wounded in the war, and his officer killed. Therefore he was giving them a holiday and their pay early.

Bless Ketchum, his manager when he was gone from the city, had been a problem: he had married a Mormon girl [against her family's strident wishes] and had told Ben he was thinking of joining the LDS Church, partly to keep some peace in the family. Fearing that connection had been made, Ben couldn't decide whether to tell Bless of their plans or not. However, if he didn't, the man would have no chance to defend himself if the Church came down on him. Finally he wrote Bless a note, saying he had to see him, and sent it by Juan, one of his stable boys, as he paid him off.

Ketchum came that evening, puzzled at the summons. Ben explained it all and his old friend, to his surprise, told him that he had suspected something was wrong but didn't know all the facts. Now that he did, he wanted to come along. His wife and he had already had numerous quarrels about his conversion and he was tired of the conflict. She could go back to her family and her Church. He would come along.

"I'll go home and hit the rack, then, when she's asleep, I'll sneak out and meet up with you on the trail. I want my money, guns and my horse. The rest of it, she can have."

* * *

After Ketchum left, Ben sat on the porch with Siccoolum a while, drinking coffee and waiting for total darkness. He looked out at the new stables, his grounds, his fields and good fences. Down there on the quarter section, he had planted corn this year. There'd be a good crop, looked like. The grass was green in the horse pasture way off to the left and down farther in the little valley, he could see the tip of the chimney of Moira's newly built house. He hated like hell to leave all this, uproot them, but it had to be.

He got up and went in and armed himself with his old Sharps and his Colt. He'd given the Henry to Freddy. With a sigh, he stepped out the door for what he knew would be the last time.

Siccoolum went out without a backward look. She had hated the place and the white people who sneered at her and made remarks they thought she couldn't understand. It would be good to be back in the mountain country again, among the tall trees and the game. To see her own kind. Her man was wise. He was doing the right thing. If they could get away.

* * *

Dawn was tipping the Wasatchs high above the road a pink when Ketchum made his appearance to their rear. He had a long scratch on his face and he was grim as he came up to Ben, riding by Hank's wagon at the end of the column.

"Abby woke up as I was saddling up and came out to see what I was doing. She saw I was leavin', Ben, and she must have heard somethin', for she was goin' to tell Haight. I had to tie her up and she was likely found, I s'pect, by now. Put up a battle, I tell you." He touched his face. "Anyhow, they'll likely be after us soon."

Ben said, "I'd hoped fer a day 'er so more to put some distance on, but we'll be ready."

* * *

Isaac Haight was a fanatic Mormon who worshipped the ground that Brigham Young and his Bishops walked on. He had designated himself one of the "Protectors" early on and done his best to keep Joseph Smith and his brother from harm. He had survived the Illinois and Ohio debacles and fought himself into the good graces of Brigham Young. As such, he was the de-facto leader of the militia that had been evolved when they made a fighting retreat out of Missouri. Over the years since, the Mormon leaders had come to rely on him and his men as their strike force against Indians and other enemies of the Church. He would go to any lengths to do their bidding and when Young had preached in the Tabernacle that he was "upset by the Gentiles incursions into Utah and would no longer extend the umbrella of protection over them, as he had in the past," Haight and his militia had viewed it as an open season on anyone not LDS.

He and some of his Iron County Brigade of the Stake of Zion had been preying upon travelers ever since. They were particular, though. Their victims had to show evidence of their wealth, either in stock, horses, money or possessions, such as the Perkins train had displayed. There had been other graves along the trails that hid luckless emigrants before that train and there would be others later, he was smugly complacent. Their depredations had made them rich and some of it was regularly passed on up the hierarchy.

The Militia members, Danites, they called themselves, masked their crimes with a pretense of moral uprightness. The Danites had men like Prime Coleman, his Sergeant, Amos Thornton, Samuel McMurdy, Albert Hamblin, all of whom were coopers. Nephi Johnson, Howard Fenton, Hall Durand, Sid Rigdon, Torry Owens

164

and his brother, Barry, who were carpenters and builders, Koyt Kirkland, Hig Doyle, John Macomb, Solomon Spalding, Zeke Hillard, Will Bateman and some of the others were all farmers.

Haight's able adjutant was Major John Higbee, and the one who had carried out the attack on the Perkins train and led it to its gory conclusion was Captain John D. Lee. like the Colonel, Lee was a Protector and a blood thirsty fanatic who hated Gentiles, particularly Missourians, who he blamed for the death of two of his children and one of his wives. These men all came running from their jobs when the Colonel's message came to form up, outside of town at his farm. The call almost always heralded blood and money.

As they gathered in front of the Colonel's fine home, Lee noted that his CO was riding the sleek new horse he had gotten him: Doctor Perkins big black standardbred stud. The men were, as they were supposed to be, all ready for extended action, be it a day or a week. They had their saddle bags full of ammunition and easily transported food like jerky and biscuits. All carried extra water bags and there was a pack horse for every five men with more water, ammo and food. They didn't talk, they listened as the Colonel addressed them in his loud, bull voice,

"Men of the Zion Militia! I gathered you today to take out after one of Hite's trains headed north! Hite loaded fourteen wagons the day before and they taken out yesterday morning. Then, when dark fell, Hite taken out with all his horses, no doubt to catch up with 'em. He must have known we was watchin' him and was gettin' ready to wipe 'im out. The man paid his Mex servants off and gave 'em a holiday. He thought, no doubt, to trick us and get a few days ahead, so we maybe couldn't catch him. Ketchum's wife come runnin and told me that he went somewhere. I went and checked and Hite's stables're empty. Well, he left his lands to us, lock, stock an' barrel. That'll all be parceled out, as usual, by random draw. Now, we'll fetch his horses, wagons and wimmen!" He pirouetted his fancy new mount and jerked it up so that it reared. "Let's go!"

Image courtesy of Bob Cherry

Chapter 24

When Bless had told him what had happened, Ben had ridden forward and halted the train, then gathered his drivers. They were mystified when he ordered them to unload half of each wagon's load of flour right there by the road, the cheapest commodity they carried, then redistributed some of the loads to Ben's satisfaction.

That done, his hand on his pistol, he faced them and told them he no longer required the services of the Mormons and would pay them off right now. They had been good men, reliable and trusted but he knew their first loyalty was to their Church. Will, Hank, Ketchum, Kittledge, Troyer, Siccoolum—even Freddy and Moira were armed and ready to back him, the Mormons saw. They took their pay meekly and some, having affection for Kittledge and Ben, wished him good luck and shook hands. Three others turned away and started the long walk back, water bags on their shoulders. Then, after they had gotten out of hearing, he hurriedly told the others, seven of them, what he had learned and what he intended to do.

"So, men, you can either go with us and mebbe git in the middle of some fightin', 'er you can head on back to Mormon country. Suit yerselves. But we're headin' out now and we're goin' fast!"

All seven were with him, as he thought they would be. The other wagons were taken over by Miles, the girls, Ketchum and Siccoolum. Freddy took care of the horse herd. Hank and Will left their wagons by the pile of flour and Hank's goodbye to his goods was to

168

douse the whole pile and the discarded wagons with lantern oil and throw a match to it. The resultant whoosh and smoke cloud billowing into the sky would tell their pursuers their exact whereabouts but that was moot. The wagons and horse herd left a trail a blind man could follow. And burning the wagons and the flour was an old army tactic of denying the enemy supplies. Ben grimaced when he saw what Hank had done. It hurt to see his flour going up, which would have fed so many people up north. Likewise, the wagons were his stock in trade and he was letting go of his livelihood. He turned away. It was the right thing to do. Wagons and flour could be replaced, but he intended that the Mormons would pay.

* * *

Haight's column saw the rising plume from far off. They had many miles to go to get to the burning pile but each man in the column knew what the smoke meant. The train knew they were coming and were trying to get away. What they had discarded was burning to keep it from lining the pockets of the approaching Danites and they felt that loss as if it were their own goods. The pace picked up a little, the horses working now in the heat of the day.

* * *

Ben, Hank and Will were riding to meet them. They had picked several sites along the trail as they had passed them and now they were approaching one they particularly liked. From its vantage point, they would start the first of their delaying tactics. The column was rapidly advancing and about two miles away. The three got down on ridges, Hank on one side of the road, Ben and Will on the other and placed their horses close but out of the line of fire. Then they waited a little. Coming up, they had set some rocks on each other by the side of the trail, then measured pretty exactly the distance to the ridge they were now on. It was just over 800 yards and open ground all the way.

Haight was riding in the front of the column, mad clear through at the profligate idiocy of a Gentile who would deliberately burn his own goods, just to keep them from the hands of those who so deserved them. Suddenly, Higbee threw up his hands and tumbled from his saddle. The column halted and several dismounted to see to the Major, who was squirming on the ground. Had he suffered a fit, Haight wondered? At that moment, another man spun off his saddle and a horse screamed and staggered, then fell. Distant gunshots then became audible.

"Shooting!! They're shootin' at us! Take cover!" Haight screamed. They peered about. Cover! But where? He looked around him. The ground lay flat and the only cover was the dead horse lying there. Lee scrambled off and got behind it, almost shouldered aside by another man, Torry Owens, then another, as they pushed to get away from the bullets whining in. A meaty smack! and another man went down, then another horse, as the column disintegrated and the men looked in vain for shelter. Haight recovered first and seeing they were in danger of being pinned down, hollered,

"WE GOTTA CHARGE 'EM! THERE CANT BE MANY OF 'EM! LET'S GO, MEN!"

He mounted, then kicked the stud in the sides and it exploded forward into a run. Behind him, the militia gathered some order and the mob spread out in a loose line that picked up speed as the men all realized their best salvation was to become a moving target.

* * *

On the ridge to their front, the distance lessened as the line came at them. Will had already turned after firing his initial three shots and mounting his horse, headed at a run for the next site they had decided on. Hank and Ben fired at 600 yards, both scoring a hit on their man, the empty saddled horses keeping the line of the charge with the other horses, leaving the men behind. Now, the line was firing, trying to score a hit on the run.

Both Sharpshooters knew how unlikely that was, shooting from the back of a running horse, and they picked their targets again and fired, scoring hits yet again. Then, they sprinted to their horses and made for Will's vantage spot.

Behind them, the charging line crested the ridge, pistols at the ready, their horses blowing from the long dash at full gallop, only to find it empty. To their front, two riders were racing away.

Haight yelled, "After those bastids! We'll catch 'em and cut their balls off!" He looked back. Five men, no six! were down. One had his head up and was waving weakly for help. Two horses were down, too, and there were some with empty saddles milling around. Men were looking about them, when one fell, his horse shying as he hit the ground. Then a distant shot was heard. This time, with cover available, men dismounted, ducked behind the ridge and began firing back.

Haight took cover, too, making sure the stud was safe. He cussed himself for riding the expensive animal and exposing it to danger. 'What was he thinking of?'

He looked about him. Closest to him was young Bateman, trying to reload his rifle while lying prone. He called Bateman to him and told the wide-eyed boy, when he crawled over,

"Take my horse, son, and ride back to the City and when you git there, you go right to Banker Rawls and tell him I need another twenty men to come out to us. Tell 'im I said, "Bring extra horses and rifles with plenty of ammo! Their best shooters."

The youngster started to crawl away and Haight said,

"Now, I don't want you to founder that horse. He's too valuable! So you take it easy on 'im and make sure you rub him down good when you git back. Not too much water and no grain, you hear me?"

He shook the boy's arm and that worthy stuttered out a "Yessir!" He low crawled down off the hill, breathing a sigh of relief when he got down from there.

Stirrups shortened, he swung up and away, as three shots came whizzing in on the men at the ridgeline. One hit Haight in the arm, whirling him over, another took Prime Coleman in the chest as he rose to shoot, the last hit Nephi Johnson in the head, spattering brain matter and bone on Lee and Durand, the two closest to him. The rest of the column had gained cover and shortly, the ridge blossomed with rifle fire as they blazed away at the second ambush site.

Up there, Will and Hank had already withdrawn to the next one to set up their rest and cool their guns a little. When Ben abandoned his position, they would provide cover for him. Then, they'd do it again. Meanwhile, they saw from their higher vantage point, a horseman ride back and away off the ridge, evidently headed back for reinforcements.

"Wonder if Siccoolum kin catch 'im. And if she kin kill 'im, if she does." Will commented, taking a long pull of his water. Hank said, "She's light and she got a couple good horses in the black and the buckskin. Bet she does."

"You're on. The usual?"

"Sure thing." The usual with them was a $20 gold eagle. Over the years, they, and Ben, had passed many of them back and forth.

Siccoolum had come with Ben's extra pair of field glasses, a twin to the pair Mrs. Bradley had given him years back. Her man had sent all the way to someplace he called England for them some years back and had given them to her to use. They were magic and brought things far away up close. She loved to look through them. From a vantage point behind the column, she had witnessed the effect of the first devastating shots, seen men fall all over the flat. Waiting patiently, she had seen the charge to its conclusion, watched the puffs of smoke from the second ambush site, saw a horseman riding that way, likely Ben as she thought she recognized Monte, then more shots and men and a horse going down on the ridge. The hated whites now were firing up on the ridge and not looking

172

back the way they had come. Now a rider had come down towards her.

Getting up, she tightened the cinch of her black and swung up on him. The buckskin following, she went down on to the trail ahead of the coming rider. Coming to the first dead man, she got down and took his hair. '*A white scalp! For her! And her man had said it was all right to do it, that she should do it.*' Then, as she came up to the second man, he brought up his head and looked pleadingly at her. It was Barry Owens, one of the men who Freddy had said had fired their stable. She got off her horse and approached him, staring down as he said, "Siccoolum! Help me! I. . . I'm shot. Here." He flopped an arm and exposed the bloody gout of bright red which stained his chest on the right side. Shot through the lung, she figured.

In a fluid motion, she pulled her knife and kneeling down, stabbed him several times, he bucking up and gurgling as she put the knife into his body. Then, she cut his throat and watching the blood pouring out on the ground, looked and saw that the horseman was coming up. She turned and pulling out her carbine, waited for him, sighting over the saddle as he approached. The black, as she had trained him, stood steady at the shot.

Bateman, who had thought the person standing by the man on the ground was one of the Militia, found out otherwise when he felt a hard blow to his chest that knocked him from the stud. He didn't feel the fall, but he knew he was off the horse, his breath gone, looking up at the sky, which was suddenly blotted by the figure of an Indian woman.

Hite's squaw. He recognized her even as she grabbed his thick blonde hair and started sawing off his scalp. He screamed then, and she stuck him in the throat with her knife. Then he felt his scalp come free to her hard jerk. The young man's sight went dim, then faded away completely.

'*Three scalps!*' Ben had said that she was welcome to scalp as many of them as she might take without getting in any danger herself. She wiped her knife

173

on her skirt again, the buckskin cleansing the knife blade, then gathered the reins of the horse he'd been riding. *'Ileee! This horse was one that filled the eyes of a rider!'* And he wasn't cut! A stud.

'This one she would bring back to her man and give to him for all he had given her.' She scurried around then, busy at her scalping chores and soon, done with her task, she hopped aboard her black and with the two horses behind her, started a wide circle back to the fighting.

Chapter 25

Haight hadn't seen his courier die. He was occupied with trying to tie a piece of shirt around his arm and stop the bleeding. The shooters were still making it hot for the Militia left on the ridge. He had more men down from the phenomenal accuracy of the riflemen, and marveled now at how they seemed able to place their shots with such fine deadliness. He was scared. Yes, he admitted his fear. He couldn't go forward now, with so many men lost.

He looked along the line and out of the twenty two men he'd had, more than half were down, and most were dead, not wounded, like him. He felt faint, the bullet had torn muscle and veins and it felt broken, also. He couldn't move it without nearly screaming. And the loss of all that blood was frightening. It kept pulsing from the large wound. It slowed, but didn't stop.

'Bastid musta used a big buffalo gun,' he thought just before he lost consciousness. A few yards away, 'Old' Sam McMurdy shot his Enfield musket one more time, looked hard but couldn't see any effect, then peered over at the Colonel, who looked mighty peakedy. *'Hmm. He'd slumped over. Was he killed? If their officers were dead, he allowed he'd skedaddle for home. Whoever was shooting at them was too damn good.'* Haight fell over sideways.

Now McMurdy saw the bloody arm and the sight made him rise to help the man, to try to stop the blood he saw now dripping heavily onto the ground. He didn't feel the bullet. It struck just above his right eye and tore most of the skull off the back of his head as he fell back, his heels drumming the earth. The bullet's impact was clearly audible to the men on the hill.

Those left now began a very cautious retreat, scrambling down to their horses. Off of the firing line and secure from the searching bullets, they counted themselves and saw seven scared men left of those twenty-two who'd followed their leader so confidently into this blood bath.

Lee, his face spattered still with the brains of his dead friend, looked at Torry Owens, who had a bullet through his hat that must have parted his hair.

"We can't advance against those men! They're the best riflemen I've ever seen! But I think we'd best take the Colonel back with us. and the rest, if we can catch enough horses. Someone crawl up and pull him down and we'll put him on his horse. Tie 'im, if we have to." He looked around. No one moved.

"All right! Ye cowards! Dammit! Come on, Torry."

Reluctantly, the other man accompanied him back up to the ridge, where they crawled as low as they could to the Colonel's legs and tugged on them until he came limply down into their arms. Then they carried him to the waiting men.

"Where's his big stud horse?" Lee asked.

The men looked about them. "Where the hell was the damn horse?" No one left alive had seen young Bateman get his orders and scurry back down to mount and ride away. They'd been too occupied themselves with getting into a firing position and trying to keep from being shot. It was a mystery they couldn't solve, except to believe that he must have spooked and run away. They put the Colonel on another empty saddle and tied the unconscious man on, then rode back the way they had come, It was Lee who saw the first scalped man, young Bateman, lying there face up to the sun.

"What the Hell! Bateman! HE'S BEEN SCALPED!"

That revelation made the men all look around, their fear redoubling. How had this happened? Indians to their rear that they'd never even seen—riflemen to their front who were the most lethal they'd ever come up against. They hurried on, more horrified yet as they saw the mutilated remains of Higbee and the others from the first minutes of the battle. Like the boy, they had been scalped.

* * *

"Should we follow 'em?" Will asked, taking a swig from his canteen. The day was getting warm.

"We'll draw straws. And which one wins gets to do a little harassin' tonight, when they stop. The other two head back to the wagons." Ben said.

Will won the draw and was satisfied. His blood lust was up and he wanted some more of the men who would kill little babies and women without mercy. 'Eye for an eye' was his motto. It was Old Testament and good enough for him. He'd grown up a Catholic in Indiana and actually spent a year at Notre Dame before the war, thinking he wanted to become a lawyer. The war had changed all that.

* * *

That night, the surviving Danites rode far but finally had to quit, the horses about done. They got the bodies down and laid out. Haight and the other wounded men needing attention, they built a big fire and did what they could for them. Haight was near death, from loss of blood, as was Howard Fenton, shot through the stomach and whining in a high squealing tone as he breathed. Rigdon was still alive but likely wouldn't last the night, with a chest wound that whistled as he struggled to breathe.

The night was dark, with no moon, and after a hasty meal of jerky, some hard bread and biscuit, and a pot of black coffee on the boil, the men were just settling down around the fire when a bullet crashed and the pot jumped from the impact, then fell over in the flames, putting it nearly out. On its heels, as the men scrambled for weapons, came another shot and a man screamed. By accident or design, he'd been shot low in the groin, the bullet breaking his pelvis, taking most of his scrotum and one of his balls away. In agony, the man kicked and in his pain, fell into the fire. No one helped him as the bullets came in, another man going down, shot in the face. Then, it was still, except for the moaning of the wounded. No one slept. they doused the fire and each crept into as much cover as they could find.It was a night that seemed to last for an eternity. The wounded men moaned and cried as those alive declined to come and help them.

* * *

Ben and Hank came back to a circled train, miles closer than they had anticipated. "What the Hell now?"

They both immediately went into a defensive mode, wondering why the train had stopped at this crucial time, when they should be miles up the trail. Kittledge was on guard and came hustling out, grinning.

"I know, Ben! But we had to stop just now! Moira had her baby. Good thing Siccoolum came back when she did. She handled ever'thing. And say! Did you tell 'er to take those scalps? She's got a bunch of 'em!"

"What is it—boy 'er girl?" Ben asked as they stepped down.

"A boy! An' guess what she named him! Benjamin Miles Troyer." He did a little dance and crowed. "Yer a granddaddy, Boss! Ye got a little namesake!"

"They okay?" Ben was unsaddling while Hank brought them some fresh horses from the remuda.

"Seem to be fine. Like I said, yer little Indian princess took care of it in fine shape. Made 'er get up outa bed and hev it Injun style, squattin' down. Seemed to work fine. The daddy passed out, though." He laughed. "Guess all those scalps and you boys back with us means ye had some good huntin', but what about Will? They still after us?"

"He's all right. Goin' to do a little night huntin'. Keep 'em stirred up. They're headin' back to the city, those who're left."

"Fine and dandy. Want some supper? Betty and Katy made a great stew fer us tonight. Say! Shoulda seen how the girls handled their teams today!"

* * *

John Lee, hunkered down by the trunk of a tree with his gun, praised the Lord as he watched the sun come up. From that day forward, he would fear the dark and sleep with a gun in his bed. He stirred, looked carefully about, then got up to see if any of the horses were left. The shooting had scared them and they had to be searched for before Owens found them grazing peacefully in a small meadow a half mile from the camp. He caught one and brought the rest in, some still with saddles on them. There were four men left of the Iron County men who had so blithely rode out to do their mischief. The Colonel, Fenton and Rigdon had all passed on in the night. They threw the dead bodies on the horses as best they could, tying them head to feet. As Lee was trying to bend poor Johnson on, he found a note tucked in his shirt. He read:

A MORMON LAMENT
The Mormon Militia rode out one day
On Ben Hite's wagons they thought to prey.
Poor widows and children they will cry
for all those fathers that had to die.
Now you Danites better listen, you better take heed
Or it's a new Mormon Leader you soon will need!
Stop your robbing and killing!
Leave the Gentiles alone!
Or us Sharpshooters will come back
and wolves will gnaw on your bones.
Signed:
  A Sharpshooter

'Bloody Hell!" The paper trembled in Lee's fingers. Young would have to see this. It was an outright threat on his life! Who the Hell were those Sharpshooters?'

Lee, in his distraught state, failed to tie Johnson on properly and he slipped off half a mile down the trail. They left his body. Another mile and another one, McMurdy, bounced off. They left him, too. The note had to get to Brigham Young and the Elders.

* * *

"Will always figured himself fer a poet." said Hank, chuckling as he poured his friend another cup of coffee. They'd listened to Will tell of the night before and grinning, he'd recited the warning he'd left. Givens leaned back against the wagon wheel. Ben had decreed that they would hold up a day to allow Moira and her newborn a little rest before they went on. "I liked the one you wrote after Kelly's Ford. Went somethin' like this, if I remember," He recited,

> "At Kelly's Ford that fateful day, Company
> 'C' was ordered to enter the fray.
> Forward we skirmished, our Sharps at the

ready,

> 'Keep your heads low, boys and let your aim be
> steady.'

Ben thought he'd forgotten the rest, and was trying to remember it himself, but then Hank spoke up again,

> "We fought on the ridge, advanced into the
> valley,
> When evening came, we reckoned the talley:
> Old Californy claimed he'd gotten six, maybe
> seven!
> Hite said nothing, but the boys knew that
> he'd bagged eleven.
> Then Givens came in. 'Thirteen,' said he.
> And Kernzy showed up, with his usual three."

Will said, with a chuckle, "He always gets the last part wrong. That's supposed to be,

"Then Kernzy showed up. 'Thirteen,' said he.
And finally **Givens** *came in, with his usual three."*

Hank grinned, "Well, I knew it was somethin' like that. By the way, Will, you owe me $20. Siccoolum took that messenger's hair."

* * *

Siccoolum was smug and proud as she showed Ben each of her prizes—six fresh scalps which she intended to use to make him a suitable war shirt, trimmed with the trophies of war. Ben smiled nervously. That would be something he would do his best **not** to wear. Then she went out to the herd and came back with the stud. He was astounded. The wagon train stud! This wonderful horse had been ridden by the dead courier, he gathered. He took in the lines of the beautiful animal and was saddened when he thought of its dead owner. The doctor had been so proud of this horse, and it was that very pride that had likely gotten him killed. Siccoolum told him, "I give this horse to my man. He is a great warrior. He should have the best horse."

Ben shook his head. "Listen, luv, this here is the horse thet likely got thet whole wagon train killed. I'll take it for now but we need to be damn careful. It could lead them to us. It could even be used by the Mormons. They could say that <u>we</u> were the ones who killed all those people and that the horse is proof of our guilt. Take it out and cover it with mud, then turn it back into the herd 'til we figure out what to do with it."

* * *

They went on unmolested. When the train topped the Continental Divide, Ben went back for one last time and searched the backtrail with his glasses for half a day, seeing nothing but emigrants they had passed or noted on the way up. They had fought clear but he knew the LDS Church was like a big spider, with a wide web. They would never know when or where the Mormon Militia might strike.

"Bison" courtesy of Dan Rick

Chapter 26

They forded the Beaverhead and passed the curious stone ridge called "Beaverhead Rock" as they went on to Bannack. Arrived there, they found the town almost deserted. Mapes was just finishing loading his wagon as Ben rode up. "H'lo, Hite! Was hopin' you'd show up before I left. I was goin' to leave you a message on my door. Gold's 'bout done here, except fer a little smatterin' and most of us are headin' fer Last Chance Gulch. Got the receipts fer us?"

"Right here, Gus." Ben handed them over and Mapes took them with relish. "This'll be a godsend fer the boys. Thanks, Ben!" He stashed them in his vest.

"Well, guess that means you don't want any of your shipment? Just as well. We had trouble on the trail and had to drop half our loads just to make it through."

"The hell you say! Injuns?"

"Mormons."

"Hell's Bells! Thought the Army had taken care of 'em!"

"They were after us because we knew about them killin' off a whole train of emigrants to steal their stock."

At Mapes's stunned look, Ben added, "We had to fight our way through and it cost 'em."

Ben had decided to tell as many people as he could about the Militia's preying upon travelers, so that if they did kill him, at least some record of the massacre might be left.

* * *

They headed back to Sheridan, where Randall watched them come in. He was his old self and shocked as Mapes when Ben told his story of the Perkin's train. He went off to inform the Committee and deliver the receipts. A crowd gathered as they off-loaded the cargo designated for the store. He had to tell his story several times before they cleared for Nevada City and on to Alder Gulch.

There, they repeated the tale, and their loads delivered, and Ben's remaining stock sold, they headed on back to Sheridan to their customary camp. It was taken over by emigrants cattle and a train nestled where they usually parked the wagons. Ben decided to go on to Bozeman and camp there.

Because of their forced shedding of weight back on the trail, Ben had used his own invested cargo to fill out the orders of his merchants. He had sold the rest in Virginia City, so the wagons were light as it was not time yet to think of what to do about shipping the Committees' gold. In any case, Ben was done with Salt Lake City and that route. Now, it would have to be transported by the steamboats. They went on to Bozeman and Fort Ellis.

* * *

They camped on a long bend of the Gallatin where a small hill allowed a clear field of fire for the circled wagons. Seated by the fire, Ben tried to decide what to do. He had twenty teams of heavy draft horses and needed at least sixteen more wagons and tack to be well enough equipped to use them on the Helena route to the Missouri. Would there be enough freight though, from the steam boats to warrant adding twenty-six wagons to those fourteen he already had working that trail? Should he go to the banks and ask for money on his horses, get into debt again here in the Territory, or have a sale and shed himself of some of the beloved teams? Asking for a loan was distasteful and made him think again of fat Banker Rawls. He would have a sale.

Also, there was the question of the stud: should he deliver it into the hands of the Army? That body owed him a considerable amount for scrip they hadn't honored, when the train had given some of their precious freight into the hands of Colonel Carrington at Fort Kearny. Now, he would be turning over a valuable animal to them, which would likely go into the stables as a personal mount for the fort's CO. He decided he would rather keep it for what they owed him, at least for a while.

* * *

He, Hank and Will rode in to the noisy camp on a beautiful sunny morning and found a burgeoning city. It had a main street that was wide and busy. There were quite a few new store fronts and the boardwalks had been extended several blocks farther in the months Ben had been gone. Will headed for a saloon, the Silver Dollar, and Hank decided to go with him. On an impulse, Ben decided to ride over to Fort Ellis and ask if the Army would honor the scrip he had gotten from Colonel Carrington. If they would, he would turn over the stud. He would also deliver the letters Miles had written telling the tale of the Perkins train.

A new commander, a Lt. Colonel Watkins, had just taken the post over and he was only willing to receive the scrip if Ben would discount them 50%. Ben rejected that offer as too penurious. The officer listened to his story of the Perkins train and said it was out of his jurisdiction but he would pass the information along. Ben gave the letters into his care and went back up town to see what interest there might be in his horses. Walling, at the Bozeman Emporium, told him he would buy two teams and knew of some others who might, as well.

At $150 a horse, on average, he had considerable money on the hoof. He had money in his pocket, and more when he got to Carroll, where Lakey Steele, his friend and partner on the Helena Route, should have considerable cash ready to hand over to him from the proceeds of the last six months. He proceeded to the Advant Courier, a newspaper which was publishing twice weekly now, and inserted his sale ad. The sale day would be next Saturday, which would give him time to clean the horses up and do a little grooming.

That done, he went to the Montana Armory to stock up on ammunition for his rifle and pistol. To his consternation, he found that they had no paper cartridges for his old Sharps. Walling grinned when he said,

"Nope. Won't find any, neither. None in town, I bet. Your old Sharps is outdated. Here's what's new."

He went to the counter and pulled down a shiny new rifle. It was a breechblock Sharps, but without a percussion cap nipple on the receiver. Double set triggers. The barrel was as long as his old 1859 but the fore end only went part way, with a nice German silver end cap. Ben examined the ladder sights, which went to a thousand yards. He saw the caliber was .45/90. He hefted it. A heavy rifle but not any more than others he had shot, maybe three pounds heavier than his .52. Say twelve pounds. A beautiful weapon. He handed it back reluctantly. Was it time to discard his trusted rifle and upgrade? The Henrys used metallic cartridges and now, it seemed, the Sharps Company was converting to them, also.

"What the hell does the cartridge look like?"

"This." Walling handed over a shiny brass cartridge topped with its heavy bullet. "This'll go plumb through a buffalo an' kill another one out the other side."

"Humph. Don't need that much punch. What 's the bullet weight?"

"500 grains, but you can get lighter bullets fer 'em. Got another one here. Last ones left right now."

He handed another rifle over the counter—almost a twin to the first but with less weight. Hite turned the barrel to read it and found it was marked .45/90, also. It had a curious part round/part octagonal barrel but it was shorter.

Both rifles had good balance to them and Ben instinctively knew they would shoot and handle well.

"Well. . . .Got plenty of ammo fer 'em?"

"Plenty of about every caliber."

"How much?"

"Fer you, $50.00 each. Ammo is $25 a case.

"Make it two cases."

"Got one other thing to show you. This one you'll like, fer sure." Reaching down under the counter, he pulled up a pistol and passed it over. Ben took it and felt it carefully, then examined it. It was a Colt. 45 revolver with a 5 1/2 inch barrel. Like the Sharps rifles, it took metallic cartridges. Walling showed him one— .45 Colt.

"Caps are built right into the shell, just like the rifles."

"How much?" Ben asked. Like the long guns, this one had the feeling of a keeper. He'd upgrade his old pistol, too. And he'd need to show these to Hank and Will. They'd be damn envious.

Image courtesy of Bob Cherry

Chapter 27

Torry Owens was still shaking as they made it into the outskirts of Salt Lake. He couldn't seem to stop. The sight of the line of horses packing dead bodies and those with empty saddles was such that people had come to their doors or watched out their windows as they had passed. Lee took them down the lane to his farm and they unloaded the tired horses there, the corpses already starting to get ripe. They laid them out in the shade of the barn and covered them with a tarp. Not a wounded man had made it home alive.

They trooped into the house, where they sat in a stupor about the table, while Lee's fearful wives set a table loaded with the food they had thought would be fed to the triumphant returning Militia. The men had little appetite, their minds still on the ridge, out on the flat or filled with the night before.

Lee sat, looking out the window at the barn, idly touching the checkered cloth tablecloth and sipping his tea. He thought of the poem he'd found. It mentioned the widows and the children of the dead fathers. He'd never totaled up the exact number of wives or the children left without their fathers but the amount would be considerable and the Church would have to take care of them. They'd all be parceled out to other families. He thought of Young and what he'd say. He realized then, that he was the last remaining officer of the Iron County Militia, a now dubious honor. He supposed he'd be promoted but wondered now if he really wanted to have the distinction of leading such a decimated troop. 'The *funerals. . . .'* He sighed and got up from the table. The message had to go in to Young, along with the story of what happened.

"Koyt, you ride for the coroner, old Jennings. Tell 'im what's doin'. Torry, guess you and me got to go to see Brigham, much as I hate to face him. Hig, stay here and take care of the horses. Don't let the dogs or the hogs get to those bodies. And you wimmen! Clear this off and get yerselves to the widows and break the news." They strode out.

* * *

Brigham Young was incredulous at the tale Lee had to tell. *'God in Heaven! Eighteen men gone, just like that! They hadn't had such a mess of killin' since they'd fought the Utes and other tribes when they crossed the desert! And the threat in this poem—was it to be believed? From Lee's account, it would have to be taken seriously.'*

"What do we know about this man, Ben Hite?"

Lee told him what he knew, just that he was a successful Gentile freighter who had built his company into a formidable transportation business, with routes that went every direction. Bless Ketchum, he knew, was running the one out of the city to the railhead. Hite had a nice farm out of town just to the north where he raised and trained his draft horses, big Percherons. Other than that, Owens had mentioned that he thought the man was a veteran Union soldier who had served in many campaigns.

"Get Owens in here. I need to talk to him right away."

* * *

Hank and Will were not envious. They had been in the store before Ben and purchased new rifles and Colts for themselves. They laughed at Ben when he showed them his new guns, then brought out their own and compared each to its merits. Expert riflemen that they were, they couldn't wait to sight them in and get the feel of the new weapons. It was decided that they would help Freddy and the rest of the drivers groom horses in the morning for the coming sale the next day, then, in the afternoon, hold a shooting contest. The whole train took on an aura of anticipation at the contest.

Bets flew that evening and not all were made by the men. Siccoolum loved to gamble and she staunchly backed her man, to the delight of Kittledge and the others. Ben had to forbid her putting up her scalps, her black or her guns, though she bet all the money she had accumulated, her buckskin, along with another horse she had, some moccasins and a white buckskin dress Betty had coveted.

The youngster hated to bet against Father Ben, but did, in the hope of getting the beautiful garment for her own. She also bet a horse on Hank Givens, on whom she had a little crush. Moira bet Ketchum a gold eagle against doing his laundry for a month, she backing Ben, also. Freddy was undecided, and decided to play the middle: he bet on Ben with one of the drivers, who took Givens. He bet on Givens with Kittledge, who took Ben, also. The other drivers had a field day, betting on Ben or Hank Givens, to a man.

Troyer was the lone advocate of Will Kernzy and took him against all the others, at considerable cost to his pocket. Ben, Hank and Will put up their usual pot of $20 each. They would shoot their new rifles: ten shots any position, ten shots standing, at 200 yards. The contest would begin after each man had sighted in to his satisfaction.

Ben had them up early, and Freddy and he ran the horses in and the work started right after breakfast. Each had a curry comb and a heavy brush, with pails of soapy water and rags. Freddy caught the horses and they brought them in to the groomers while Ben wrote remarks in his little notebook about each one, making a close inspection and coming to a decision as to whether he wanted to turn him back to the herd to keep, or if to sell, deciding how much to ask for it. He intended to cull the older stock, and since Ketchum and Kittledge knew each horse, ask their opinion if he was uncertain. Both were old teamsters and he valued their expertise.

With some organization, it went well and the men and the girls had fun with the big animals, who seemed to catch their enthusiasm. Draft horses, particularly Percherons, were not the dull animal of drudgery many seemed to think they were, rather they were intelligent and without the negative qualities a horse could have or acquire: viciousness, laziness, lack of spirit, physical weakness and no endurance. They epitomized the very best of what the horse should be in every sense. Ben was proud of them and it hurt him to let any of them go, but he was horse poor right now and it just made sense to sell some.

That big cleanup chore done and the horses looking their best for the next day, they knocked off for lunch, then went out to the range they had marked off, each of the shooters with their new weapons. Sighting in took less than an hour, off a table rest they had set up.

* * *

Weighted wooden cracker boxes were placed out at the stepped off distance and the men got down into their favorite prone positions, Ben with a coat used as a rest, Hank with his rifle propped between his feet, Will with his barrel resting on a stump. At Ketchum's "fire when ready," the men sighted in an instant and then sent a bullet down range. Long schooled by years of practice and the experience of war, where targets of opportunity flashed for an instant into view, a successful sniper had to be able to let off a round quickly or it would likely be too late.

Ten rounds went by quickly and then the boxes were retrieved. Each box, about the size of a man's chest, had a group within it. Counting the rounds on each, all had ten shots through the back of it. Measuring the groups, Ben's was nine inches across, Hank's was eight and half, Will's was a tight seven and half, which was incredible to the bystanders. Will, they knew had been drinking yesterday and his eyes were red rimmed yet. At breakfast he'd had a tremble in the hand that held his coffee cup. All of them now, with the exception of Ben and Hank, who knew him too well, were astounded at his shooting.

The standing position was next. New boxes were placed down range, and the size of the group there would be added to the prone one to give the winner. The men stepped up to the mark and taking their aim, fired, brought the hammer to half-cock, then jacked the breech lever down, and slipping in a new cartridge, brought the lever forward and up, cocked the hammer back. Bringing the weapon up to their shoulder and finding their aim again, they almost as one, pulled trigger on another shot. This went on for less than a minute, as prescribed by their late Colonel—ten shots in less than sixty seconds. Expert as these three were, the time lapse was about forty-five seconds.

Bringing the boxes back, it was seen that though the groups were spread farther about the boxes, still a man would be dead or grievously injured for each of those bullets—all thirty rounds had hit the boxes. The measurements were taken and this time, Ben's was tightest: another nine inches across. Hank had a group of nine and a half, Will's was ten. The two scores gave Ben eighteen, Hank eighteen, and Will seventeen and a half— the winner!

Miles was ecstatic at his dark horse's win, the others glum over their losses. The two losers shook hands with a grinning Kernzy and paid over their money. "Guess I'll have to write another poem 'bout this shoot. Not often I beat the best of old Company 'C'."

* * *

The next day was the sale and as a crowd began forming, Kittledge, who had agreed to act as the auctioneer, began warming them up by telling a few jokes. Freddy and the drivers began haltering the first horses and bringing them in to the rope ring, where they paraded them around. In each case, they tried to match them with a team mate to make a working pair.

The women had decided to do concessions and had cooked a barbecue, with beans, biscuits, and coffee. They served out of the end of a wagon and had to constantly wash utensils and plates to keep up, as the crowd got bigger.

Ben had decided to sell fifty head, if the market stood it. In the event, with Kittledge at his best form, they sold them all. Ben was surprised at the fluctuation of the sale, some went for more than he thought they would, some for a little less. Overall, he was well pleased and the money box was full. The women, too, had sold out of all their concession articles, and Ben told them they might keep that money to use as they saw fit. That got them excited and a trip into town was planned to do some spending.

"Buddies" courtesy of Dan Rick

Chapter 28

"Now, Torry, Lee tells me that you know something of this man, Hite, from doing work for him. I want you to tell me everything you can remember about him."

"Well, Sir, I know from one of his blabby drivers, that he was a Union vet, that he fought in a lot of engagements and battles, and that he was in one of Berdan's Sniper regiments. I was told that he was one of their best, and that must be true, yer Honor, because we got shot to pieces out there! At long range! And he musta had some of those sharpshooters with him, because there was at least eight or nine, maybe more against us. Seemed like it, fast as they shot. What I don't understand, is when he could of got them to help him. I never did see any strangers out at his place when I was working there."

"What about this ridiculous poem? You think I should take it seriously?"

"Well, sir, we found that note on Johnson's dead body. Yes,sir, it seems to me we should take it very seriously."

Young was silent for a minute, thinking, then said, "What I will do is put a $5,000 reward on his head and any other so-called sharpshooter, if it can be proved that the man is one. That kind of money should flush them out. Spread the word, Torry, and you too, John. Get it out to every County Militia that these sharpshooters are enemies of the Church and Brigham Young will pay it in gold when proof they are dead is given me!"

The word went out to the Militia, then spread through the communities and soon every Mormon in Utah was on the lookout for a Ben Hite or somebody who called themselves "Sharpshooters." Then came the successive funerals: one after another, each attended by multiple wives and numerous children. Eighteen men dead! The reason for the great reward was soon a topic of conversation at every meeting place the men congregated. Owens, Durand, Doyle and Lee were questioned at length and their story was ever more embroidered as it was retold again and again. The numbers that had fought against them grew proportionately. The consensus, though, was that the sharpshooters had cleared out of the country after the Militia had fought so hard against them. The number dead on the other side was unknown, but according to the survivors, it was high.

Banker Rawls heard the news and he was ecstatic. The man, Hite, was long gone and with the loan on his business, he could foreclose without a qualm. He gloated as he thought of the new stables, the houses, and the land, good bottom land with a coming corn crop that would go, Hite had told him, thirty bushels. Also, then, he remembered Hite's route eastward to the Head of Track. There'd be wagons and stock, tack and equipment. How could he get all that, too? It would require some thinking. Maybe a new loan against the collateral might be found.

* * *

When the Sioux closed off the Bozeman Trail, the northern route through to Salt Lake City had to be used, a long, torturous, one, 450 miles along, with steep inclines and snow filled passes that filled up early in the year and stayed closed through late spring. The route was unreliable and merchants cast about for another way to get supplied. In 1869, after Red Cloud's triumph, Captain E.W. Clift led a reconnaissance from Fort Ellis by Bozeman that established a wagon trail to the Missouri.

It ended at the mouth of the Musselshell and at first was called Musselshell City, Later Carroll City.

That opened the door for the steamboats who could struggle up the "Muddy Mo." Though it was 2600 miles from St. Louis to Fort Benton, the desperate need for supplies and equipment up in the gold mining communities made it imperative that those needs be met.

The river was treacherous with Indians, hidden gravel and rock bars, and in many places, snagged so bad that the boats had to winch through. Enterprising captains braved the hazards and if successful in their run, made enormous profits. So big were the returns, in fact, that if a boat could make just one trip up and back, it would usually pay for that craft twice over. One such was the *Waverly*, which was built in 1866 at a cost of $50,000. Her first trip paid for her plus making a profit. She made three trips before snagging at Bowling Green Bend by Yancy, Missouri.

Passengers and freight were the main paying cargo upriver. Then, if a boat could bring back returning passengers and that precious commodity, gold, they realized small fortunes. Another paying cargo was the furs of the tribes who traded for the white man's commodities, though the time of the beaver hat was past and the mountain men left eked out a living, like the Indians, with buffalo robes and other pelts. The *Waverly* brought 508 bales of robes and other furs down on her third trip, along with paying passengers and gold. Her profit was enormous.

A steamboat that made a good run downstream was three or four times faster than the slow moving wagons, slowed by a long trail, weather and possible road agents. The *Waverly's* third trip was completed in just thirteen days. The problem for the boats, then, was how to insure the miners that their gold would not end up on the bottom of the Missouri, like the *Waverly* when she attempted her fourth trip.

For a while, the mouth of the Musselshell River was the head of navigation. Later, as boats improved further, it was Cow Island, then finally, Fort Benton, itself. From the unloading points then, wagons would take over the freight and passengers and get them to the camps by way of what was first called the Helena Trail, then later, the Carroll Trail, named after one of the major partners of the Diamond 'R' Freight outfit, a major transportation company, who was now Ben's competitor.

* * *

A week later, Ben headed the train and the trimmed down horse herd northeast towards Carroll's Landing. Before he left, he cautioned Hank and Will about the retribution he expected would come from the Mormons and Hank laughed and said, "It's you they know and will come after. Will and I are a mystery to 'em."

Ben had to admit the truth in that but wondered if they might want to part company and go on to the gold fields. Will slapped him on the back and said, "Don't worry old coon, we'll tag along for a while to save your bacon again, if the need arises."

* * *

Hite's train intersected the freight trail thirty miles south of the Gap, a low pass through two small mountain ranges, the hills around them dotted with little bands of buffalo. Antelope gazed at them as they passed, flocks of prairie chickens rose ahead of them, and twice, they saw bears, one a black bear that rose on its hind feet and gazed at them, the other time, a big grizzly trundling along a ridge that looked back at them a long time, then disappeared. It was mid-July and the days were long and hot, the nights warm and the stars above an endless swirl of bright lights. That high, there were few mosquitoes and so they sat around the fire for a time after the day's travel.

Ben had covered this ground several times and knew the trail, though there were enough wagon tracks over it now, all headed in the general northerly direction they were headed, that they had no trouble following it.

They'd known that they were crossing the contested hunting grounds of several tribes, the Crows, the Blackfeet, The Cheyenne and the Sioux, including the Metis from Canada. These were a cross-bred conglomeration of Indians, interbred with Huron, Athabascan and French Canadien who had somehow become a tribe of their own and came down to make their yearly buffalo hunt, to the frustration and anger of the other tribes, who begrudged them the many animals they killed, into the hundreds and sometimes thousands.

As more and more tribes found themselves squeezed into less and less country, old hatreds and friction between tribes became outright warfare and an attempt to annihilate each other, with alliances made and broken as they sparred back and forth for territory. Therefore, the Metis were doubly unwelcome, but they had persisted in their incursions across the Canada/American border because of their need to hunt their winter supplies. Their spoken language was French intermixed with Indian patois and their religion was Catholic, with a priest traveling with them to perform baptisms and marriages. They usually traveled in large bands of sometimes as many as a thousand two wheeled carts pulled by oxen. With them would be their buffalo running horses and various other livestock. Women and children would ride or walk alongside and their gaily colored clothes lent a carnival atmosphere to the whole proceeding. At night they would fort up like the emigrant trains for defense against attack, with all their livestock inside for protection. The big game rich area from the Missouri south down to the Yellowstone was their favorite destination, bounded by the Mussellshell on the west and as far east as the Missouri again, which made a long curve to the south.

* * *

Thus it was that when Hite's train topped the low divide that led into the Judith Basin, they saw a hunters' paradise, with many bands of buffalo, antelope, deer and even elk visible across the prairie. However, the animals were on the move, largely westward, away from what the train could hear were gunshots far off to the northeast.

"Circle up!" Ben called and gestured to Ketchum, driving the lead wagon. Bless whipped up his lines and started the train into the well-known curve that would become a tight circle, the horses brought inside and close tethered behind the boxes, to provide some shelter from enemy fire. Meanwhile, Ben rode out to see what the shooting was all about.

He pulled Monte up on a rise that overlooked a bench where it looked like about a hundred Metis carts were barricaded in a defensive circle of their own, their horses and stock inside. The firing was between them and the circling Indians, which looked like Sioux. Some bravo riders were making feints at the besieged defenders and it looked like all eyes were on them, which was good for Ben. He backed off until just his head was above the skyline. From where he was to the defensive circle, he estimated the distance was five hundred yards. There was close to two hundred Indians down there and his little train was vulnerable against that number, even more than the Metis. What to do?

He considered: He had fifteen shooters, with Hank and Will. Freddy had his Henry, as did Gus Wicke, Jim Custis, and Blaine Wickersham, three of their drivers. He had vowed that he would arm every driver and himself with such a repeater when he could find them to buy. But Bozeman had only four available. They were a hot commodity in the west and everyone wanted one. He galloped back to the waiting wagons, drawn up in a tight circle. He gathered them all and told them what he'd seen.

"There's about two hundred, give 'er take ten 'er so. Enough to run over us if they care to. But I don't think we can just go around without drawing attention to ourselves and havin' them come after us. Better, I think, to go right after 'em and shoot the hell out of 'em right off. That likely will take the fight out of 'em."

He looked around and felt good about the determined faces. These were men—and women— who would do what needed to be done, besides Hank and Will, who merely looked ready for anything, especially a fight.

"We'll get up to the ridge above 'em. What I want you boys to do, is you men with repeaters fire quick and fast. Put lots of lead in the air. Hit the horses. They're big targets and the Injuns set a lot of store by their war horses. Hank, Will and I will pick our shots and try to put some Injuns on the ground. My hope is all the shootin' from the ridgeline will convince 'em we're a bigger threat than we are."

He didn't wait for questions. Talking seemed to just take the fight out of men going into battle.

"Grab yer ammo. Hank, Will, anything to say?"

"We need to hit 'em hard and run 'em off with their tails 'tween their legs." Will said. Hank nodded. "Yer show, Ben."

* * *

As they reached the ridge and looked at the scene below, Ben was struck by the fact that it looked as if the siege had been going on a while. There were horses and oxen down inside the cart circle, and as he used his glasses, he saw a fire arrow arch up and over into a cart. The Indians outside were having fun at the Metis' expense. Time to see if they couldn't turn the tide. He picked up his rifle.

"Ever'body ready? Then fire away!"

He himself took a bead on a brave who was shooting from behind a dead horse, about three hundred yards from the circle and close to the same distance from him. He shot just as the repeaters got going, making racket with their rapid fire. On the other side of them, Will and Hank got into action and down below, the heads of the Indians between them and the circle swiveled around to their direction. Horses fell and Indians hit the ground. The Indian behind the dead horse slumped over his weapon.

The distance was not too extreme for the repeaters, and after the initial volley, Ben could see the effect, with Sioux turning to meet this new danger. Shots began coming back up at them. Ben swiftly reloaded his new rifle and fired at a warrior on horseback, a brave who had a flowing feather headdress on, who had just completed making a bravo run across the front of the encircled train. The man flipped off the back of the horse and it kept running as the Indian lay still. From the corral, the fire redoubled. The Sioux milled, uncertain of just what to do. The ridgeline blossomed with more rounds going downrange.

Now, the Sioux below were regrouping, gathering into a loose group to talk it over, which was a mistake. Those on the ridge had more targets clumped up and they poured bullets into the horde as they milled about. Indians fell and horses, hit, screamed. Someone down there used his authority to bring order to the war party, and under fire yet from both sides, a group broke off to begin a charge up to the ridge. That was fine with Ben and the experienced vets. The targets were just coming closer and easier to hit.

"RELOAD AND GET READY! POUR IT IN WHEN I YELL!"

The charge of about fifty yelling braves quirting their horses, was trying to get some impetus into the headlong uphill attack when at forty yards, Ben's yell to 'let 'em have it' swept horses bare of their riders and broke the assault into individual braves either continuing to try to reach the ridge or, like most of them, turning away to save their lives. Only two made it to the top and those both fell as they attempted, on the one's part, to fire a cap and ball revolver which sputtered and misfired, and the other, who wielded a tomahawk that came crashing down on Wickersham's head as he tried to block the club with his rifle. Both braves fell from multiple hits as the other men used their rifles or pistols to good effect, but Wickersham was dead when Ben rolled him over, his skull crushed. Ben had fired his pistol at the brave and hit him, but the bullet or those of the others hadn't stopped his berserk attack until the luckless driver was dead from the killing blow.

Now, those at the ridge had a moment to reload and take stock and their situation looked grim. The warriors below were regrouping again and this time, were about to split in two and take them from either side. Their charge was about to begin when, from the cart circle came a wild yell and two carts swung apart. Spilling out from the opening came a large body of riders, making a counter-attack. Faced on either side with foes that seemed formidable and able to stand fast and inflict casualties, the Indians turned and fled, breaking off the engagement.

Some tried to save wounded comrades, but those were soon ridden down by the vengeful Metis, who dispatched them using a paired attack that took the single braves or those doubled up on laboring horses, on either side. Those on the hill above stood and watched the end of the fracas as it wound down.

Ben said then, "Hank, Will, take the others on back to the wagons and let's be ready for trouble there, in case the Sioux decide to come back and cause us a little trouble."

Hank saluted mockingly and said "Yessir, Yessir!" Clearly, neither he nor Will, who stood by grinning, were too upset by their brush with death.

Freddy said, "What're you goin' to do, Father Ben?"

The boy, like the others, persisted in calling him "Father" or "Daddy Ben." He'd told them to call him just "Ben" but it hadn't taken in their minds, he guessed, so he let it go.

"Go on down and talk with those Metis. Want to come along?"

"You bet!"

As the others mounted and headed back, Freddy and Ben walked their horses on down off the ridge and a group of Metis riders clumped together and came to meet them. One came to Ben and emotionally tried to reach across and actually kiss him—'Frenchie,' Ben thought. 'Always kissing and hugging each other.' He held out his hand and the other gripped it with both of his. The shake lasted a long time and while Ben was engaged, Freddy was experiencing much the same treatment from some other riders. The man jabbered some French—at least,

Ben recognized some of the words. "Speak English?" he asked.

"Not good. Americaine, you?"

"Sure. American. Headed for the Missouri. Carroll."

"You save us. We go together! We kill plenty Sioux!"

"Yeah. That we did." The bodies were being savaged by the Metis women, as usual. He thought of Siccoolum. Seemed like the women were more bloodthirsty than the men.

Looking around, Ben saw fresh bloody scalps swinging from several of the riders' hands. Evidently, being Catholic and a supposed Christian didn't mean they couldn't rip hair from their dead enemies and mutilate the bodies.

* * *

The two trains came together and there was wild celebrating that night, preceded by four funerals, one of which was Ben's driver. A white-haired priest did the services and after asking Ben the dead man's religion, which Ben didn't know, said that he would go ahead anyway, and give him a Catholic burial. Ben thanked him and gave the man a gold eagle to see him properly interred.

The entire assemblage from both trains attended and the service was uncharacteristically swift, as Louie Gaspard, the leader, and all the men, wanted to get on to the celebrating. Louie drew Ben and his stepson to the near vicinity of his cart, where his wife, a fat, graying motherly matron, was laying out a table, assisted by several other women. The Frenchman grabbed a bottle off those lined up on an extended cupboard of the cart and with an expert twist of his corkscrew, popped the top. He called for cups and the woman brought him some, then he poured them full and offered them to Ben and Freddy. He held his up in a toast, offering thanks to the Lord and to their timely rescuers, then upended the cup and watched while they did the same, then poured them full again.

"Aha! We drink! To the Virgin Mother whom I pray to, to the deadly aim of our new friends, to Fate, which brought us rescue in our hour of need—and to Life!"

He drank up and Ben, thinking he needed a clear head, took a small slurp. Freddy, though, imitated his host, and saw the bottom of his mug. Another bottle was opened and Gaspard did the honors again. After another gulp of the strong Merlot, Ben asked,

"So, how long you bin under attack?"

"Two day. They hate the Metis. We hate them. We all hunt the buffalo and there are just not so many as there was."

He went on to tell them of how it was when he was a child, coming on to the southern prairie from his home, Red River, up in Canada, where, if the yearly hunt failed, the people starved in the winter. How they would kill two, or even three thousand buffalo. How for the last three years now, it had been lean times in the North country. And this year looked like it would be the same, and he feared that there would be starvation in the Metis camps again, when snow came. He himself, was considering whether to travel East, instead of North— back to the Great Lakes, where a man could always fish, if he couldn't get a moose. Then he spat.

"Pah! I hate the fish!! Fish stink. Buffalo now, that is man's meat! To hunt on the back of a horse! That is man's work. Any fool can throw a line in the water, or a seine, and catch a damn fish!"

The little man looked close to crying as he talked, his sad hound eyes brimming.

"No! I will not let the sau'vages, the stinking Sioux! keep me from the buffalo! They are God's animal, sent down to provide food and skins for those who are man enough to hunt them."

He downed a last big drink, belched and yelled,

"Mama Maria! the food! She is ready for our guests?"

"Yes, yes. Come. Sit. We feed you. Eat."

Ben ate, his head a little woozy. The wine had a bite. Freddy started to fill his plate, then went off, looking green and Ben heard him emptying his stomach behind the cart. Ben was embarrassed. Louie laughed.

"The boy. He has no stomach for the wine! Come, have another!" While they ate and drank, men started showing up and more bottles had their corks popped. Freddy had disappeared, but Ben heard him, trying to talk with a girl by the cart. Once she laughed at his miserable attempt to imitate her French. Louie and Ben looked at each other and grinned.

Ben got through the meal, a highly spiced stew and rough fresh bread, and the two men agreed that Ben's train and they would camp close by that night, to give each other some security, then travel in tandem toward the mouth of the Musselshell and Carroll.

* * *

As they traveled, they camped each night together and the members of the trains got to know each other somewhat. Louie, when he found out Ben and Siccoolum were living together, thought that they should have his priest, old Father Dupree, marry them. Siccoolum flashed her eyes at him and he considered what the look entailed. They were by now, both quite versed in each other's moods and looks, and this one said that she was curious as to what he would make of this proposal: was he truly a white man, full of their prejudices against Indians and content to use her both in bed and in the tipi as a cook and washer of his clothes, or would he honor her as an equal of sorts, give her status in the eyes of those whom she respected and held dear? He studied her, in turn.

She was Indian, of course, with the high cheekbones of that race, black haired and tall for a woman, with straight nose and black deep set eyes that nevertheless could flash when she showed some emotion, though usually they were calm and quiet. She was strong and worked hard at her tasks. She had fought for him and with him, had saved his life, in fact, now he thought of it.

Why not keep peace in the wigwam, make her his woman under the White God she had come to set some store by? He would do it.

His smile and agreement brought a welcome warmth to the tent and that night was one they both cherished in their memories.

* * *

The wedding was a simple one, attended by the members of each train. Siccoolum, who had lost her horses, her prized white dress and numerous other things in the shooting contest, gained most all of them back in wedding presents, including the white dress, which Betty returned so that she would be able to use it as a wedding gown. With her shiny black hair neatly done in thick braids and tied with red ribbons, her beaded white buckskin dress and matching white beaded moccasins, she made a fetching picture and Ben was proud to stand by her side and give the responses to the old white haired Priest's questions as the ceremony was concluded.

Then the French Metis, who loved weddings as an excuse to throw a party, let loose and the wedding night was punctuated with drunken shouts and laughter and random shots in the air. It also gained the old father a convert, maybe two, as Ben, a moral man, had no objections to a Christian religion which he had seen serve as a bulwark to many men in the war. He was satisfied to embrace it, also, along with his new wife.

Emigrants on the Bozeman Trail – courtesy of Wickipedia

PART III

Chapter 29

Another week of leisurely travel interspersed by frequent stops to hunt and the two trains topped the rise above Reed and Bowles's trading post. The log fort was situated on a bend of the creek largely fed by a big spring which flowed clear and pure from the snowy mountains above it. It was appropriately called Trout Creek for the myriad big fish who lived in its clear, pure water and it wound through the hills and benches to the Judith River. The Judith Basin, a large rolling country about fifty by forty miles in scope, was surrounded by five small mountain ranges, forming a natural bowl in which the weather blew in and out, but usually left moisture, either in the form of rain or snow, to run the creeks and grow the feed for the game. The grass was thick and the game was likewise, with elk, antelope, deer and buffalo roaming the area. It was a wonderland which even Ben took heed of, looking about him with a calculating look. He'd seen some great areas of the Rocky Mountains but really none could compare to this one. Evidently the Metis felt the same, for they had come here with the idea of perhaps staying on.

Nelson Story and Charles Hoffman in Bozeman, had learned that the government planned to relocate the Crow Agency to the Judith Basin and had sent men to build a trading post there. A tight little fort had been erected only to find that the Senate had not approved the relocation. These businessmen had sold the fort to the Dawes Brothers, who had in turn sold the buildings to the present owners. These men had taken the buildings down and relocated their post at Carrol Crossing, to take advantage of the freighting trade.

Major Alonzo Reed and J.J. Bowles, his partner, were traders of a low order, using liquor to cheat the Indians of their furs, if possible, and taking advantage of the squaws when they were drunk. Ben met them at the post when they were dealing with the Metis, and he was not impressed with the men. Bowles was scruffy, dirty and shifty eyed, the type of man Ben had seen plenty of in Missouri and the war and was too familiar with. Reed, who called himself a major, was a little more clean-cut, a six footer who wore a buckskin shirt and sported a mustache and a goatee. Both went heavily armed. They were the kind of men who would smile at your face and shoot you in the back. He decided to watch his when he was around them.

The two men were expert at getting the Indians to drink their terrible whiskey and their favorite way was to promote a horse race, which never failed to get those camping near them worked into a frenzy, leading to the desire to turn loose of any inhibitions they might have. Reed had a fast bay mare which he would match against any comer and the Indians would come long distances to try to beat it. When the two trains arrived, there was a band of semi-friendly Arapahoe camped on the bench by the post. Reed laughed when he told Ben and Gaspard of how the band had matched their fastest against their mare the day before, betting everything but their breechclouts and losing.

"Even got me a couple fresh Injun squaws! Sent the ones I had back to their tribe. I use 'em up pretty fast, I tell ye! Say! I see thet one you got along with ya is a dandy! Want to trade her?" Ben declined.

"Seen any Hite wagons lately?"

"No, but they'll be along soon. Always stop just over there where the ford is, and lay over a day to fill their stock up before they hit the Gap. See you got some Hite wagons with you. Know the man who owns 'em?"

"Yeah. That'd be me. Ben Hite." He shook hands.

"You don't say! Glad ta meet ya." Reed's eyes hooded over and Ben thought he knew something that he wasn't telling.

Gaspard said, "We have good horses, too! Metis like horse race. You like to run your horse?"

"Sure. We'll put our bay up against any horse! That's a nice black you're ridin,' Hite. Want to run it?"

"Might do that. We'll see. If not the black, maybe a couple others."

Monte was fast but the horse had a little age on it and though it had a good bottom, its speed on the shorter stretches was not something he'd bet on. He'd not watched the stud run, though it had the finest lines of just about any horse he'd seen, with the intelligent eyes and the head of some of the finer Standardbreds he'd observed down south. However, the horse was a question and more, since he hated to bring attention to it. But Siccoolum's black was good and fast. He knew how she liked to gamble. The black would be in the race, if she had anything to say about it. Freddy had been with the horse herd and might have a better idea. He'd ask him. Accordingly, he rode out to the herd.

* * *

"We'll hold up here a while. Good feed and water for the horses. I'm hearing the traders want to get a race goin'. We got any animals with some speed, you think?" Freddy was enthusiastic and flattered that Ben had asked him. "Sure! Siccoolum's black horse is good for a run. Kernzy's 'Jake' is fast. The Perkins stud, though, is the best in the herd for speed, Father."

"Well, I'd rather not run it, if you know what I mean."

"Too bad. I bet he'd beat the field."

Ben considered. What to do with the animal was a dilemma. He was sure that the horse would sooner or later cause them a peck of trouble. It was a Jonas horse who'd gotten a lot of people massacred. Now it was in his keeping and maybe it would do the same for him and his outfit, too. He'd like to be rid of it. Every time he saw it, the reminder of what had occurred in that mountain meadow and what he'd seen, the three pits of decomposing men, women and kids, came back to him. Yet, the stud was such a fine animal, he, like any other horseman, couldn't bring himself to part with it.

* * *

The destitute Arapahoe pulled out the next day, and they were bothered for a couple nights with attempts on the horse herd by their warriors, who wanted to regain some horses, be it the post's, which was heavily guarded, or anybody else's. The Metis were old hands at the game and they too, kept their band of horses under strict guard. So, some shooting and yelling was heard about the camps but finally, the Arapahoe gave up and things quieted down.

Major Reed [he self-styled himself a Major but Ben privately questioned whether he had any actual credentials as such] visited the camps several times, as did Bowles, who had an eye for the ladies, but with a gut-ugly countenance and a surly demeanor, most avoided him unless they were drunk. Evidently, Gaspard knew them both and he kept his young ladies under cover when they prowled about. Both had an eye for Siccoolum but she ignored them. Ben, seeing them bothering her, finally called them on it and they left, trying their best to make a joke of it.

Betty, and to a lesser degree, Katy, were coming of an age to be interested in any man who paid them some attention. Ben found himself doing some talking to them about just what kind of men he would allow them to be around and why they should keep away from the other kinds, like the two traders. That brought questions and he ended by referring them to Siccoolum or Moira and fled the situation, taking Monte out for a hunt. After all, the pot needed meat continually.

* * *

A few days later, a band of Indians came in to the post to trade. With trading posts who would supply them

216

with powder and lead and other white man's commodities few and far between, the surrounding vicinity of the posts were considered neutral territory by the tribes, though not always did that hold true. Mortal enemies such as Crows and Sioux might leave the post's people alone but often they themselves would attack each other, though later the chiefs of both tribes would decry the incident. This post was so situated that it was in the middle of the buffalo country and various tribal hunters were always in need of more ammunition. This time, it was eighty tipis of Northern Assiniboine, hard fighters, good hunters and not very friendly to the white man, at best semi-hostile, according to the situation.

Ben saw them coming and alerted his men and they doubled up the guard on the horses again. Then he went with Gaspard to meet the chief and have a smoke. At the same time, he saw Reed and Bowles heading for the new arrivals. They met at the edge of the village being erected and together, approached the pipe carrier, who was attended by some of his older warriors. They raised their hands in greeting, and grunted various welcomes, as did Reed and Bowles. Louie rattled some French and Indian patois and Ben just listened. Somehow, with signs and various languages bandied back and forth, some communication was effected and when the newcomers heard of the race, their faces for the first time, became animated. "Yes! Yes! They had some horses they would run! Good ones! Fast as the wind!" Reed turned his head and looked at Ben.

"You decide to put a horse or two in?"

"Sure. We'll have a couple, three, I guess."

"Good enough. Looks like we'll have a big field, then. We'll run three races. A short, a medium and a long. The short will be a sprint—six hundred yards. Second one'll be a half mile, third'll be a mile. How's that suit?"

"Sounds like fun." Actually, Ben was looking forward to some fun. Couldn't remember when he'd had any. And he decided that he'd run the bay stud. What the hell. If the horse won, he'd be good trading material and he'd foist the damn thing off on someone else. If he lost, he still might trade him. He just wanted him gone. Besides, Freddy had said that he'd covered several mares in the herd and he'd have some colts out of him that might be keepers. It would remain to be seen.

* * *

Reed was right about the Indians and how they worked themselves up about horse racing. It was an addiction. Siccoolum was beside herself. She would race the black, of course, and it was going to win. Then she thought about the stud. Would he race it? Against her black?

"Yer black is fast on the short run, Luv. Why don't you run it on that one? I'll put the stud in the long one. Hank is going to put his horse in the middle one."

That satisfied her. She would have a horse to bet on in each one. Now, Ben had to restrain her a little. He gently told her that she couldn't bet guns or powder or shot. Moccasins, dresses, bead work, knives, pots, even some money and commodities that he would let her have, all these were all right to bet.

"I will bet my buckskin and the pinto," she said.

"I guess that would be okay." He said indulgently. They had horses to spare and either was expendable. For himself, he'd gamble hard cash. He had plenty right now.

* * *

The post people had the courses well laid out already and he had no doubt that they knew to an inch just how well the bay mare and the two other horses they ran would handle the distances. Likely they had run them in practice many times. The bay mare was a classy looking animal that he would have liked to get a colt out of from the stud. She had clean legs and a long back that spoke speed.

The other horses they had were a funny looking sorrel that had a bucket head and yet somehow, with its big chest and strength of loins and withers, might be one to not overlook, and a cream colored stallion that was leggy and powerful, almost of draft horse proportions.

Ben, looking at them, thought that his wife's black likely had a good chance against the trader's mare and the stud might take the cream. Maybe. The traders had beaten the Arapaho, who must have had some decent mounts to put up. The men had been at this game for quite a while. But he'd bet on his horses anyway.

Chapter 30

Race day on Trout Creek

Ben had forbidden Freddy to groom the stud and he looked a little shabby against Siccoolum's shiny black and Jake's big roan, which both had washed and brushed until they shone. Yet, watching the eyes of the other men, he could see them taking in the lines of the horse that he'd privately named, 'Jonas.' As magnificent as the animal was, elegant and trim, Ben could arouse no feelings for it. He asked Freddy to ride it and he gratefully consented. Siccoolum would ride her black, and Givens his own horse.

As they made ready, Louie came over.

"Ben, have you walked the tracks?"

"Wal. . . no. I haven't."He cursed himself for having overlooked such an elementary precaution.

"Then, as a friend, I tell you that a favorite trick of these evil men is to have their riders push the other horses against the north side, where there are many gopher holes that can break a horses' leg. Whatever they do, do not let them push your riders to the north side of the two long tracks."

"Why, Louie, you tellin' me—that's being friendly. Thank you." He went to tell Freddy and the others of what Louie had said.

* * *

With a pistol shot, the first race was started. Ben noticed that the trader's mare was steady at the line and broke very fast. She was neck and neck with the Arapaho favorite, a leggy pinto, and just in front of the Metis' lunging grulla. The three other horses in the race were left behind, to fight for fourth place. The horses charged down the stretch, with Siccoolum coming on, quirting her black, lifting him into the third spot as they thundered across the line. First by a neck was the trader's mare, ridden by a gnarled little old Indian who looked like he was born on a horse, second was the Metis' grulla and Siccoolum, third, just in front of the Arapaho pinto. Ben, seeing the swiftness of the mare and the others, was glad he hadn't entered Monte. He would have been dusted.

Siccoolum slid down off her horse, a chastened loser. She had put up her buckskin, a beaded dress which she'd worked on the whole trip from Salt Lake, numerous pairs of moccasins and nearly all the money that Ben had given her. Ben tried to comfort her but she wanted to go sulk, so he let her be for the moment. The excitement of the next race might bring her out of it.

The camps were abuzz with the race just run and money and goods were fast changing hands. Louie came to Ben, with his sad face matching his eyes. The Metis had counted on their horse and bet heavily. Reed and his partner were smug and gaily raking in their winning bets. Ben had bet $50 on his wife's horse and went over to pay them off.

Reed smiled as he took the money.

"Our little bay is damn fast, isn't she?"

"Have to admit that she's the quickest horse on the short run I've seen." Ben agreed easily.

"You gonna put up anything on Givens roan?"

"It's a good horse. I'll go another $50 on 'im."

Reed wrote the bet down on some wrapping paper he was using for a tally sheet.

"Was hoping you might bet yer squaw. Some Indians do." He leered.

Ben said shortly, "This Indian doesn't." The man was a sharper and a womanizer. He shouldn't let him get under his skin but he was fast doing so.

* * *

The second race had seven entries. Givens' roan was heavily bet on by the Hite contingent. Hank himself rode it with a stripped saddle and bootless feet. The trader's horse was the ugly bucket headed sorrel with the little Indian aboard. The Metis had two in it: a long legged black and an appaloosa with some pretty color to it. The Indians had three: a good looking bay, a black, and a pinto. As they jockeyed for position at the starting line, the ugly sorrel reached over and took a bite out of Given's horse, which kicked and whirled as the gun banged. That tangled the line and a second shot brought them all back for a re-start. This time, the sorrel kicked out at the Indian's black and as the pistol banged, the horses sped away, Givens' sorrel in the lead. He kept it until past the half way mark, when the bucket-head seemed to shift into a new gear and surge past the field, taking the race by a length and half.

Ben was amazed that such a misshapen, ill-proportioned brute could run like that and thought it was worth losing the bet to see it. However, the rest of the Hite group and the Indians were highly incensed about the horse's conduct and thought he should be disqualified. That didn't happen, as there were no hard and fast rules and again the traders cleaned up, gloating as they did so. As Ben paid off his loss, an Assiniboine who owned the black the bucket-head had kicked, showed up and there was a fresh row, which Reed finally settled by letting the Indian off his bet, slightly mollifying the irate brave.

As Ben got Freddy up on the stud, he reflected that he had no idea of its ability and would keep his bet to the $50 he had bet on the others. Siccoolum bet her pinto, her last valuable possession. Then at the last moment, to Ben's chagrin, she put up her little black, saying she was mad at the horse for losing. Freddy and the others had just about lost everything already but their clothes and so the Hite contingent was reduced to being onlookers as the field assembled. Freddy and the stud, Ben noticed, was attracting quite a lot of attention as they approached the starting line. Bowles came up and tried to get him to up his bet, which he, at the last moment, decided to do, making it $200. The man strode off with satisfaction in his face.

Ben stood watching as the other horses came up. The cream stallion was fighting the little Indian as he struggled to get it under control. The Metis' entry, a piebald sorrel, looked speedy, as was that of the Indian's, a strong looking big buckskin ridden by a young Indian boy who seemed proud to represent his band. The field came forward in a ragged formation, and when the line was reached, the shot sounded and the horses surged forward, the stud behind the group. Ben thought that it was the first time it might have been run against other horses.

The Metis' piebald was in the front, setting a fast pace. Right behind and working hard, was the Indian's buckskin, the boy flailing away with his quirt. The old Indian had the trader horse running third but keeping up with the leaders, setting a rhythm that would eat the mile up. Freddy had the stud lined out and it was finding itself, and starting to run smoothly, reaching out in a long stride that Ben, seeing, liked despite having taken against the animal. He watched as the field faded away then a few minutes later, came surging back, the cream now in control of the race it seemed, when Ben saw, with a thrill, that the stud was coming up fast. As they thundered past, Ben saw Freddy kick the stud hard and it was well ahead of the trader's horse at the line, the others straggling in after them. He reflected that the bet paid off his losses and that Siccoolum would have horses again, at least. He went to congratulate Freddy on his good race. The boy was ecstatic at the win.

Going to gather his money up, Ben enjoyed seeing the glum looks on the faces of the two men. He was folding his money when Reed said, "Say, Hite, want to sell that stud?"

At the same time, Gaspard came forward and asked Ben the same thing. He looked at them both and the thought surfaced that here was a good time to get shut of the bay, for the right price.

"I might look at a good offer for it." He told them, not seeming too eager about the idea.

"$500 cash." Reed said, looking at his partner, who nodded. Ben turned to Gaspard, who said, "$550, by Gar."

The two parties bandied numbers together until finally, with an effort, Reed said,

"$900 and most any animal we got except the little mare 'er the sorrel. Take the white one, he's a good horse."

"Tell me about yer ornery buck-headed sorrel, the horse makes me curious."

Bowles said, "Well, we got it from a band of Pawnees comin' through. They took us fer about ever'thing with it 'til we put the bay mare against 'im. She took it on the short track by a nose but if it had gone on much longer, even another hundred yards, woulda been different. But the old Indian is the onlyiest one who can ride 'im. Bucked me off. Reed, too. He's got a twist to 'im thet'll put ya on the ground afore ya know it. Tell ya somethin'! He'd likely take that stud of yers in a real long run. He's got a world of bottom, could go all day. But he's got a burst of speed at the half mile that's 'bout right against any Injun's horse. They like the shorter races and lots of bettin'."

The two partners looked at each other and Bowles said reluctantly, "Tell ya what. We'll give ya $1000 and the brute fer yer stud."

Gaspard jumped in, "We got horses, too, my friend! I'll give you the pick of our herd and match his price plus fifty dollair. Wat you want that evil-lookin' beast for, anyways?"

Ben smiled. "I'll tell you later, Louie. Right now, I got a deal goin' here." He turned to Bowles and said. "Mister, you got a deal." Gaspard's face fell.

The traders handed over their money and the deal was struck, the stud led over and the reins handed into the hands of a triumphant Bowles by a visibly reluctant Freddy.

"Go gather the jug-head sorrel from their herd, Son. I made a trade today."

"You traded the stud for that . . . that. . . bastard of a thing!" It isn't even a horse! It looks like a big snake!" The boy was as mad as Ben had ever seen him. Ben shushed him.

"Just go get it and bring it up to the wagons fer me!"

Freddy went away, still mumbling. Ben took Gaspard by the arm and led him away.

"Listen, Louie. I didn't want them to hear it but that stud is a. . . it's a bad luck thing, an animal with a curse on it. I see that horse and all I can think of is dead folks. Its owner was killed by the Mormons for it." He went on and explained what had happened and how he'd come by the horse. "So, I didn't want you to have it because we're friends and I didn't want that bad luck to come to you."

Louie grumbled, "Still, that horse is an animal that fills the eye with beauty, he runs like the hawk flies and I would have chance the bad luck, my friend." He sighed.

"But you may be right. The Metis have enough bad luck without gathering more. I will forgive you, if you have a drink with me."

"Well now, that can be arranged, just as soon as I get done dealin' with my people. The rest of 'em will be just as upset as Freddy was and I better go talk to 'em. And, Louie, you may not know, but I saw the stud cover a few of your mares. Just by accident-like, I know."

Ben had observed the Metis sneaking some of their mares that were in heat over to the train's herd to have the stud cover them, a service that would have cost hundreds of dollars had they been east of the Mississippi. As it was, he had let it go. He liked the Metis and a few colts from the stud was a gift he could give them free.

Louie had the grace to look embarrassed about it. Ben laughed. They went back to their trains.

Siccoolum had heard the news and she was furious. The others had also gotten the news and were aghast that Ben should make such a terrible trade. He endured some ranting, whining and grumbling before he gathered them together and did a forceful job of explaining just what he felt about the stud, the money he'd gotten to boot and the relief he felt about seeing the bay gone from the herd. Siccoolum thought about it and finally said, "You think the horse was bad medicine? For you, for us?"

"That I do, Luv. I'm sorry. I know you thought you were givin' me a heap gift. But I think we're better off without that bad luck animal. And here, I see somethin' in that bucket-headed snake, as Freddy called it, that bodes good fer us."

Chapter 31

Snake was a horse who liked his privacy. He would run off other horses, when most all horses liked the herd and chose up friends to swish flies and chew the grass together. He was a picky eater, and when he found a spot of particularly succulent grass, would chase the other horses so he could eat it himself, eyeing them as he ate, as if to say, 'I dare you to come try to eat it.' They came to fear his teeth and hooves and left him alone. However, he did make a friend, Brutus, one of Maxxus's pups out of a Mormon Pit Bull bitch who was now a grown dog in his prime. Maxxus was gone, he'd died in his sleep back at the farm one night, devastating the whole family by his death. They'd buried him under a spreading apple tree in the yard and one of the things Ben and the others held against the Mormons was that his grave was back there, that he was not with them. Some day if things went well, and they found a permanent place to dwell, Ben had decided to try to have him dug up and brought to rest with them. He said nothing to the others, though, it was just something he wanted to do.

His pup, Brutus, was a copy of Maxxus, which was why Ben had kept him. Like his daddy, the dog was intelligent and a fighter. He'd also been an exemplary watch dog, and Ben credited him with saving the horse herd, maybe even the train, a couple times at least. He'd been a favorite of the Metis since the two trains had gotten together and Ben knew, that like the stud, there'd be little Brutuses with the cart families in the months to come.

The dog and the ugly horse seemed to hit it off. Brutus wasn't scared of man or beast and maybe Snake knew that and respected it. Whatever the reason, the two started spending time together and soon were inseparable. It was a curious friendship. Ben watched it with puzzlement. Louie explained it as "the two are soul brothers." He'd seen it, he'd said, with other animals: chickens and pigs, horses and chickens, even a goose and a moose, once up north. Dogs and horses friendships were not so uncommon, he said.

Ben talked with the old Indian and for little more than a bottle of good whiskey, got him to tell him just why the horse would let him ride, when he bucked the rest off.

"Horse lets me ride 'cause he knows I give him some t'ing." He explained with a drunk whisper.

"You mean you pay him fer the ride?"

"Always." The gnarled little rider said. "He give me ride, I give 'im somet'in he like."

"Like what?" Ben snorted. 'Payin' a horse to ride!'

"Apple, if I have. Corn cob. He like to chew 'em. Biscuit, piece bread, piece hard sugar. Always somet'in he not get udder-wise. He like 'bout anything. But I not tell anyone else. They try ride 'im, he just twist 'em off 'cause they no pay."

He belched and Ben poured him some more. The tin cup bottomed up and Ben thought he'd maybe given him too much but no, the old man came awake again and said,

"You pay, he let you ride. You see."

The next day, a couple apples in his pocket, nearly the last in Siccoolum's barrel, he went on out to the herd and approached the horse, Brutus laying by as the animal grazed away from the rest of the bunch. He pulled out the fruit and advanced, talking soft as he went. The animal watched him with what Ben thought was a decidedly vicious eye. But he stood as Ben came up and offered his treat, then took it from his hand, munched it contentedly and nudged him for more. Ben gave it the other one and patted him over his powerful body, thinking that he was a horse in a thousand and that was good. You wouldn't want too many of them. In fact, one of Snake was plenty.

That first week, Ben was content to just get acquainted with the animal, bringing treats, some sugar, once a doughnut that Moira had made, and some fried bread, which for some reason, Snake seemed to prefer. Then, he brought out his saddle and after, giving Snake his treat, threw it on, the horse watching alertly. He cinched it up without complaint, then gave him another treat, this time, a piece of hard candy, which the horse rolled in his mouth as Ben got aboard. The ride went well, though Ben did not kick him into a lope, just trotted him about a mile or so, then got down, pulled off the saddle and gave him one more piece. Ben continued the practice religiously and the friendship seemed to be cemented.

* * *

A train came in from the Missouri and Ben saw some Hite wagons in it. A rider looked familiar and Ben recognized Lakey Steele. Ben was riding Snake and as the two came together, he heard Lakey laugh.

"Hello, Ben, they said you was here waitin' fer me. I'da been here sooner but I was waiting fer the *Helena* to come in. Where'd you come by that ugly damn critter?"

"This ugly horse will outrun anything you got, Lakey. Good to see you." The two shook hands.

"So tell me what happened down in Salt Lake. I heard some things."

Ben told him, leaving nothing out. Steele whistled.

"Eighteen men? Good God, Ben, They'll be after you and the others for that! What about your place down there, Ketchum's route to the railhead?"

"Lost it all, Lakey. But Ketchum's here. And I did manage to get most of my horses out. Sold half of 'em at Bozeman." They talked of other matters. Lakey's end was going well and he had money for Ben along with him.

"Thought you might need it." He explained.

"Nope. I'm flush now. But I'll take it, just the same." Ben rejoined. What's goin' on with yer end at the Missouri?"

"The last few boats made it up to Fort Benton. Looks like, if the new boats have decent luck, that should be the place to make a headquarters. There's a big bench across the river there that makes good horse feed, but not like I see here. Too bad this place isn't closer to the Missouri."

"You know, Lakey, I'm wonderin' if I might just go in to raisin' horses. I've got forty head of the best workin' horses you've ever seen. Come look."

Together, the two men rode out to the herd and Lakey, seeing what Ben had saved from Utah, was deeply impressed.

"Too damn bad about Atlas. He sure threw some nice colts. Most of these are his."

"Yeah." Ben's memories of that great horse still hurt. He had unfinished business down in Utah that he intended to someday take care of.

Snake

Chapter 32

<u>**1878**</u>

Ben looked about him with some satisfaction, drinking coffee on his porch. The big log home was situated on a low hill above the big spring creek, a mile below the trading post and in the midst of some great natural meadows that yielded succulent grass hay. He had a great view of the surrounding mountain ranges from the wide porch, and he was close to the Helena route that used his wagons, could actually see the ford they used. He'd let Lakey continue as the manager and concentrated on building up his holdings on Trout Creek. Miles had their own house just about finished now, too.

The Basin was a snow hole, he'd found, with lots of weather blowing through and the winters were tough, but the ground was fertile and with hay to put up and feed out, the half-finished log barn he hoped to soon have up, his family and his animals should be well cared for the next winter. He hoped so. The winter had been a tough one. They had kept the stock deep in the willows and all had worked hard to keep the big horses alive, going out on snowshoes to cut the willows and drag them in to the horses, breaking through the ice for them to drink. The stock had come through all right but it had been a hard one, not to be repeated, if he could help it. He had hired the Metis laborers to help as they could, for most had decided to stay in the country, forsaking their north country and had settled on the bench land where they were going to raise garden produce, wheat and oats to sell to the miners west. He had helped them, loaning them teams and letting them borrow money as Louie needed it to buy equipment and seed stock. They, too, had gone through the hard winter but they were used to cold weather and were doing all right.

* * *

Mid-day the middle of May, Hank and Will arrived from Fort Benton, where they had gone to establish a saloon business. That had busted. Will kept drinking up all the profits, Hank said with a wry laugh. That worthy agreed that a bar wasn't the best business for him or them to be involved in. They both had spent too much time in front of the bar, instead of working sober behind it. They'd gone broke and thought they might come and see what Ben had going.

"Hell, boys, come on up to the porch, have some coffee and we'll kick it around." Ben said. Looking at them, he thought both looked the worse for wear.

They settled into chairs and Siccoolum, grinning, brought them big mugs of coffee, laced with cream. The cow Lakey had brought had come fresh. There was milk, butter and cream for coffee, a great delicacy. They sipped appreciatively. They talked for a while, then Ben said,

"You could go huntin'. This is great buffalo country. I'll stake you to an outfit complete with a wagon and team, ammunition and grub. You hire a couple skinners from the Metis and with hides worth $3.00 to $4.00 at Benton, you'll have a good stake in one year's huntin'. You're both shooters and with any luck at all, you should clear a thousand or more each, come fall."

Hank slurped his coffee and looked at Will. "That sounds good, Ben, and we might take you up on it, but we got some news fer you. Better tell you before we go to makin' plans. It's really why we came to visit. We mainly just got tired of the bar business."

"What's doin'?"

"Miles's letters must have stirred things up back east. The U.S. Army come waltzing out to Utah nosin' around and the Mormon Militia sent 'em home with their tails between their legs. Brigham Young's bin doin' some heavy braggin', and sayin' 'bout how they might just secede from the Union. An' we hear he's got a $5000 reward out on us—you particularly, by name. Surprised you haven't had anybody here after yer scalp, yet."

Ben's face turned grim. "That bastard needs to be reined up some!"

"We thought you'd say that. We're comin', too. The huntin'll wait."

* * *

He left Freddy and Miles in charge of seeing the barn completed, the stables started and the hay put up. Freddy wanted to come but he noticed that Miles was relieved he didn't ask him to accompany them. That was fine with Ben. Miles was a good father and a caring husband. But he wasn't a fighter.

Siccoolum and Freddy, who both bitterly opposed not being included, insisted that they take her black and Freddy's roan, which he'd bought from Hank the year before, and three of their other best horses. Ben left Monte, which was getting too old, and took Snake, Siccoolum's black, and the big grulla that he'd bought from the Metis. Hank rode his new bay, Will had a horse he'd gotten in Fort Benton, a palomino with a flowing mane that looked classy and had a wonderful walk but seemed a little slow. He selected two other horses from Ben's herd, good horses with some proven bottom that Freddy recommended. They used one of their three for pack horses and loaded them with food and ammo, with a bed roll topping it off, their clothing rolled inside. That left a horse free and they would change off all around as they needed to, usually each day. They traveled fast and made Helena in two days. There, they stayed just long enough to replenish their food, then went on.

* * *

Ten days later, they were deep in the Great Salt Lake valley. Torry Owens' farm was three miles out and they scouted it carefully, using a heavily treed, sheltered wash about a mile from his place. Ben worked his way forward to a vantage point that allowed him to see the house and barn, and using his glasses, looked it over carefully. The corrals were visible and he was puzzled when he saw what was in one of them. He thought he recognized a horse, maybe two, that he was sure had been lost in the fire. Both mares. That made him look harder and after a while, he recognized another one. Three horses from the stable that he'd thought were ashes. *'What the hell!'*

After two hours wait, he glimpsed Owens coming from the house.

* * *

Torry Owens was resigned and almost relieved when he saw the men riding into the yard. For months, he had a recurring dream that Hite was coming for him, that he was talking to him, that he was holding a knife to his throat, or that of his children's, or one of his wives. Now, here they were, Hite and two strangers, getting off their horses and walking unconcernedly up to his porch while he stood there, frozen.

"H'lo, Torry. Guess you knew we was comin'."

"Yes. . . .I. . . Ben, I'm sorry. The men you've killed. . . My brother. . . can"t you just let it be?"

"No, Torry, I hear there's a reward on our heads. That makes me mad and I come back to see about it."

"I had nothin' to do with that. It was Brigham Young's idea! Ben, I. . . got somethin' to give you. Come on out to the barn."

"That might be better, anyway, Torry. Don't like to scare the young folks."

Ben had seen children's faces peeking out the windows, along with a couple women's frightened white countenances. "Tell 'em if we see anybody goin' fer help, you'll be a dead man."

"I will. You, Mary, Helen! keep the kids here and stay inside. Don't leave or they'll kill me."

Privately, he thought he was a dead man anyway. But he didn't want to have it happen in front of his family. He walked out to the barn, the others following alertly, their pistols out.

Inside the cavernous structure, he took the lantern down and lit it with a trembling hand, then said,
"Back here."

The others followed and they heard Ben give an exclamation of surprise. In the far stall, was a huge horse.

Atlas! It nickered, clearly recognizing his smell.

"Fer God's sake! Atlas, old boy!" He gathered the horse's head to him and the familiar smell of the horse was nearly overpowering to him.

"Ben, I want to tell you how sorry I am about ever'thing. It was wrong and I know it. I don't know what I can do to repay you but I'm willing to try. Here's Atlas. There's three of his mares out there, too. I've got some money. It's yours. That ride after you, those dead men. . . my brother! Ben, you don't know how many widows and orphans resulted from that day! Fifty-one kids and twenty-seven women without husbands. Now, if you kill me, there'll be another four women that'll be widows and nine children. Please, don't kill me! I'm askin' for my family."

Ben's eyes were luminous in the lantern's bright glare as he stood and stroked the big horse's soft nose.

"We'll see, Torry, but first, you're goin' to give us some information. About yer boss, Ole' Brigham Young, King Beezelbub of the Mormons!"

"You'll have a hard time killin' him, Ben. He's got a swarm of bodyguards around him since you men sent that poem. He thinks you're after him."

"We are, but there's other ways to skin a skunk."

* * *

That evening, Torry, Will and Ben rode out while Hank, with the party's horses and gear in the barn, stayed in the house to make sure those inside were kept quiet and not leaving to spread an alarm.

Torry guided them to another farm four miles away and they again reconnoitered silently before riding in to the place. Ben turned to the stricken man.

"Now, I'm taking you at yer word, Owens. Yer certain sure this Young's place and that all these people are his wives and kids. Twenty -six wives! What a passel."

"I swear that it is and they are, Ben. The ones you want are in that yellow house over there. The boy's name is Brigham Junior and the girl's Abigail. They're his favorites, It's common knowledge." The men rode down and up to the house. Ben gestured to Owens.

"Get on up there and knock on thet door. Git 'em out here."

Owens complied and the woman who came to the door opened it timidly.

"Melissa. . . These men need to talk to you." He stepped aside as Ben walked up on the porch. The woman came out the door, a tall slim blonde with a fearful look.

"Howdy, Ma'am. I understand you to have two kids?"

"Yes, that's right. Why do you ask?"

"A boy named Brigham Junior?"

"Yes." Her voice trembled. Somehow, she divined the intent of the men. 'Could this be. . . Ben Hite?'

"Tell him to come on out here."

The boy, a youngster about six years old, came out on the porch and Ben said,

"Come on, Son, we're goin' fer a ride." He took the boy by the arm.

With a scream, the woman threw herself on Ben, hammering at him and trying to wrench the youngster from him. He threw her back and taking the boy in his arms, handed him up to Will, who took him in front of him, the child starting to struggle.

Ben swung back to the woman and said,

"Now, the girl—Abigail, right?"

He turned and went in the house, returning with a young girl of about four years in his arms. The woman stood, clinging to the doorway for support as she watched Ben hand the little one up to Owens, who took her and put her in front of him in the saddle. She was wide eyed and starting to cry. The mother, nearly in shock, was weeping as she said,

"You men, you'd take my children? What kind of men are you?"

Ben thundered back, "The kind of men who believe that a terrible deed shouldn't go unpunished, ma'am. I'm talking about a hundred and twenty men, women and <u>kids</u> —the Perkins train, who had many children in it who were killed and mutilated by Injuns! And <u>your</u> husband put them up to it!"

His eyes drilled into hers and he saw realization of what he'd said come over her. '*The Perkins train!! The Mountain Meadow Massacre!*' Was there an adult Mormon who hadn't heard the truth of that epic tragedy, that didn't feel guilt in their heart for those who had died because of the greed of the leaders of their church?'

He saw it in her face and she slumped to the floor as he turned and swung up in the saddle. He gestured to Owens and he handed the girl over to Ben, who tucked her in the saddle before him, she crying and holding her arms out to her mother.

"Tell yer man that he needs to come meet us where the road forks at the head of the valley. He best come alone if you or he wants to see yer kids again. If he does what I tell him, they might live."

They reined their horses around and galloped off.

* * *

Back at Owens farm, they swung down by the barn. Ben whistled and Hank appeared at the door of the house with a boy, Torry's oldest, at his side. He looked to be about ten years of age. Hank brought him to the barn. Ben turned to Torry, whose white face shone in the moon's light.

"Now comes <u>yer</u> time to pay what you owe me, Owens. I figure the stable, the horses and the lost business at $30,000. You got that much?"

"Ben, I don't. But I can give you $5000 and send the rest as I get it. The crops look good this year and maybe the next. . . ."

He looked about to cry as he saw Ben take the boy from Hank and a knife appear in his hand.

"Not good enough, Owens. Yer hands are as bloody as yer Beezelbub king's. The men, women and children in those three pits they were thrown into are cryin' out for revenge. You ripped their lives from 'em and it's retribution that you and the rest of the killers git yer punishment! Too bad yer wives and kids have to bear it, too!" The boy was quiet in Ben's iron grip.

" Please, Ben. . . !" The silence lengthened.

"All right! Here's the deal! I'm takin' these kids with me. You'll get <u>your</u> boy back when I get paid my dues. He'll work off yer debt 'til then. Say goodbye to yer Pa, son."

The two embraced and Torry whispered, "I'll get it paid! Somehow. We'll get you home, son!"

Ben looked at the boy, who gave him a direct gaze in return. "What's yer name, son?"

"Thomas Owens. I'm not scared. I'll come with you."

"Good boy. Git on old Atlas there."

The cavalcade got started and rode through the night.

Chapter 33

At the forks of the road where the northern trail headed off to the Territory over the mountains and the eastern route went off to Fort Laramie, they held up and waited. The three men alternated guard duty and kept in readiness to make a swift exit if pressed by pursuers. The boy, Thomas, made himself useful and seemed to be enjoying the situation. He showed no fear and was already an expert horseman. The two little ones were terrified at first but the men liked kids and it was soon evident, for they saw to their needs and paid attention to them, answering their questions and reassuring them that they wouldn't really hurt them.

* * *

A day later, Brigham Young rode up on a beautiful dark bay horse. Ben covered him with his rifle. He was a well-built man, just under six feet tall. His hair showed to be light brown, and his eyes were a penetrating blue-gray. He had a full beard that matched his hair. Despite the circumstances, he seemed to be in control of himself and his demeanor showed outrage.

"You're Hite? I want to know if my kids are all right!"

"Hank, bring up the boy." Givens let him see his son and the boy waved at his father. The sight of his son unnerved him.

"Now my Abigail!" He choked out.

Will held the girl up and she screamed when she saw her father. He started forward, then stopped as Ben raised his rifle. Young stopped and faced Ben.

"What do you want, you murderer?"

"Git down. Walk up here."

Young, a commanding figure normally, seemed to shrink as he stepped down from his big bay mount and walked toward him.

Ben sat down on a rock, his rifle across his knees but pointed at Young.

"Stand right there, you bastard. Well now, King Beezelbub Young! Emperor of the Mormons! The Lion of the Lord! The man who thumbs his nose at the Army and the U.S. government. The one who thinks he's above the law and can do what he wants to—kill who he wants to, rob whoever comes down the road, just because they ain't of his creed.

Like I told Owens, the blood of the wagon train and the others who've been killed by you and yer crew of cutthroats cries out fer justice! Don't you think they loved their kids, too?"

Brigham Young stood silent like a statute, the words seeming to wash over him like water around a rock.

"Now, it seems that justice is slow comin' to you, so we thought we'd come back and see some punishment handed out fer what surely was as bad a deed as any written up in the bible. But first, say it!"

"Say what, murderer?"

"Admit yer guilt."

Young looked to the sky, the clouds were thick and rolling, possibly it would rain. A weight seemed to fall and land on the shoulders of the blocky man. He looked at Ben.

"What you'll do to my kids if I don't? They had no hand in anything."

"'The sins of the father'. . . ever heard that one preached?"

"And if I have?"

"Admit yer guilt, you sonofabitch! Before I do somethin' like shoot yer balls off!" The rifle came round and centered low on Young's body. The man stood firm.

"I do admit I should have known enough to rein in the Militia. What they did was. . . .not right."

"Not good enough! You primed 'em and pointed 'em in the direction of thet train, sure as God!"

The rifle fired and Young jumped as the bullet plowed the ground between his legs. Just as quick as he shot, Ben reloaded. Young's face turned a dirty white.

"Yes!! I did! But please, please don't hurt my children!" Ben got hold of his anger.

"That's better, Mr. King of the Mormons."

Ben sat back. "Now, here's what's goin' to happen. We don't want to hear of any more Gentiles havin' trouble when they're in Mormon country. You'll take care of that. The Perkins train I figure was worth at least $100,000. You, King Young, will gather that up and send it on to my account at Fort Benton so's I can hand it over to those relatives we can find. I figure Banker Rawls owes me $40,000 for the farm and my rollin' stock on the railhead run. He kin have 'em but he sends me that sum to my account at Fort Benton. That all gits done, I will send back the little girl. The boy I'm goin' to keep until I know fer sure you've pulled the reward offer on me and my friends. Maybe that'll take a while, a year, like, before we know fer sure. When we do, and if there's been no trouble, the boy might kin go home.

Then! Just keep it in mind that you've more to lose by comin' after me and my friends than we do. Yer kids are the pawns in this here game. Your word, I hear, is good. Right now, you'll promise me that all this gits done, you and the Militia will leave us alone."

Young looked dazed, a tic worked in his left eye.

"I'll swear, if you'll keep your part of the bargain."

"That depends on you, Mr. Head Mormon."

* * *

243

It was a strange cavalcade which wended its way down to the big log house in the meadow days later. Big horses and little children, pack animals and mounted riders, all strung out as they came into the yard and those within came out to see the procession. Ben saw Siccoolum shade her eyes and then wave as they rode up. Moira was there, with Miles packing their new baby girl. Betty was holding little Benjamin and Katy and Waterwheel came running from the barn, with Freddy right behind them, Brutus running alongside.

Ben, stretching in the saddle, with little Abigail in front of him, reflected that his outfit had surely grown since those solitary mining days at Sheridan. Here they would stay, in what was surely a western paradise. He got down, deposited the little girl on the ground on her wobbly legs and Siccoolum came running into his waiting arms.

ABOUT THE AUTHOR

Dave Lloyd is a 4th generation Montanan whose great-grandmother came up the Yellowstone on a steamboat to the head-of-track outside Miles City. She knew and told her family stories of the men and the women who lived at the time. Dave grew up listening to her and his grandmother, the first white baby born in the county, as they reminisced of that era's rowdy times.

As a young man, Dave was a working cowboy and became assistant ranch-manager on one of the largest ranches in the state, Western Cattle Company, with hundreds of sections of land and cattle numbering in the thousands. The harsh Montana winters gave Lloyd the incentive to leave the rigorous ranching life and get a higher education.

After attending college and becoming an educator, then school superintendent, Lloyd began to write of the early beginnings of the state he loves. He researches his books and tries to make them historically accurate, with their characters true to the times.

Now retired, Dave Lloyd and his wife, Donna, divide their time between Lake Havasu City, Arizona and Helena, Montana, where Lloyd continues to research and craft his novels.

THE STORY CONTINUES

Read book two of the Ben Hite Series, THE HUNTERS, and book three, LEGACY.